NEW YORK REVIEW BOOKS

CLASSICS

THE OPEN ROA

D0562580

JEAN GIONO (1895–1970) was born and lived most of his life in the town of Manosque, Alpes-de-Haute-Provence. Largely self-educated, he started working as a bank clerk at the age of sixteen and reported for military service when World War I broke out. He saw action in several battles, including Verdun, and was one of only two members of his company to survive. After the war, he returned to his job and family in Manosque and became a vocal, lifelong pacifist. After the success of his first novel, *Hill*, which won the Prix Brentano, he left the bank and began to publish prolifically. During World War II, Giono's outspoken pacifism led some to accuse him, unjustly, of defeatism and of collaboration with the Nazis; after France's liberation in 1944, he was imprisoned and held without charges. Despite being blacklisted, Giono continued writing and achieved renewed success. He was elected to the Académie Goncourt in 1954.

PAUL EPRILE lives on the Niagara Escarpment northwest of Toronto. His translation of Jean Giono's *Melville: A Novel* (NYRB Classics) won the French-American Foundation's Translation Prize in 2018.

JACQUES LE GALL is a professor of literature at the University of Pau and is one of France's foremost interpreters of Jean Giono's works. He contributed extensively to the monumental *Dictionnaire Giono*.

THE OPEN ROAD

JEAN GIONO

Translated from the French by
PAUL EPRILE

Introduction by
JACQUES LE GALL

NEW YORK REVIEW BOOKS

New York

THIS IS A NEW YORK REVIEW BOOK
PUBLISHED BY THE NEW YORK REVIEW OF BOOKS
435 Hudson Street, New York, NY 10014
www.nyrb.com

The translator acknowledges the generous support of the French government's
Centre national du livre.

CNL

The drawing on page 4 is by Claude Boutterin.

Library of Congress Cataloging-in-Publication Data
Names: Giono, Jean, 1895–1970, author. | Eprile, Paul, translator. | Le Gall,
   Jacques, 1949– writer of introduction.
Title: The open road / by Jean Giono ; translated by Paul Eprile ; introduction
   by Jacques Le Gall.
Other titles: Grands chemins. English
Description: [New York] : New York Review Books, [2021] | Series: New York
   Review Books classics
Identifiers: LCCN 2020047546 (print) | LCCN 2020047547 (ebook) | ISBN
   9781681375106 (paperback) | ISBN 9781681375113 (ebook)
Classification: LCC PQ2613.I57 G813 2021 (print) | LCC PQ2613.I57 (ebook) |
   DDC 843/.914—dc23
LC record available at https://lccn.loc.gov/2020047546
LC ebook record available at https://lccn.loc.gov/2020047547

ISBN 978-1-68137-510-6
Available as an electronic book; ISBN 978-1-68137-511-3

Printed in the United States of America on acid-free paper.
10 9 8 7 6 5 4 3 2 1

INTRODUCTION

JEAN GIONO was born on the thirtieth of March, 1895, in Manosque, a small Provençal town in the south of France, midway between the Alps and the Mediterranean. He was the only child of a shoemaker of Italian ancestry and a laundress. To his father he owed his taste for books and the fictive world, his love of nature and liberty, and his passion for healing; to his mother his exceptionally blue eyes and blond hair, his sensitive nature and a certain sense of balance, and an indomitable spirit. Was his childhood impoverished? Yes, one could say so, but it was nevertheless pampered, dreamy, happy. The "real riches" (windstorms, rainstorms, snowstorms, sun, mountains, rivers, forests) were right there, close at hand, magnified twofold, tenfold, by the mysteries that the imagination and sensuality of a child can invent "out of thin air."

> *Childhood granted us, once and for all, our share of poetry.*

At the age of sixteen, Giono left high school and entered "the lunar world of the bank." He copied out addresses, delivered letters around town, opened and closed doors, politely greeted lady and gentleman clients. But he led "a second life," one which enabled him to envision Ulysses in a pig merchant who'd come to make a deposit. He earned a modest wage that gave him the means to establish an embryonic library and to help his family out financially. At the same time, he read (mostly classical Greek and Latin authors), tried his hand at writing, escaped to the hills, and formed his identity:

> The greater part of me, nothing could touch. It was called Jean-le-Bleu.

This golden age came to an end with the Great War. Conscripted in 1914, assigned to an Alpine Infantry Training Unit in 1915, he was sent to the front in 1916. Verdun, Les Éparges, Chemin des Dames, Mont Kemmel ... Uttermost tragedy. Unforgettable. Unforgotten. From the Sixth Infantry Company to which he belonged, Giono would be one of the rare survivors. Many of his childhood friends would not return. Nor would a large number of already established French writers: Charles Péguy, and so many others—almost seven hundred of them—would have less luck than Giono, who nevertheless lost so much, even if he didn't lose his life:

> I was twenty-two years old. Gone: my belief in myself. Gone: my magnificence.

Demobilized in 1919, the young man returned to earning his livelihood at the bank. His father died. Giono married Élise Maurin. Aline, their first daughter, was born in 1926. A second daughter, Sylvie, would be born a few years later. He wrote some prose poems that would be published in a review in Marseille. A first novel, entitled *Naissance de l'Odyssée*, was refused by the publisher. On the other hand, *Colline* (translated into English, it received the Prix Brentano in the United States; it has since been superbly retranslated by Paul Eprile) received immediate acclaim. Members of the French literary world, like Jean Paulhan, were enthusiastic, and André Gide paid a visit to the "New Virgil." So Giono decided to strike out on an adventure. He gave up feeding from the manger at the bank. He would attempt to live by his pen, while staying put in Manosque; in other words, far from Paris, the place where, so often in France, "everything happens." He bought a modest house called Le Paraïs—on a hillside covered with olive trees—overlooking the roofs of his native town. He would spend his whole life there, right until his death on the night of October 8–9, 1970. And there he would write the greater part of his life's work, a gigantic oeuvre, seething with life force:

> Right away, I wrote for the sake of life, I wrote life itself, I wanted to make the whole world drunk on life. I would have liked to have been able to make life boil over like a rushing stream and to make it crash onto all of those dried-up, desperate men, hit them with cold, green waves of life, make their blood rise to their very surface of their skin, stun them with freshness, with good health, and joy, tear up their leather-shod feet by their roots and carry them away in the torrent.

Toward the end of 1950, Giono temporarily suspended writing one of his most ambitious books, *Le Hussard sur le toit* (*The Horseman on the Roof*), and embarked on the composition of what would be the fourth of his *Chroniques romanesques* (Fictional Chronicles): *Les Grands Chemins*.

He had been pondering this title since the 1930s. Without question, it derived from Whitman; Giono had read him, passionately, since 1924. So, there is a good reason why the English translation of the title *Les Grands Chemins* echoes "Song of the Open Road" from *Leaves of Grass*. The novel's evolution had followed a long and sinuous road. On the other hand, its drafting seems to have been free of obstacles (the manuscript shows few deletions or revisions). It moved ahead full speed, taking just a little over two months, from October 10 until December 22, 1950. The first excerpts from the novel would appear in print in January 1951. They were headed by an epigraph from *Hamlet*: Giono had read widely in Shakespeare, no doubt guided by his daughter Aline, who had a degree in English, and by Henri Fluchère, one of his closest childhood friends, who had become a translator and a specialist in Elizabethan theater. *Les Grands Chemins* was released by Gallimard in April 1951. In the same year—and this attests to Giono's remarkable creative powers during the years following World War II—*Le Moulin de Poulogne* (*The Malediction*), *Monsieur Machiavel ou le Coeur Humain dévoilé*, and, finally, *Le Hussard sur le toit*, would all appear. This last novel takes place during the nineteenth century, in a Provence ravaged by a cholera epidemic. It was completed in April 1951 and met with a triumphant reception. The books that would follow, up to his very last—*L'Iris de Suse* (1970)—would confirm Giono's status as one of the greatest novelists of his time.

With *The Open Road*, we are at the antipodes of the romance and sublimity of *The Horseman on the Roof*. At first, the chronicle seems straightforward, made even simpler by seamless narration in the first-person present tense, as well as by syntax that feels loose and a predominantly oral style.

The storytelling is linearly chronological, without chapter divisions, fairly close to stream of consciousness. Landscapes, cameo portraits, episodic happenings, meditative pauses, directly or indirectly presented dialogues, interior monologues: all of these succeed one another and merge in a continuous movement that connects the momentary with the permanent, and the spoken present of the narration with a completely different present—that of popular proverbs (sometimes discreetly altered) or of aphorisms (ostensibly well known).

When he began, he definitely had the notion of drafting a large-scale, picaresque novel along the lines of *Don Quixote* (Cervantes being one of his favorite authors), or of Fielding's *Tom Jones*, or of Sterne's *Tristram Shandy*. But Giono's novel might be closer to a "thriller," in the vein of American titles in the French Série noire (the collection of noir fiction published in French by Gallimard; Giono particularly admired Dashiell Hammett). In *The Open Road*, two marginal characters will cross paths, in every sense. One, who can only be called the Narrator, is a vagabond who wanders freely, wherever the wind takes him. Endowed with a reassuring physique, he seems equipped for every form of enjoyment. He switches jobs according to circumstances and the seasons. One would trust him implicitly. The other, by contrast (he, too, nameless, until the last pages of the book), has an ugly face and an ugly character. Let's call him the Artist, with a capital "A" that doesn't appear in the text. In the Artist's view, to work would be to lose his dignity. He plays the guitar expressively, and card games and tricks with consummate skill, all the more so because he cheats with virtuosity. Short of making love (but what do we really know in this regard, exactly?), these two characters attract each other magnetically, and

Giono, while letting us glimpse that they're two sides of more or less the same tarnished coin, and two personae of the novelist himself, sends them out on the road.

The action of *The Open Road* takes place in a geographic space that the author is careful to shuffle (in the same way that the Artist, the unnamed Narrator's counterpart, shuffles his cards): to start with, the Alps; then, the Provençal south; and finally, a village close to a provincial capital designated only by the initial D. Conversely, this action is bounded (from autumn until the first stirrings of spring, and with particular emphasis on winter, the season of desires) and quite clearly defined in temporal terms. It unfolds during the period when Giono was writing the novel, in the aftermath of the Second World War. There are several markers of this, among them references to women's right to vote (in France, women were not enfranchised until April 1944); the "surplus" goods left behind by the transatlantic Allies (from the "American Army raincoat" worn by the Narrator; the Artist's American cigarettes; the jazz that Madame Edmond—one of the owners of the walnut-oil mill where the Narrator works for the winter—listens to; and "the American make of farm machinery and tractors" that the Narrator demonstrates at a country fair). There are also numerous allusions to explicitly French historical events, as well as to global phenomena linked to the Cold War and decolonization, which were two of the outcomes (consequences) of World War II: a political crisis during the presidency of Vincent Auriol (who was president of the French Republic from 1947 to 1954); a suicidal jump, by a Russian schoolteacher (Oksana Kasenkina), from a window at the Russian consulate in New York; and the Indochina War (which preceded the Vietnam War). There is good reason to think that the action of the novel takes place precisely in 1950, the year of the outbreak of the Korean War and of the evacuation of Cao Bang along the RC4 (Colonial Road 4), a disaster which became known in France on October 10, the same day on which Giono began writing *The Open Road*.

A road generally knows what it's about; you just have to follow it.

The lighthearted tone of the opening pages seems designed to bear the reader away on a sort of "road novel," easygoing and picturesque. But very early on, and by fits and starts, things veer off track. In this adventure, the pair of vagabonds seems curiously ill-assorted. We're far from what Giono had previously invented in the novella called *Solitude de la pitié* (*The Solitude of Compassion*), and most of all in *Un de Baumugnes* (*Lovers Are Never Losers*). Particularly when it comes to the question of friendship, *The Open Road* can be read as a recasting of the latter novel, published twenty years earlier. With a minimum of attention, one can realize that upheavals have been signaled from the very first pages of *The Open Road*, long before the spectacular tempest toward the end and the denouement it presages. If there's a need for "reconstruction," if "there's jobs for masons . . . and for every trade" (including, no doubt, for writers), it's because the country has just been devastated (by the war); if the truck that picks up the hitchhiking Narrator is "hauling acid," it's because the author has a bunch of accounts to settle. From one page to the next, a mounting ambiguity never stops undermining the ostensible Euclidian simplicity of the story. Often cross-country, more or less steep, more or less washed-out, snow-covered or flooded, dirt or asphalt, open to the sky or forest-covered: manifold roads branch off from the "main highway." In the final analysis, aren't the majority of them roads that only lead nowhere, like the *Holzwege* of Rilke or Heidegger?

Clearly, it's not our business here to recount what comes to pass along these roads, nor to reveal the denouement of this "hard-boiled novel." Let's list only some of the themes that are interlaced through the chronicle: that of the road (a metaphor for an internal evolution); that of friendship (and its ambiguities); that of love (so much less tangible than hatred); that of gambling (and marked cards); that of solitude (incurable); that of boredom (especially in the Pascalian sense); that of security (in contrast to taking risks "without a ceiling"); that of the *libido dominandi* (which can manifest itself either in protectiveness or in ritual violence); that of *Homo mechanicus* (modern civilization has drained the world of delight and produced a human race devoid of worth and beauty); that of freedom ("How to change the way things unfold isn't something just anybody can pick up"); that of nature (men are denatured animals cut off from Mother Earth to the point where they have to gnaw at the bones of their own desires); that of truth (when it's so much more fun to lie); that of happiness (happiness?); and even that of narrative structures (subverted by an author who projects and mirrors himself through the two characters whom he's sent out on the road).

In the guise of the contradictory, dialectically opposed traits of his two vagabonds, Giono portrays his own self yet again, while also depicting the temper of his times. With *The Open Road*, he mingles personal experience (first and foremost, that of the two world wars—in the course of the second, he was imprisoned twice) with his reading, or rereading, of Pascal, La Rochefoucauld, de Sade, Hobbes, Cervantes, Nietzsche, and Machiavelli. Ennui, "mutual self-interest," cruelty, "perpetual war," disillusionment, the "will to power": these are what he retained from the first six of these. As for the towering figure of Machiavelli, he is the acid-bearer par excellence: of the acid hauled by the truck into which the hitchhiker Narrator climbs on the novel's first page. Like the Italian author of *The Prince*, Giono the novelist unveils the human heart, stamps out received ideas, deflates the moralizing verbiage of windbags: "It's impossible to move ahead when you're up to your knees in righteousness. All of them tell you they've marked the trail. But ... just try. With the first step, you'll sink up to your waist."

What's disturbing, despite the realism of this fictive mode, is the strangeness and ambiguity of everything and everyone. Who is the Artist? An extreme restriction of point of view causes us to see him only through the eyes of the Narrator. And so, between fascination and repulsion, attraction and mistrust, empathy and antipathy, the latter character swings in bewilderment. Besides, who is the Narrator himself? A good guy or a scoundrel? A defender or an assassin? A small-time hedonist? A sage? A cynic? An ordinary fellow? From this point of view, the adages that the Narrator continually draws on are also deeply disturbing: They're based on the aphorisms of the French moralists whom Giono surely had in mind (La Rochefoucauld, Chamfort, Vauvenargues ...), but it's impossible to draw from them an unequivocal meaning ... even harder to discern a message or a philosophy. In principle, a maxim serves to convey a complete, precise meaning, carved in stone. But here, by dint of accumulation, the aphorisms of the Narrator end up battling and negating each

other. What a job faces the translator who must, at one and
the same time, render the clear-cut aspect of these sayings,
while conveying their ironic distance.

The task is all the more difficult because, whether in
subtle traceries or in unspoken references to the space "between the lines" (Giono often drew attention to such *inter-
lignes*), the writers with whom the novelist invisibly engages
are everywhere. (In this respect, too, the Narrator—who
"jumps" on the chance to illicitly borrow a copy of *L'Esprit
des lois* by Montesquieu—resembles his creator.) We have
already mentioned some of them. There are others, and many
are American. Having been entranced by his reading of
Whitman's poetry, Giono developed a passion for Melville,
whose *Moby-Dick* Giono translated in collaboration with
his close friend Lucien Jacques and Joan Smith. Paul Eprile
is well aware of this background: after translating *Colline*
(*Hill*), he also translated *Pour saluer Melville* (*Melville: A
Novel*), the marvelous introduction Giono wrote to accompany the French version of Melville's masterpiece. Is it an
accident that the Narrator of *The Open Road*, in search of a
Friend (with a capital "F"), says that this quest is as difficult
as trying to find a great white whale? Is it possible to believe
that Giono, in citing this proverbial phrase, didn't have in
mind the great white whale that Captain Ahab pursued?
Furthermore, in addition to Whitman and Melville, Giono
showed himself to be a brother in art and arms of the great
William Faulkner. Giono's Provence? A Yoknapatawpha.
An imaginary South. Finally, and specifically in connection
with *The Open Road*, Giono clearly had in mind *Of Mice
and Men*, the novel by John Steinbeck, first published in
English in 1937, whose French translation by Maurice Coin-

dreau was released by Gallimard in 1949 under the title of *Des souris et des hommes*.

There is even one more writer who should be mentioned here: Jack Kerouac, the American author, of French Canadian ancestry, of *On the Road*. "The Original Scroll," that long ribbon of paper so similar to a road, appears to have been typed out in four days in 1951; the novel itself was published in 1957. Of course, at the time when he wrote *The Open Road*, Giono could not have known the story of "[t]wo guys hitch-hiking to California in search of something they don't *really* find, and losing themselves on the road, and coming all the way back hopeful of something *else*." Giono (a member of a Lost Generation) could only have read this cult novel of the Beat Generation some years later. But this is beside the point. Beyond the differences, there are an astonishing number of intersections between the two texts. And they actually share a certain set of common references: Whitman, for example, and Melville as well ("Whale on the horizon!" Neal Cassady cries when he arrives in Frisco).

Translation is a meticulous labor, patient and passionate at once. It's not within everyone's reach to translate Giono. How can one open the gates to the world of this native of Manosque, in a language other than the French he used so beautifully, but in ways so often out of the ordinary? Whether we're speaking of *Hill* (a poem-novel), of *Melville* (an elegy), or of *The Open Road* (a chronicle laced with acid), three books whose translation Eprile has tackled, the difficulties could appear insurmountable. In the latter novel, for example, how not to lose the poetry of certain descriptions, seeing as they are so delicately ephemeral? Is it possible to replicate the countless nuances in the figures of speech—

whether familiar or highly colloquial—that pepper the dialogue? Is there a way to translate the "pulse," or the "gestalt" of certain pages? How can one draw the reader into the "marmot hole" of elliptical allusions? Is there a way to make us see the reverse, the negative of the photograph placed under our eyes? To make us feel the delight that Giono felt while he played with the fire and the slow-motion cheating of that infernal Gambler, that heavenly drifter, the Artist? To render that mixture of liveliness and sadness, of bitterness and tenderness, of deadpan delivery, of irony? Can one make all of this come to life? And, besides, what does it mean to live? How can one live? Eprile's translation shows us a way.

The sun is never so beautiful as on a day when you take to the open road.

—Jacques Le Gall

THE OPEN ROAD

Let not thy mother lose her prayers, Hamlet;
I pray thee stay with us; go not to Wittenberg.

First thing in the morning. I'm by the side of the road, waiting for the van that collects the milk. I see it coming and I stand up and wave. But the guy doesn't even look, just leaves me in his dust.

I fill my pipe. Autumn's been my traveling companion for weeks. The orchards are red with apples.

A minute later, I hear another engine: It's a big tanker hauling a trailer. This one picks me up.

The guy's on his own. He shoves a packet of shag across and he wants a cigarette. I roll him one. I ask if I should lick it. He says "Lick it."

He doesn't care where I'm from—a good sign—but he does ask where I'm headed. I say I haven't made up my mind.

"Job?" he says.

"Yes, and no."

For a while we ride along quiet, the way I like it.

"There's reconstruction going on around here," he says.

I say yes, to be polite.

"There's jobs for masons."

"Yeah."

"For all the trades."

"Yeah."

We're passing through a good-sized town, where every-body's still in bed. Even so, a few cafés are already open. We don't stop.

"Gotta stick to the timetable," the guy says.

He's hauling acid for a factory. He has to cover eighty miles, at least three times a day if he's able to.

"And I better be."

Four trips or more, and he starts collecting bonuses. But as he's telling me this, he breaks up laughing.

In spite of my looks, he asks, in so many words, if I'm on the road just for fun. I put him at ease. I tell him I'm in no hurry to find work at the moment, but any day now I'll have to get back down to doing something.

"What's that?"

"A bit of everything. A hundred trades, a hundred head-aches."

This little jingle works every time, this one included. He's pleased as punch.

On our way out of town, we go by a stadium. A big yellow poster announces the game of the week. He brakes and stares at the billboard.

"They're all pumped up in this hick town," he says. "Un-believable."

Next, he launches us full tilt downhill. The golden poplars whiz by at top speed.

We're following a narrow valley. On both sides, the slopes are blanketed in beech woods, almost completely rust-colored. Then the country widens out, and I can see a fork in the road ahead.

"Drop me off here, pal."

He stops. I've rolled him another smoke, and I hand it to

him. He thanks me like I was giving him a real gift. He asks if this is where I was headed. I tell him I'm going to give it a try, and he pulls away.

I like it here. I walk up to the signpost and read the place-names. They mean nothing to me. There's a village a mile away, probably too close to the main road for my liking. I can see it from here. Not bad. The roofs are in good shape. The clock tower is fancy. There are signs of wealth. The orchards are red, like where I just came from. But what really gets to me are four or five patches of cosmos flowering out in the fields. I notice some quince hedges loaded down with fruit and some vines with unripe grapes. They must be for homemade wine—this isn't vineyard country.

The fields are all broken up. The biggest plots are less than a hundred yards across. Even so, they've grown wheat, not barley. Everything sits on layers of silt dumped by the river. They've dug a channel through the stones in the riverbed. There's a little black water winking down there now. It looks like whoever's in charge of the roads keeps on top of things, and the local coffers must be respectably full. They've built a bridge that's worth a second look. About five miles away, it seems, there's another village. The name of this one is a whole saga in itself. It must be hidden in a pass—somewhere over there.

I have nothing on my mind. The morning moves along. There are already a few bees. I cover the first mile at an easy pace. This road is more to my liking. It's a village lane, barely fifteen feet wide, nice and springy underfoot. It steers clear of all the private estates. If you drove a stake in its path, this lane would give it a wide berth. And that's just what it did when they first laid it out. It's bordered by kitchen gardens on both sides, and I notice they like flowers around here. Too bad it's so close to the main road. These zinnias might actually persuade me to be friendly and polite.

From close up, it's a village like any other, except for one thing that scares the shit out of me: a château with turrets. There are no châteaus with turrets in my state of mind. I've had it up to here with châteaus and turrets.

Past the fountain, I make a sharp turn and I head toward the place with the famous name, five miles away. The road follows the stream, and I get real pleasure from it for more than an hour. I'm overlooking the ravine: It's wide and loud, choked with alders and birches. I love this season. It's fresh. A thrush is singing in the woods. What it's saying fits perfectly with the gold-colored leaves on the ground and the chill in the breeze. It's an unassuming bird, but one who knows its business.

I walk for a few more minutes, and here's a house that does reach close to the road. It's a low-slung chalet in a chestnut grove. I get closer. The stable door is open. I notice two or three things I like—one of them's a bench in a choice spot, with a view. There are a few tools carefully stored inside, and they have solid-looking handles.

There's a dog, but he's just a shepherd mutt with a sleek coat. He barks because he's supposed to. In fact, he's just fooling around. He doesn't look like he'd scare too easily. All the same, he holds me off and makes it clear he's laying down the law. Lucky for him, I have great respect for dogs' law. I give a shout. The mutt lies down and keeps his eyes on my feet.

The owner is a short, heavyset guy. He has the well-meaning look of a bachelor who lives alone in a forest. I ask if there might be any work for me around here. He tells me no, politely, with a touch of regret. He's kind. His chestnut trees are magnificent. And now that I'm on the terrace in front of his house, I can see how well-placed that bench really is.

We exchange a few words about the weather and the season. He offers me a cup of coffee. I turn it down. He already has a bench, a dog, and piles of things it would take too long to list. No point in adding another pleasure on top.

I ask him about the village, the one that must sit inside a pass. He says yes, it does. It's a couple of miles farther on. He doesn't think anybody there would hire me. To do what, anyway? he asks.

The country he's looking at while he tells me this—and I give it a glance too—doesn't look like it needs anyone or anything at all. The little bit of farmland would barely support a child, and the rest is just forests on mountainsides.

After I bid this fine fellow farewell, I take stock. I still have almost all of my final pay. This gives me at least five or six days of easy living, and if I'm careful, a lot more than that.

The village looks bad. Nothing you'd call picturesque. It's at the far end of the famous pass, but it sits in a bowl ringed by mountains as bare as porcelain. I was expecting more. There are only five or six houses. I make a turn past an outcrop of rock. Now here, facing due west, things look a bit better. There's a grocery store, a post office, and a bistro with a terrace for playing boules.

What do they charge for a coffee around here? Ten francs, like everywhere else? I'll go in and find out.

It's neat and tidy inside, and today's paper is lying on the table. It looks like they're well served by public transport. But how? I didn't see the mail truck go by.

A woman greets me from the kitchen doorway, but a young girl comes out to serve me. I call out to the woman. She's raking coals in her woodstove. I ask if by any chance there might be some work around here. This seems to interest her. She comes out, wiping her hands on her apron.

She's a redhead, with freckles. A pleasant face. She's young and well-endowed. I put on my innocent look.

She says a guy named Chanton was doing some logging in a valley higher up, but she thinks he's done. It's been a few days since she's seen him. Anyway, she doesn't know if he needs any help. Apart from that, she can't think of anything.

She knows her own worth, and she pushes herself forward to fill out her chest. It's a pretty sight. The girl steals a glance at us.

I ask if you get anywhere by carrying on from here. She answers in a tone that indicates, precisely, that the world exists anywhere else but here. According to her, you only have to leave this place to arrive in the promised land. That's one way of looking at it, I guess.

Her coffee is good.

I check the time on her clock. It says ten, but she tells me it's slow. Nothing to worry about. I'm not in a hurry. I gather some information about the region. I come to the conclusion that these people live off honey. There are lots of hives. Honey, timber, and hauling them both around.

I'm trying to hold up my end of the conversation. The business of her chest aside (she's dwelling on it), the lady is nice. I ask her what they do here on Sundays. She tells me they dance and play boules. I like this program. I tell her so. She agrees. She adds, "There are better things to do, but they cost more." I remark that she's hit the nail right on the head.

On this bright note, I take off again into the sunshine.

The road climbs, without letting up. It's good for the locals, who have the legs for it. But it leaves me a bit breathless. I take two or three breaks and look at the bare slopes rolling down toward me. The pastures are rusty brown, and they're covered in white thistles. There ought to be mushrooms under the larches, but where are the larches? Inside all this, there's me: a speck, nothing more. The rest is just grass, rocks, and the thread of the stream. It must be cold, judging from its color, and how silently it runs.

I reach a hollow ridge in the grasslands. It's a saddle. The view from here to the north is terrific.

Horsemen, dismount!

The air is sparkling. I'm feeling good. I have a bite to eat. At the same time, I look around. It's a pretty sight in every direction. Mountains, mountains as far as the eye can see, and forested valleys—this one in particular. And because I'm here, this is the one I'm going down.

I don't know what I enjoy more: eating, or thinking about the pipe I'm going to treat myself to at the first digs I find. Miles and miles surround me, like anywhere else, but here you can see them. The valleys lift your spirits just to look at them. But best of all is the air. You can't get enough of it. It's been a long time since I've been this happy.

On my left but far off, there's a flock of sheep. Their bells are ringing faintly now and then. They're slowly getting closer. I watch how the shepherd is moving. He's seen me. He wants to know who I am, but he doesn't want it to be obvious. He's pretending to follow his sheep, but he's herding them.

He's a shepherdess. A skinny, upright old lady. Tanned from head to foot. She reaches the other side of the road and comes to a stop. We say hello, and then I add, "It's beautiful around here."

"Yes, people say so."

After this, we carry on in each other's company, with the road between us. She's seen enough of me, but she's glad to stay. This goes on for a while. She has her thoughts, I have mine. We're getting along just fine.

Finally, I say goodbye. She climbs back up her mountainside, and I head back down the slope, but I slacken my pace. I'm in no hurry to get to the bottom of the valley. I'll have to, because it's not likely to be warm here at night, but it's a shame. Like everything: as if regrets make any difference... After a minute, I'm back on stride.

Just before I get to the next hamlet, there's a woman picking apples. I'm in good spirits. I say, "Greetings, Your Highness," and I compliment her on her fruit. Like me, she's keen to talk. She comes to the bank by the roadside.

"Do you want some?" she asks.

"Toss me one."

She tosses one. I catch it in midair. She laughs. So do I. It doesn't take much to get us going... We chat. She could be any age, so could I. I chomp through the apple, right to the core.

"Do you happen to be hungry?"

"No. Just a fantasy."

"Everybody needs one."

We start laughing again like fools. It must be the air.

"Would you fill me in on something?"

"Why not, if I can?"

"Would there be any work for a guy like me around here?"

"What do you do?"

"Whatever I'm asked."

"You wouldn't know how to weave baskets?"

"Sure, I'm good at it."

"What a shame. We had the basketmaker here the day before yesterday."

"So I've turned up too late."

"Not if your intentions are good."

"I think they are."

That wasn't clever. Now she's on guard. She goes back to her apple tree.

"Go to Agnières," she says.

"Is it far?"

"Three miles down."

"You wouldn't know if there's any place to stay there?"

"Sure. Ask at the Café Sube."

"Anywhere else?"

"I couldn't say."

So if there's nothing else, I'll settle for the Café Sube. I'm inclined to pay for a bed for the night unless it costs more than thirty francs. That should be close to the price around here unless they're used to rich tourists. Hunters, for example, who come to have fun and might pay as much as fifty.

I see from the clock tower that it's already three. In this closed-in valley, it'll be dark by six. I'm not afraid of the dark, but people are scared of strangers passing through in the night.

At Agnières there's nothing. I don't even dare to go into the Café Sube. It's definitely not for me, that's clear. The country would suit me though. I've arrived here well ahead of dusk, and it's pretty. Too pretty, even, seeing as there's a Café Sube.

A guy comes out wearing boots and a leather jacket. He takes a good look around and lifts his nose to the mountains. He looks like he's passing them in review. He's holding a cigarette case, and it's an instrument that serves him well. He raps it with his finger as though he's beating on a drum. He gives everybody the once-over, and he gives me the once-over.

I talk with a guy who's watering his horse. According to him, I don't have a hope anywhere in the whole district. As for a place to spend the night, it's a delicate matter. You can't just ask for it point-blank, especially at this hour. I know the score.

As soon as his horse has finished drinking, he heads off. What should I do now? The guy in the boots is pacing back and forth in the square like Louis XIV. He looks bored stiff. I feel like telling him it's not my fault. I'd like him to pay attention to a small, white house with hollyhocks, underneath three birch trees. It's a distraction for me, anyway. It's hard to believe how many thoughts it stirs up, both pleasant and unpleasant. Too many to choose from.

I hang around in the village. There's not much to it. It has a cozy side, like all villages in the evening.

It's hard to approach people at this hour. They're locking their doors. The deadbolt was invented at night, a long, long time ago. Fear is such a big deal! It takes the right sort of people to go against instinct, and the right sort of people, they're few and far between.

By wandering back and forth like this, I'm making my situation even worse. People start giving me sidelong glances. If I was sure I could get them to settle for thirty francs, I'd be glad to go in and ask at the Café Sube. But then I'd have to have something to eat, and it's not the sort of place where I could spread my papers out on the table. A bowl of soup would likely cost its weight in gold. If there is any soup.

Now, here's something I shouldn't be thinking about: I'm seeing heaps of potatoes and leeks in boiling water, with a gleaming streak of oil. There's an El Dorado at every turn.

I make up my mind, and I walk up to a cocky-looking young guy, putting my best foot forward. He, too, tells me about the Café Sube. I chuckle and point out it's not the right place for me. While we're chatting, I roll a cigarette. This casual gesture doesn't seem to affect him. Maybe I've caught him at a busy moment...

At night, it's old people who are the most open. The frustrating thing is, they don't hang around outdoors. And nine times out of ten, once they're inside, they're no longer in charge. Unless they're rare birds. And rare birds are precisely what I'm looking for.

I do something idiotic. I knock on a door and ask straight-out for a bite to eat and somewhere to sleep. I'm blunt, but I lay my friendliness on thick. I say I can pay. They're polite like everybody else, and they suggest the Café Sube. I say, and I'm polite too, that it's too expensive. So no, they can't think of anything else.

There are four of them inside: the woman who came to the door, a man who was rummaging in a toolbox, a little girl who was writing in a notebook, and an old woman who was ladling soup from a corner of the cookstove. They're all racking their brains, with the best of intentions, but aside from the Café Sube, they can't think of anything. Neither can I. I bid them good evening.

I take to the woods again, and night falls fast. The road drops down and disappears into a narrow valley, thick with undergrowth. On my right, I hear water leaping over stones. But the stream plunges deeper and faster than the road, and a minute later, I don't hear it anymore.

I thought I might run across a sawmill. You can bed down nicely in the sawdust under the sheds. But as far as I can make out, I'm in a ravine where there's only enough room for the road and for the stream running silently, way down below.

There's nothing to be done but to walk on. And that's what I do, while I nibble on a crust of bread and my last piece of hard cheese.

I usually have good night vision. Here, the forest looks dark and dense, even with my eyes peeled. All the same, at a bend where there must be fewer trees, I see a star facing me. Then I realize it's not a star but a light fixed in place, way up on the mountain. I catch sight of two or three more next to the first one. They're making less of a glimmer. Masked by the foliage, I guess. There's no question, they're the lights of some kind of settlement. I realize I must have burrowed deep into the ravine, to be able to see the lights of a village so high up above my head.

But I'm still sticking to the road. A road generally knows what it's about. You just have to follow it.

It's been ages since I've tried to pick up the scent of saw-mills. I don't sense anything particularly human around me right now…on the contrary. In the first place, there's the smell of emptiness. To my right, the forest must drop down hard and fast. From below as well, every so often a sort of sigh rises up, the kind a sleeping man makes. There must be a wide channel at the bottom, with a torrent scouring over heavy gravel. I also catch the resinous scent of pines and the smell of bird droppings. There must be a cliff face nearby. They usually smell like this.

I see other stars, but they're lower than me. A compact set of fires, staked out in the shape of a Big Dipper. But below my feet. Always a funny feeling. I try to see the stars in the sky. There's no way. All you can see is the constellation of the village up above and the constellation of the village down below. And there's nothing connecting the two of them. They're separated by maybe thirty miles of roads like the one I'm on, full of twists and turns, that must veer off all over the place. Between the two of them, tons and tons of leaves of every shape and size, each and every one of them blacker than the shadows. And in the midst of all this, I'm floating.

Your legs always feel weaker at night.

I wonder if I've got four hundred francs left, or five. Must be four, that's what Old Man Machin owed me when I left. Aside from that, just some loose change. I think I had about a hundred francs when he paid me off. Since then I've only bought a few snacks.

I'm beginning to feel fed up, but I have to make an effort to find anything at all—a farm, a village. I'd be happy to hear a dog barking. I stop and listen.

I think I hear footsteps behind me. Now I'm sure of it.

I wait. It's a guy who's keeping a brisk pace. When I figure he's close enough, I clear my throat. He asks who's there.

I tell him it's me. This should hardly keep him coming forward but he does. His voice is young. He looks a bit shorter than me. What I can see in fact is a black man in a tunnel.

I get straight to the point: Is there anywhere to bed down, not too far away, in this neck of the woods? The guy answers yes, for sure—that's where he's headed. It's still a couple of miles away. I suggest that we go there together. He repeats, "for sure," and we start walking again.

Right away, something's puzzling me. I end up having to say so. I put it a certain way because . . . really, it is something strange. I know I'm not mistaken: it's the sound of skirts.

"Are you a man or a woman?"

"I'm a priest."

I say, "Shit!" He has a good laugh.

"Isn't it a bit late to be out on the roads, Father?"

"You're doing all right, aren't you?"

He's a cheeky devil. I could be anybody at all, and it wouldn't take much to complicate his life. He adds, "People around here are partial to dying at night. If that's what suits them, what am I supposed to do?"

He politely explains that he'd gone to help out a grandmother. I ask, "To do what?" He answers, "To die like a Christian."

There are times when you don't say a word; this is one of them, mostly because of the darkness, the quiet, the scents in the air, our footsteps falling in unison, the constellation of village lights (I can still see it, high up on the mountain, through the shadows and the leaves), and the certainty I now have that I'll be able to sleep soon, with a roof over my head.

I haven't posed the question yet. I'm not as concerned as I was a few minutes ago. Even so, I bring it up. He says if I'm not too choosy, I don't have to go any farther than his place. This is what I was counting on.

He takes me on a side road. We skirt around an outcrop of rock, and I see a light. We carry on a while longer, turning this way and that, before we arrive. There's an electric lamp on a pole at the entrance to the village. It lights up orchards, gardens full of cabbages, flowers. I look at my companion: He really is a priest but a very young one. I could easily be his father. I can see seven or eight houses at least. He pushes open the gate of a pocket-sized cemetery. We pass through. All at once, we're at his place, in front of his doorway.

He turns on a light. He's a short guy with a dome-shaped head. Like me, he has a good inch of beard. He says, "It's not luxurious, but . . ." There's no need for the "but." Besides, it's just fine.

The cookstove fire hasn't died out yet, and there's some soup.

I look at his books: Catholic stuff and a beginner's guide to chess.

He asks, "You're interested in this?"

"Yes."

"You read?"

I tell him the story of my time at Dr. Ch.'s. He says, "He was crackers!" I tell him, "Well yes, he wasn't completely right in the head, but living out in the country did him a lot of good." For obvious reasons, I've skipped over the business of women. He doesn't need to know everything.

I compliment him on his soup. He's glad. He offers me tobacco, and we each smoke a big pipe while we drink a glass of wine. This is what I like the most. I'm happy to be with this little guy. It's barely nine thirty on his alarm clock.

He says that in a minute we'll put a straw mattress down on the floor. He asks if that's all right. I tell him it's heaven. He claims that heaven is even better. For my part, I think this is exactly what it is. I ask him about his work, whether it's easy or not. According to him, it's great. The people around here are neither pro nor con, except the old folks, who are definitely pro, but there are only three of them. When there's nothing better to do, the young people go along with the old ones. Which is true all winter. The men are peaceful; they don't quarrel. As far as money goes, he couldn't care less. Or more precisely, he says it doesn't matter, and they have plenty of vegetables and firewood. He serves four hamlets on the mountain. He skis. It seems like he's contented, and I'd believe him for sure if he had a steadier gaze.

He's sharp. He can tell what I'm thinking. He says he's found a good way to get the young ones involved. He concentrates on the little boys and girls. This year he managed to send them to summer camp. The kids came back three weeks ago, after they'd made a trip to the sea. Since then he's been king of the castle. They talk about nothing but the sea. But he also has six teenagers to look after, fifteen- to seventeen-year-olds. He bought a soccer ball and got them practicing in a meadow. They couldn't be any keener. They're trying to start a team. As for him, his love is rugby. But naturally he's steering them toward soccer.

He asks what I do. I tell him. He poses some specific questions. I pose some of my own because he seems to know which end is up. It's clear, for example, when he talks about work—and how it connects to the happiness you feel or don't feel—that he knows what he's talking about. He's the youngest from a family of six, still farming in a mountain valley. He reminds me of Thomas, especially when he drinks. Like him, he grips his glass firmly and he has the same way of licking his lips. He enjoys his second pipe, the way you should. I do the same.

He hears my confession, discreetly. But not because it's his job. I'm willing to expose my weaknesses. I can tell he has something at the back of his mind. What interests him is that he's found somebody like-minded. He wants to know why I left my last job. It's no mystery: From time to time, I like to move on. It's that simple. He asks me, "But what about winter?"

"In the winter, I manage to stay in one place."

For a minute, he smokes away in silence. I sense he's about to change the subject. I wait. It comes from an unexpected angle. He talks about people who are completely at peace.

Are there any? I don't ask him straight-out. I tell him an old tale in a casual way, leaving out all the unsavory details (for obvious reasons).

If I knew just what sort of peace we were talking about, I could do better, but I'm watching my step. I don't tip my hand in any direction. The fellow I describe (it's me) is truly at peace. I go even farther. I portray this fellow as having been plagued by all sorts of problems, in specific places. I name names. I end up singing my own praises without getting to share in any of the glory. My pipe—I'm drawing on it gently—helps me relax into such modest states, given the right surroundings.

He's not convinced. He wonders if it's fact or fiction. Even so, I'm sure I've hit the right note. He wants to hear more, but he's being extremely cautious about saying so. He goes so far as to look for an answer from God. I believe it's because he's lost his composure or run out of patience, or he's on the verge of throwing caution to the wind. Because there's something he wants really badly. I can tell.

Up until now, we'd been talking and passing the time like a couple of countrymen. Now it's different. If we made ourselves clear, things would move along briskly, but each of us has his own personal interest. I get the impression that virtue isn't really what he's after. But I'm not going to be the one to tell him so.

He uses big words. Now that he's keeping his eyes fastened on me, he seems very timid. I'm sure he's wondering if what he's saying would go over well with his father and his brothers. I don't move, I listen, I even drink in his words. But he knows it wouldn't go over well with them, and it doesn't go over well with me either.

At last, he stands up and says we'll put this straw mattress down on the floor, you must be tired.

We lay it out alongside a chest of drawers. I'll be just fine. While I'm bending over, arranging my jacket as a pillow, I take the opportunity to say, "If you happen to know somebody who needs a man who's truly at peace, Father, I might fit the bill. Winter's not far off."

"Would you like another glass?"

"Yes. Gladly."

He tells me about a lady who lives alone in the country, who might need a truly peaceful man to do heavy chores around her house.

It's right up my alley.

"How old is the lady?"

"An old lady."

He might not have a clear idea of the age when a woman starts to be old. But no, I'm the one who has it wrong. He tells me she's almost eighty. After her stroke, her doctors recommended quiet and country living. She lives in a pleasant spot.

We go to bed and we sleep.

In the morning, while he says Mass I split some firewood. He comes back. He's made the coffee. We drink it. I ask him for three or four raw potatoes.

"They'll keep me going. I have nothing left to snack on. I can roast them. Once you leave here, where do you get to? Is there any place to pick up some supplies?"

I turn down the bread and cheese he offers. I have some money, I show it to him. I take only the potatoes.

Given what he says about the road ahead, I figure I can get away from here pretty quickly and find some open country. I put the key question back on the table. "About the lady, would you write a note on my behalf, Father? I'll stop in and have a look on my way and see if the job suits me. Why not?"

He sits down at the table and writes.

A priest's letter: It's always a good thing to have. He hands it to me, unsealed. "Seal it, please, Father."

Morning agrees better with this little guy. Last night on the road, he'd turned my stomach with his talk about *Christian death*. All in all, he's been very kind. I thank him in a tone that fits perfectly with the books I've seen on his shelf.

His village isn't bad either. It clings, along with some trees, to one hell of a slope. They've built low stone walls around the houses to hold back patches of soil where they've planted flowers. Right now, in one of these hanging gardens, a young woman is pinning laundry to a wire. This brings things back down to earth.

I think about the woman with the apples, from yesterday evening. I enjoy seeing people in the prime of life. When she tossed me the apple, she looked like a twenty-year-old.

After I get through a bit of underbrush, where it's chilly and damp, I make it back to the highway. It slopes down through a fir plantation managed by foresters—a real park.

Fall keeps on being good company for me today. I scan the mountain on the opposite side, in vain, for traces of the hamlet whose lights I saw last night. Everything's covered in beech forests. Seen from here, the world is made of copper from top to bottom. Through the trees in front of me I catch a bit of really blue sky. What more do you need? In the morning everything's beautiful.

I stroke my beard. It's the season when I let it grow. But it's still only five days' worth. This happens on its own without my having to think about it. So I'd be wrong not to count my blessings. In two weeks, I'll look magnificent.

I come to a clearing and I sit down. For a while, I watch leaves falling from some beech trees, one by one, without any wind. They're red and they glide down very slowly. More had fallen in the past few days, and the grass is covered with them. They've soaked up moisture, and they're giving off a scent that makes me think of heaps of soothing things. I could stay here all day.

Slowly but surely, the sun brightens and warms this spot where I'm resting. As the light reaches each tree, it touches off a shower of leaves so dense, they sound like rain. Here come the birds. There's the famous blue one with the fat beak, the one that searches for beech nuts. It flits through the golden canopy so fast, all you see is a length of thread. A robin, with its winter plumage on already—it looks like a chunk of brick—hops around in the grass. I'm enjoying myself. Most of all, I never get tired of this scent of dead leaves and mushrooms. It's almost better than the aroma of tobacco.

After this, I head off. And while I'm heading off, I smoke.

The road finally reaches the floor of the valley. It runs through trembling aspens to a little bridge. I already hear the water purring.

I see a guy sitting on the boulders next to the rushing stream. At first, I think he's fishing. Seeing how early it is, this would be surprising. As I get closer, I can make out he's holding a guitar between his legs.

I ask him, "What are you up to?"

He raises his head; he has a nasty gaze. A moment later, he answers, "I'm fixing this, see." He's carving a tuning peg with his knife. He's a young guy. I don't like the way he looks. But I'm watching his skillful hands, and I stick around.

He asks if I'm going to the fair. I tell him I didn't know there was a fair. I want to speak nicely to him. He's tanned. His hair is curly. He looks like a girl and he's strong. Right away, his gaze was so off-putting, I want to see it again. I don't think he made it nasty on purpose. It was just his natural look.

I'm standing next to him. Just like I felt a while ago in the clearing, I have no desire to leave. He's pushed in the peg he carved, and now he's checking the strings, one after another. While I'm listening to the notes they make, I really enjoy watching his hands.

"You want me to play something for you?" he asks.

"Yes, go on."

I regret that I'm not wearing my full growth of beard.

I like what he plays, a lot. It feels like it's me talking. This is how I talk sometimes. Right away, I have a heavy heart, and it feels good.

Finally, he stands up and says, "Come." And I go.

He's slung his guitar over his shoulder. We walk side by side. The road climbs through alpine vineyards. The grapes aren't ripe. We try eating some. They're sour.

"Do you work on a farm around here?" he says.

"No."

"What do you do?"

"I look for a job wherever I can find one."

"Have you found one?"

"Not yet."

"If you want, I can give you one."

"What would that be?"

"Come with me to the fair."

I gather some details about this fair. According to him, it's the biggest one of the year in the whole region. I'd like to find out more about him too, but I hold back. For sure, he'll only tell me lies. In a way, that's what I'd prefer. If he told me the truth, I'm afraid it would make me sick.

He asks if I know the score. I say no. He answers, "That's amazing for someone your age."

"It has nothing to do with age. I've never learned."

He laughs. He's not talking about sheet music.

He's been drifting around the district for a couple of months. He runs dance parties in the hamlets. He rakes in more than five hundred francs on a Sunday, with nothing but his instrument. But it's his dealing on the side that nets him the most. He asks if I play cards. I tell him yes. He says I don't. I insist I do. He says, "I'll show you later."

We keep climbing through the little vineyards. I say it's a blessing to be out in the sunshine. I even tell him it's nice to be together. He tells me this part of the country has had it. He's not interested in hanging around here any longer. I don't see anything not to like about this red and green hillside we're climbing in no particular hurry. He disagrees.

He tells me he spent last night in a little bistro. And from what he says and where he points, it could be in that mountain village—the one whose lights I saw twinkling last night. They were whooping it up until four in the morning. He tells me about two women: a mother and daughter. That high up, he says, it's always a cinch. The loggers had been paid that day. Everything ran like clockwork.

He's reached behind his back, and he's drumming his fingers on the belly of the guitar. It's so much easier to walk to a beat!

We come to a village where people are getting ready to head out for the grape harvest. They must be the owners of those vineyards we've just been climbing through. They've brought horses and wagons out from every stable. They're hitching up, and van engines are roaring. In front of the houses, they've piled crates, baskets, basins, and big glass vessels. The women are wearing headscarves of every color.

If it wasn't for him, I'd be happy to stick around here for a while. There'd be enough to do to earn your room and board for a day or two, working at something enjoyable and satisfying. All the same, it's not what's on his mind, and I'm not about to mention it.

The girls find his guitar fascinating. But we take off. I must say, I'm so glad I willingly give up the idea of buying a few slices of sausage.

Once we're far enough past the village, he makes me stop at a spring, underneath some willows at the edge of a meadow. "I'm hung over," he says. He takes huge gulps of water, enough to bust his gut. He's choking on it. I have all the time in the world to admire his nasty look.

He asks me if I noticed the girl in the headscarf, when we went by just now. No. I just saw them all together as a group. He did notice her and he describes her to me. If she's like he says, then yes, I missed out on something. But I doubt it. He avoids looking straight at me. There are plenty of things about him that annoy me. I wouldn't want this kind of man as a friend.

The road runs level through meadows covered in crocuses. I love these flowers and the thoughts that come to mind when I see them. There are some fairy rings too. I go and do some digging, and I come back with a fine bunch of white mushrooms.

"What the fuck are you going to do with those?" he says.

"Eat them, my friend."

"You'll get the runs"

"You must be joking! I know them inside out. I've been eating them for ten years now."

I tell him that all field mushrooms are as good as gold. It's safe to pick any of them. I wish he'd ask me to fill him in about mushrooms—I could amaze him.

Now we're skirting along some groves of mountain pine. Their trunks are the color of red wine. Everything about autumn makes me feel good.

A motorbike is coming up from behind. My guy plants himself in the middle of the road and waves. It's a big motorcycle. It comes to a stop, and the rider puts a foot down. He's young. My guy comes up and says, "Give me a lift." "Hop on." In the blink of an eye, he's gone. He has just enough time to call out, "Come to the fair."

I'm dumbstruck. He's been whisked off from right under my nose...I can't get over it!

I walk on for a while. I'm starting to get tired, even though the road goes downhill. At a bend, I can see I'm almost directly overlooking the roofs of a village. I'm going to buy some bread.

And there he is: right on cue, in front of the bakery with his guitar.

"You thought I was leaving you behind?"

"I didn't think anything. This is as far as the guy was going..."

"No, he was going a lot farther. But I jumped off to wait for you."

This isn't true, because I notice the motorbike on its stand in front of the café on the square. Unless it happens to be a different bike. And he sees that I can see it.

I go into a grocery shop. I buy a bag of black olives, some sausage, a tin of sardines, and a liter of wine. They take a ten-franc deposit on the bottle, and I don't put up a fight.

He's waiting for me outside. He hasn't picked up any bread. I'm going to go look for some.

We choose a wonderful spot. We're sitting side by side in the shade of a beech tree at the edge of a meadow, at the foot of a spring. The wine is cooling in the basin. Life is good!

"Cook up your mushrooms," he says.

I explain that they're better raw, with a pinch of salt.

"I want to see you eat them."

I do, right away. I peel one, slice it, add some salt, and I eat it.

"Again."

I start another one. What's he's waiting for? They're really good. I eat them all the time. I'd like him to taste this fragrance. It's like roses. I hold one out to him.

"No, you go ahead."

He says something about poison mushrooms, but he doesn't know what he's talking about. I tell him you don't always die instantly. Sometimes it's a day later.

He sees one that's different from the others. He points to it. "Eat this one."

I do, gladly.

At last, he gets tired of the subject. He pulls a switchblade out of his pocket. It makes a loud snap. He opens the tin of sardines.

We lay out a meal fit for a king. I have only one concern: We might be short of bread. But we make do. Same with the wine—we pass the bottle back and forth two or three times. I load up a pipe. He smokes an American cigarette. I'd like to ask him to play a little on his guitar, but he says, "So you think you know how to play cards?"

"Not just think so, I know so."

"We'll see."

He rummages through his pockets and pulls out a deck. I say, "Wait five minutes. We're smoking. We're doing fine."

He spreads his jacket out on the grass and says, "Watch."

He lays out the three-card trick, lickety-split. I break up laughing. I know how this works. I let him cool down a little; then as soon as I can tell his fingers are up to something sneaky, I pounce on a card like I'd pounce on a rat.

"What's your bet?"

"Ten francs."

"The house does not deal in petty sums."

He's ripe for the picking, but I'd rather not rob his cash. I refuse to raise my bet. He calls me a hick and a skinflint, but I stick to my ten francs. I don't want any of his money. I'm sure of my card.

We turn it over: I've lost.

He plays the trick five or six more times. Every time, I'm sure of my card. Every time, I lose. I know he's cheating. He takes me for a hundred and seventy francs. On the last round, I bet fifty francs. Now I'd like to win, but he's too quick and I lose. I quit. I would have been happy to have a thousand francs in my pocket—I'd have bet them all just to watch him play.

He says, "That one's just for kids. Do you want to see the grown-ups' game?"

Of course I do. He asks how much I'm staking. I'm tempted to tell him a hundred francs and impress him. Poverty holds me back. He tells me he's never seen anybody so stingy, and he asks what I'm planning to do with my cash. When he talks, pure white saliva builds up in the corners of his mouth. I feel sorry for him and I think, since I've come this far, I might as well risk another ten francs. "I'm going to call you 'Ten Francs,'" he says. "I've never worked for this little. Never mind. Watch."

So now he starts shuffling his deck of cards like he's pushing and pulling on an accordion. He bangs it, squeezes it, slaps it, strokes it, opens the bellows, pushes them back in. He calls out, "King of spades, seven of diamonds, three of hearts, king of clubs, queen of hearts, nine of spades, two of diamonds." Every time, the card he calls out falls. He flings the deck at the basin of the spring, and just as it's about to fall in, it reassembles in his hands. He spreads it out under my nose, like a fan, a horseshoe, a wheel, an arrow. He makes cards flow from his right hand to his left, like showers, like drops, like waterfalls. He talks to them. He calls them by name. They stand up all on their own, away from the rest of the deck, advance, retreat, hop. He tells some dirty jokes to the queen of hearts, and the queen of hearts jumps right onto his drooling lips. He says the king of clubs is jealous, and lo and behold, here he comes. He really does look jealous. You could even say he looks like a fighting cock. Then there's a big dustup between the kings, queens, and jacks. It's a high-speed comedy!

I'm slack-jawed.

He goes after the queen of diamonds; she's up his sleeve. He mentions the jack of spades, and pulls him out of his shoe. He answers the queen of clubs, who looks like she's filling his ear with secrets; and yes, she's actually sitting on his ear. Other cards peep out from under his shirt, his collar, the fly of his trousers, his belt. They flash their suit—heart, diamond, club, or spade—go in, come out, disappear, take off to who knows where. I'm not sure which way to look anymore. He claps his hands, and the whole deck is there in his palm.

Then he clicks his heels, closes his eyes, and makes himself as stiff as a fence post.

"Name the suit," he says, "and I'll give it to you."

While I'm calling out the cards, I don't recognize my own voice anymore. No sooner have I asked for one than he hands it to me or else drops it at my feet, or else the deck he controls drops it at my feet of its own accord. I've never been as satisfied as I am right now. And this lasts for so long, I almost can't bear it and I tell him to quit. But he carries on as though I don't even exist. And in the end, I enjoy seeing him take pleasure in it.

When he stops, I pull twenty francs out of my pocket, but he says, "No, hold on to them."

I do hold on to them, but it doesn't feel good.

In the evening, we arrive in G., where the Saint Luke's Day fair starts tomorrow. It's a big market town built on a mountainside. The highway passes right through it. There's a lot of traffic. My pal and I watch the comings and goings. They have nothing to do yet with the fair. Tour buses are pulling in to a narrow square for a ten-minute rest stop. The passengers get off and go to ask the serving girl at the café if they can use the toilet. Afterward, they sit and have a drink while they take in their surroundings.

During the short time we stay in the square, some long-distance buses arrive and depart. They're luxurious and they're all different colors. Some are bound for as far away as Paris or Milan. Inside the ones headed for Paris, everything is spotless—the equipment and the drivers, as well as the passengers. The cabins are filled with electric light, and the buses drive slowly down the narrow street, barely making a sound. They glide away, bearing their cargo of women and men, all of them colorful and gleaming.

I go into a public urinal to count my cash. I'm almost broke. I rejoin my buddy and I ask, "What now?" He answers, "Do whatever you want and leave me the hell alone. I've had my plans for a long time, and I don't need to drag a hick like you around with me." We quarrel, but he easily has the last word and he takes off.

I watch him leave. I follow him for a few steps, to see where he's headed. He goes into the same café as the bus passengers.

I look for an inn where the market vendors stay. I find one in a side street. I have enough cash left for tonight. I ask how much a room costs. I can afford it. I'm not hungry. I drink a glass of wine. There aren't a lot of people around. I notice a tall guy who's ordered a bowl of soup. I try to figure out what he sells. I stop the waitress. She's an older woman, and I know how to talk to her. She tells me he's a regular. He sells needles and thread from a little stall, and he doesn't need a hand, that's for sure.

The other people in here don't look any more likely to help me out. I'm peeved because after I've paid for the wine and the room, I won't have enough left to buy a packet of tobacco. I lost more than I realized at cards. I can still get two pipes out of the shreds I have left. I decide I'll smoke one in bed and the other tomorrow morning. I make the glass of wine last a little longer.

I shouldn't have chosen this respectable inn. The people who stay here must be farmers from the district who've used tomorrow's fair as an excuse to come to town the day before and have dinner served to them. They have no need of me— on the contrary.

So this is my situation, and I couldn't possibly convince anyone that there's any wine left in my glass, when I see a dapper gentleman step into the room. He doesn't belong here at all. He's wearing a smart overcoat, and a hat that looks like it landed on his head all on its own, without ever being touched by human hands. He walks straight up to the waitress. He talks to her. She listens to him with attention. Then she turns and looks at me. The gentleman looks at me and comes in my direction.

He asks if I want to *keep busy* tomorrow. I say yes. He studies me. Do I know how to drive a tractor? I'm very good at driving tractors. I also have my trucker's license and I show it to him. The gentleman pulls out a chair, sits down across from me, and fills me in. He's the agent for an American make of farm machinery and tractors. He has a whole line to exhibit tomorrow morning at the fair. To start with, I'd have to get there early. He explains what's involved. It's easy, and I tell him I'm really good at this sort of thing. At first, I'd be passing out leaflets. After that, he's rented a field and I'd have to do some demonstrations.

Do I want to take this on? It fits me like a glove. So agreed, and he gets up. I tell him there's one thing left to sort out: the money. How much? He offers two hundred francs. But I tell him trucker's licenses don't grow on trees. He tells me he could find as many young guys as he wants, to try out his machines for free. They're red, they're beautiful, and they stir up a lot of interest (now he's really giving me the sales pitch). I tell him I'm familiar with the make he represents, and I know if you don't go easy you're likely to bust some fragile parts. I mention one of these, and I also mention a maneuver that his excited young farmers will be certain to screw up. He can tell I know what I'm talking about.

He sits down again, orders two glasses of wine, and says he'll go as high as four hundred. I sigh and tell him I want the daily rate for a specialist, no less, no more. And what would that be? That would be eight hundred francs. He kicks up a fuss and makes out like he's going to get up, but his glass is full. He isn't about to leave it. But seeing as he isn't drinking, I figure he's staying for a different reason altogether, and I hold firm. We end up agreeing to six hundred and fifty, from seven in the morning till seven in the evening, because we'll have to return the machines to his hotel garage after the demonstration. But there's no chance for an advance.

In spite of everything, I feel better. If nothing else, this business has given me some credit in the establishment. The waitress, who seems to be the owner after all, asks me if I've taken the job. I tell her yes and I rise in her esteem. I decide to smoke my two bowls of shreds right now. I'll buy some more tobacco before I go to bed.

I allow myself the luxury of glancing at the newspaper headlines, but I can't concentrate. I watch two guys playing a game of checkers. The waitress asks if I'm going to the movies. I tell her no, I'm going to bed in a minute. In fact, I'm not sleepy. I'd be capable of walking all night. But when I think about it, this makes no sense, because I want to stay here.

Next thing you know, in comes my guitar-playing buddy. Unbelievable! How did he know I was here? Or did he come in just by chance? It's not just by chance that he's searched high and low for me. I'm overjoyed. Things couldn't be better.

Before I know it, I've ordered a liter of wine. It's only when I see the bottle that I think about paying for it. I say, "Hang on, I'm going to take a leak." I leave the room, and in a corner I count my change. I have enough for the liter of wine as long as I don't buy any tobacco. And above all, as long as they'll let me have until tomorrow evening to pay for my room. But I don't think this should be a problem.

I come back in. And I'm happy as can be to realize my

buddy was worried about me disappearing, that he's glad to see me again. I ask what he's been up to in the meantime. He says, "I went looking for you." I feel good, really at peace. He's smoking his American cigarettes. I say, "Toss me one."

"Not for your kisser. They cost me thirty francs a pack."

I say to him nicely, "You lovely bastard."

He doesn't drink like Thomas or like me. He picks up his glass with a kind of grimace, and each mouthful of wine seems to go down sideways into some sensitive place. Apart from that, he knocks it back like everybody else. If he finds the wine acidic, he must like acidic things, because he funnels it down just as fast as I do.

I confess: At this time of day, I go at it with the best of them. Wine fits my state of mind. I have a nice, easy job tomorrow, and tonight my buddy's here to keep me company. I don't need anything else.

Finally, eleven rolls around, and it's time to go to bed. I ask if he's found a place to stay. He tells me no, everything's full. I go straight up to the waitress. "Come over here for a second, we have to ask you something." She comes, and I explain that this guy's my buddy and he hasn't found a room. Is there any way around this?

It's awkward. Everything's full. Unless I have him share with me.

"Not in my bed—no way—but in my room, why not?"

"If you sort it out between yourselves, it won't bother me."

We go upstairs and we sort it out. I pull the mattress onto the floor for him, and I take the box spring.

The light hasn't been out five minutes before the springs start digging into my side. I have to turn over, and this makes a hell of a racket.

"What are you up to?" he asks. "Where are you going?"

I was already pretty foggy. I come out of it and I say, "What? Where do you think I'm going? I'm turning over, and that's that."

When I'm half asleep, I hear his switchblade snap open. What an idiot this guy is! And I doze off.

A nightmare wakes me up. I was dreaming it was raining. My job was completely screwed up. No dough, no tobacco, debts to pay. Obliged to skip town. And worst of all, do a bad turn to the waitress, who had faith in me.

But no, it's dawn. And it's not raining. It's a fountain down in the square making the sound that fooled me.

He's even more of an idiot than I thought. Isn't he sleeping with his knife open in his hand?

The gray light of dawn is on his face. He's not a pretty sight. The girls might be attracted to him but surely not the guys. A thread of saliva has crusted on his lips. They're clenched like when he's getting ready to play a card trick. Even so, he's asleep.

I doze for another half hour, bounced around like I'm in a dump truck jumping over cobblestones, and then I get up. I don't make a sound. I slip out. I'm not taking off for good. I leave my rucksack behind. I'm going to work.

Downstairs, I have the waitress all to myself. The rest of the house is fast asleep. She's making coffee, and she looks much older than she did last night in the lamplight. I stretch myself beside her stove. She doesn't mind having a man standing close by, warming himself, first thing in the morning.

We chat. I talk about the work I'm going to do. She tells me the gentleman in the spiffy hat can be trusted. She agrees to let me wait until tonight to pay my bill.

I'm in fine form, and I talk about how I'm going to let my

beard grow and keep it on all winter like I usually do. She says it will suit me well.

I go out. It's chilly. The sky's clear like it's been for days, and it's a pleasing shade of green. The lane smells of vine shoots and coffee. On the main square, the market vendors are already pitching their tents. At this early hour, the canvas makes squeaking sounds, like mice. There's a strong odor of corduroy and tin.

I get to the meeting place. The machines are here. They're Mathewsons. Their clutches are a bit stiff. I'm used to these tractors. They're stripped down to the limit. They tend to flip over when they're going uphill. In my opinion, they aren't built for the kind of country we're in. They belong on flatlands with no ups and downs. Apart from that, they're not bad gear.

I'm circling around these red grasshoppers when the gentleman in the spiffy hat arrives. He shakes my hand. He seems like a decent guy. Last night, I hadn't noticed his dazed look. It warms me to him.

He asks what I think of them. I share my thoughts, backed up by experience.

Have I ever operated Mathewsons before? Yes, I worked with these rigs at Mas-Thibert in the Camargue. In light soil they run like a charm. But I get him to see where, in my opinion, they fall short. I point out the hitches—they're flexible, perfect for level ground. But can he imagine drawing an implement with one of these on an upslope? What will happen? I point out how narrow the engine is. Doesn't that tell him something? Get up onto the seat. He gets up and tells me he can see very well what will happen. The tractor will rear up off the ground.

It will tilt back. And if the guy who's driving is too sure

of himself and pushes it too hard, he'll find himself on his back, with his four hooves in the air and a ton of scrap metal on his chest.

But there's a way around this. I haven't lost faith in this system yet—I'll be able to keep flogging it until tomorrow. I guarantee him: For today, it will do the job. But in the long run, he should warn his customers to have a sturdier hitch forged: a bar of steel that will slide in right here under the pin and fasten here with a nut. Then there'll be no more chance of rearing back; it's like a crutch for the tractor.

He's an experienced guy and he really gets it. He asks if I smoke. Yes I do, when I have tobacco. On the spot, he gives me a hundred francs, and I race away. I come back. He's taken off his fancy hat and he's stuck his head sideways under the hitch. He pulls his head out and offers me a swig of white wine. I keep a close eye on the way he picks up and holds his hat. I've noticed that he handles it on the inside. He has a few tricks up his own sleeve too.

Buses and cars are arriving every minute. People in their Sunday best are getting out. There's a big crowd and lots of activity. The gentleman gives me detailed instructions on how to hand out his leaflets. He tells me to go back and forth through the fairgrounds until ten or eleven o'clock. After that, we'll head off in a convoy to the field where the demonstration is supposed to happen. It's on the edge of town, right at the turnoff.

We go back to our machines. There's a heavy trenching plow. This is the one I'm going to operate first. One trench will do. The toughest job will be the four-furrow plow. Naturally, we won't be doing anything with the reaper-binder. All of the equipment is pretty and it's lined up nicely in full sunlight. The colors leap out—they tempt you. There's already a big crowd. The gentleman is quick to hand me my bundle of leaflets, and he starts in with his sales pitch. I'm going to stroll around.

There's a huge crowd. I stuff leaflets into everyone's hands. Women, girls, children, old people—they're all passing by. I wander down lanes lined with every kind of stall. My mind is on my tractor. I'd like there to be lots of people there to watch me do my maneuvers. So far, so good—they're fighting over my leaflets like they're hotcakes, but that doesn't mean a thing. I know they can't resist a handout, especially one with a picture, and even better, with a picture of any kind of machinery.

I wonder what my artist friend is up to, whether he's finally woken up and discovered what an idiot he is, all alone with his switchblade open in his hand.

I get a good blast of fairground air, and now it smells of face powder. I see girls of every shape and size, every height and color. Some arm in arm, some in gangs, some with mothers dressed in mourning but also very determined, who head straight to the kitchenware stalls. There are two or three loudspeakers blaring out a god-awful racket of brass-band dance music, and hucksters are squabbling and interrupting each other over the heads of the crowd.

I play my role in the midst of all this, savoring a nice pipe at the same time. I get jostled around. People elbow me in the side and step on my feet. But I'm the kind of person who knows how to enjoy being in the thick of a crowd. We're all looking at each other from so close up—both men and women—we can't take anything seriously. And I actually break up laughing. I hand out my leaflets cheerfully. I have a word for the grandfather, a word for the mother, a word for the daughter. They all take me for what I am: a guy who's ready for action and good at heart. What a pity I'm not wearing my full beard!

In one corner there's an accordion meowing like a cat, and I think again about my artist. Shouldn't he be here too, strumming away on his guitar? Something tells me he's not. And in fact, I cover the whole fairground, but I don't see him.

I keep on going as far as the inn. They tell me he came downstairs and went out.

I still have some time before I start. For a while, I stroll along the side streets and the boulevards. You can feel the excitement everywhere. They're selling exceptionally fine-looking pigs in a tiny square full of squeals and shouts. The cafés are spewing and swallowing batches of men in tall felt hats. Shop doors are opening nonstop. Clerks come every second to take away items on show in the storefronts. Every window display is magnetic and attracts a whole cluster of onlookers, like iron filings. I listen, all around me, to the come-ons of the hawkers. They're selling whetstones, lighters (which, by the way, do appeal to me), bundles of rope, ballpoint pens that can write underwater (young guys get excited by gadgets like these), American overalls, army surplus fur-lined jackets (another of my weaknesses; they make my mouth water; I feel like I'm already wrapped in one of them, warm and snug, but they're fifteen thousand francs, so no way!), safety razors, perfumes, even books—all of them ten francs apiece—which I allow myself the luxury of rummaging through, but nothing interests me. I don't see my artist anywhere. And now it's time to climb in the saddle.

A lot of people have gathered around our machines. As soon as he sees me, the gentleman gets the crowd to let me pass through, and I join him in the middle of the circle.

They're all looking at me like I'm some kind of rare specimen. And when I get up on the seat, I do feel like a real somebody. I get off to a smooth start, and we head to the field for the demonstration.

I (or let's say, to be more exact, it's this huge, red grasshopper I'm riding, and the two plows trailing me with their shares rearing up like angels' wings)—I'm the most powerful magnet in the whole fair. I drive across the grounds. People step aside and then fill in right behind. The barkers fall silent as I go by. There are only the loudspeakers providing me with a little brass-band accompaniment. For anyone with a romantic spirit (like yours truly) this is a moment to savor.

And I make the most of it. I maneuver around in the midst of all this like God the Father himself. I'd give my whole day's wages if my artist buddy, with his guitar and his decks of cards, could be somewhere nearby to get an eyeful of this rare spectacle.

The field where I'm supposed to perform my drill is surrounded by towering poplars. The ground is flatter than I imagined. My gentleman has good instincts. Right away, I can see the direction where I'll have the most success.

There's a little speechmaking, and then it's over to me. A first go with the trenching plow. At a glance, I've seen that the soil here is easy to work. It's going to go along with me. I get myself into position. I activate the gigantic plow, and it lowers to the ground. I set my sights on a red mountain ash directly opposite, and I make a beeline for it. All this has happened in a matter of seconds. Nobody should notice that I'm here. The machine has to do all the work. I believe I've played the game to perfection.

At first, I'm all alone out in the field. To my rear, everybody has quieted down. All I hear is the smooth sound of this obliging soil opening up just the way I dreamed it would. Then out of the corner of my eye, I see a man in a big felt hat come up—his head and mine at the same level—and he keeps on walking beside me. Then another comes up on the other side. And now while I don't lose sight of the mountain ash I'm using as a target, my side view is completely cut off by a billowing cloud of more than a hundred felt hats. I've pulled everyone along with me. They're all leaning over the plowshare and the deep trench it's digging. When I reach the end, I swing around. Now we get to see how well I've done. I've cut a trench as straight as an arrow. Hats off all around. I let go of my grip on the wheel.

After this, the furrowing plow is child's play. The whole crowd keeps escorting me back and forth for hours. They can't get enough of the sight of this soil as it slices open and flops over like butter.

We take a break for a snack. I wonder what my artist is up to. I would have been glad to give him an idea of what it means to work. He could have taken my slipping out this morning the wrong way, even though I was only trying to let him sleep—him and his idiotic knife. Maybe he's hit the road again.

I'm feeling blue. Like they do everywhere, the roads from here lead everywhere. It's impossible to hold on to anything or anyone. We grow attached, but we can't hold on.

My gentleman is sitting next to me on the grass, in the shelter of the hedge. He's bravely peeling the sausage with his fingers. Each of us has a glass, and we're drinking the hotel wine. It's not bad.

I ask for a short break, just a half hour, and he agrees. I race over to the inn. The artist hasn't shown up to eat. I go to the room. He hasn't left anything behind. This makes sense—today's a good day to make use of his guitar.

I head back to my red grasshoppers. Another crowd has already gathered to watch, but it looks like they'll be more relaxed this time, at least as far as I'm concerned. It seems as if the ground I've already worked—it stands out clearly in the field—will do for now. The big felt hats go and lean over the furrows, then come back and lean over the plowshares, the gears, the cables, and the levers. People ask me questions, and I say what I think. Well, not exactly.

It's almost three o'clock before they ask me to take off again with the four-furrow plow. I start up. I can tell this ground's a little less forgiving. I set my sights on a maple, all copper-colored and shiny, but I have my hands full just keeping it in front of me. I also feel that my tractor's less stable than it was this morning. Whatever the case, I get through it, and it turns out just as well as what I'd already done.

A short guy is negotiating with my gentleman. As soon as I've finished swinging the machine around, he calls me over and I join in the conversation. The short guy is looking to buy. He weighs the pros and cons, backed up by a tall woman who's thin but tough-looking. She's dressed in black like an old lady, even though she can hardly be forty. It's her I enjoy looking at. Her eyes are fastened on me, but they aren't seeing me at all. She steers her husband with nothing but little movements of her head. (I envy men who are this lucky. Call me a fool, but that's how I see it. And this after lots of mature experience and reflection.)

I feel a crazy affection for this stocky little man who's been kneaded into a ball by who knows how many winters and summers, just like his parents before him. When it comes to tractors and plows, he knows what he's talking about. He just has to resist getting carried away by the bright red paint and the straight, deep furrows I've dug.

They're what really interest him. He goes and checks them out. And then he draws me aside. He seems like he's wrapped up in warm wool. His way of talking is calm and full of feeling. He looks straight ahead with beautiful, chestnut-brown eyes. We begin to get a little friendly. His wife keeps an eye on us and lets things move along.

I explain the operation of the tractor before an audience where my little guy is king. After I'm done, he climbs onto the seat. I join him, on the running board, and he starts up. He gets all the way to the far end, following my orders like a kid, but you can't say he's made a very good job of it. Compared to mine, his furrow looks bad, but nobody makes fun of him. They realize you have to get the knack of it. And in the end, everything works out on the farm the way it should, if you make the effort.

The deal is done. It costs a bundle: a hundred thousand francs. I like this couple. He's as good as gold. And she adds just the right alloy to make his gold stand up to everyday wear and tear.

My gentleman calls me over. There must be a snag. He asks if I'm free. Free for what? It's about the little guy, who'd like to hire me for eight or ten days, maybe longer, if we get along. I say I like him well enough and I give my gentleman a smile. He gives me one back. The question of freedom, that's something else. Sure, I'm free, free as the wind. In reality, I didn't plan to hang around here. Plans and actions, they're two different things, I know. But he's taken me a bit off guard. It's often best not to think too far ahead. I know that too. He asks me what's the matter.

Nothing's the matter. It's a young guy I met yesterday.

Just a kid, but I'd rather not leave him behind. I'm kicking myself, hard. This is the kind of thing I come out with only once in a blue moon. I'm so ashamed, I accept the job. I'll go tomorrow. The short guy gives me all the directions to get to his farm, the time of the bus, the name of the crossroads. I'm pinned down. Happiness is a lonely pursuit.

All in all, we've had a runaway success. I drive the machines back to the corral. The fair is over. Night is falling. A bitter wind is stripping the dead leaves off the lindens. The vendors are struggling with tarpaulins, poles, and ropes.

I'm confronted by a sort of lumbering giant, strong as a Turk, wearing an oil-soaked beret. He's drunk as a skunk, but he's staying stupendously upright by keeping his legs spread apart. He tells me I give him a real kick and, well, on a day like this ... Anyway, he still hasn't gotten over seeing the machines in operation. I don't know how he managed to see any of it through the glories of the wine, but judging by his eyeballs, it must have been quite a spectacle. He asks me to help him paint the town red. And right away, I make this my own plan. "Hang on, I'm going to collect my pay, and I'll be back."

My gentleman hands me seven hundred francs. Tomorrow, he'll be delivering the plow and the tractor to the little guy. He suggests he could bring me along. I say, "All right." He'd be more than happy to launch into a glowing description of the farm where we're supposed to be going, but I cut him short and turn to leave. He grabs the tail of my coat and hangs on, mainly to tell me the farm is a true land of plenty. I answer politely enough to get him to loosen his grip.

I've barely gotten away before my big elephant in his beret takes me by the arm. I wonder if I'm dreaming or if I'm already seeing double. There are two of them, each one incredibly tall and wearing the same ridiculous getup: a beret and cavalry pants. I didn't think this sort of thing existed anymore except in the movies.

I find out right away that they're carpenters working for a company that builds timber chalets in the mountains. They proclaim they're inseparable. If I ran into one of them on his own a few minutes ago, it was only because the other one was pissing against a tree. This explanation makes perfect sense to me. They can't stop asking for more details about the red grasshoppers. Anyway, they're so far gone, they wouldn't listen even if they were being blessed by the pope. All I have to do is stay quiet. If the tractors were parked in the town square, this pair would be capable of kicking them around like soccer balls, they're so fired up.

We decide to go all out. There are four bistros around the square, and we're taking on all four of them headfirst. To begin with, we treat ourselves cautiously, with anise. It's only when I'm knocking back my tenth shot that I realize I've hardly eaten anything today, other than the snack of sausage at noon.

I have a brilliant idea. Let's suppose my artist didn't take off but had the good sense to go about his business at the fair. It's most likely I wouldn't have spotted him in that crowd. He could also have signed up with some dance band. I know, I always tend to imagine the worst. Let's suppose instead that the little lamb is sitting peacefully right now waiting for me at the inn, worrying about me the same as I'm worrying about him. This seems as clear as day to me, blinding even. And ever so nice.

For the time being, I'm feeling fit as a fiddle. The anise has barely started steaming in my whiskers. When it comes to keeping balance and passing muster, I could outdo a whole squadron of police chiefs. I could walk a tightrope thirty feet off the ground. In this spirit, and with me in the lead, all three of us head for the inn. I'm a bit shocked not to find the little lamb there. And then it causes me a lot of grief.

I introduce my two elephants to the waitress. Even though she pretends to ignore us—me in particular—she serves us some rosé that's not hard to take. We go at it in good faith, with gusto. I hear the artist hasn't been sighted since he left this morning. Screw him! I couldn't give a damn. So why am I asking about him all the time? Who's asking about him all the time? You. No, you! My two elephants and the waitress stare at me without blinking. I think I'm telling them to go fuck themselves ... and then it all goes blurry and confused for a second or two. Nothing serious, because right away my eyes fill with tears, and everybody's concerned about me. The elephants crush my shoulders with their jabbing. They make me seasick. I bolt outside and throw up. This is followed by a long, chummy conversation about people who can hold their drink and people who can't. I claim I can hold mine, but that they shouldn't have shook me up the way they did. The elephants claim they can be shook up like bottles of Epsom salts. At this point, I pummel them with a vengeance. A dreamy look comes over their eyes, and before you know it, they're belching like bullfrogs. We get thrown out like trash, in the nick of time, and the two of them go into an alleyway to finish retching. I go back at it with them, shoulder to shoulder.

Right afterward, we feel better. We decide to get drunk like men instead of like boys. I should definitely have a bite to eat. We go to a place called Ma Lantifle's, in a narrow lane, off the back of a courtyard. She has some cabbage soup that whets our appetite. No sooner have we sat down in front of our three bowls than I start to talk. My heart is melting.

It's hard to be a world all on your own. There are days when I get there. Tonight I feel like I'll never get there again.

The elephants are upset. I tell them the story of a wonderful buddy of mine—affectionate, loyal, and all—who'd let himself be drawn and quartered for my sake. I crown him with every virtue I can think of. And I reel off deeds he's done where he was brave, honest, sensitive, considerate, caring. The more I talk about him, the more my heart melts.

The elephants are green with envy. It's even made them forget about their cabbage soup. They overwhelm me with questions. What's he like? I tell them. When I talk about the guitar, they run out of breath. I describe the card trick. I lay it on thick, with all my heart. I feel sick.

Suddenly, I don't say another word because I feel, as plain as day, that the glorious buddy I'm talking about is in reality the slimiest bastard on the face of the earth: absolute scum, thief, liar, in it for himself, nastiness incarnate, capable of swindling his own parents, happy as a pig in shit. No matter how thick I lay it on, I still miss him.

We decide to take heroic measures. We're going to search for him. Starting here. We'll comb through the neighborhood. If we don't find him here, away we go. We come up with the most terrific plans. We figure if he took off this morning, walking two or three miles an hour, he couldn't have gone too far. Assuming he must have stopped once or twice, and that by this time of night he must be sleeping like a log in some flophouse, it's easy. If we join forces to catch him, we'll catch him. The elephants declare they can do five miles an hour. I say that's a lot. They say yes, but insist, in all modesty, they can do it. Well, for that matter, so can I. And

I go one better. In the present circumstances, I'm capable of doing six or seven miles an hour. This seems harder for them to digest. So I chew them out. Which makes me feel better. I call them every name under the sun. They're slack-jawed. So am I. I know I'm capable of a lot of things, but at the same time, what I come out with shocks even me, ever so slightly. I say to the two of them, "I had you figured out from day one. You're nothing but a piece of shit. Friendship? Did you think I'd fall for that line of crap? I'd seen through all that before you were even born. Do you know where I'm at now? I'm at the point where phony is all I need. I buy phony stuff. That's where I'm at. I have a ball with phony. I've made it with phony, with my eyes wide open. Figure it out, you piece of shit. You're the one whose pockets are empty."

They're less drunk than I thought. They pretend to stare off into space. They know what it means to be downhearted. They say they can't understand a word of what I'm saying. In any case, we've been stewing long enough inside here, where it stinks of cabbage, and we're going out to get some air.

Being outdoors sobers me up. I say, "Don't pay any attention to my blather, it's just the wine talking." They share this opinion. And at the same time, they have one of their own: That it's now time to get seriously plastered.

We get right down to it. We launch an attack with shot glasses. We line them up like pieces of artillery. And the bombardment commences. We cover the town from top to bottom, from side to side. There isn't a bistro or bar that can boast of escaping our notice. We even hit the sleaziest dives, in blind alleys, under porches, in the depths of courtyards packed with bleating goats. At one point, we wind up in the shop of a low-life dressmaker who serves us a disgusting brandy from the base of her sewing machine ... We're fucked if we can say why we're in this place or how we got here. Or how we've managed to get out.

Every once in a while, we cross a boulevard where the tall trees are more ink-black than the dark sky. Where nothing's happening. Nothing. There's a foul wind dragging its pile of dried grass and leaves around just to show off. My two buddies and I know only too well what it's like to be treated this way, day in, day out. When we pass under streetlights, I see our ugly mugs and nobody's laughing. We go into some private houses where my two guys supposedly have friends. It's late, and everybody's gone to bed. But as soon as we knock, and they realize the kind of shape we're in, they get up and open the door. They bring us into the kitchen and serve us—on our feet—shots of brandy, one after another, and they charge us a fair price. After that, they try to find ways to throw us out, and they always succeed. We go from house to house and from bistro to bistro. What is it we're hoping to find?

Now I've really hit my stride. I'm wide awake from head to toe. I'd be capable of counting the feathers of a quilt in the blink of an eye. I feel the paving stones giving way underfoot, and I lean into the wind. There's no need any more to stand up straight; I can get by very well on a slant.

Now we're in deadly earnest. This is the moment that really counts. There's nothing more glorious than walking full tilt, not giving a flying fuck about anything or anyone else in the world. You are somebody.

We've been in this bistro ten times already. We come in again. This time, the door at the far end is open. There's a ruckus going on in the back room. You can't seriously think we'd miss the chance to get involved. All three of us get closer and—oh my, do we ever like what we see! A bunch of guys are brawling, or more to the point, they're all beating up on one guy. And that one guy is the artist, flesh and blood! I have to admit, when I realize it's him, for a split second I'm glad to see him getting socked right in the kisser. But a second later, I'm already next to him and I've shoved him behind my back, out of harm's way. I couldn't be prouder. We've turned up at just the right moment.

I must have taken a punch. It feels like it. But I'm not sure. My side facing the brawlers is numb. On the side the artist is clinging to, I still feel something. I can tell his hands are clutching my jacket.

I'm too far above crude shenanigans, right now, to concern myself with taking or giving punches. I simply shove back the fanatics, and I talk. I talk loud. And for sure I talk well. I'm dousing the fire. I just have to fend off one of the more ferocious ones, who looks like he wants a little more action.

My two elephants are helping us gain the upper hand. They're thrilled with this interlude. And they're acting like it's child's play. They've hurled their big paws right into the thick of it. I see two or three cowboys who've been bucked right off their saddles. They're trying to shake the ringing out of their ears.

Now it's a matter of making ourselves understood, relying on our God-given power of speech. Everybody's talking at once. I take advantage of this to take a look at the artist. He's as white as a sheet and he's bleeding from the nose. I couldn't be happier. I say to him, "So what now, shithead?" But with great kindness. He's glued to me like a louse. He'd give anything in the world for me to keep protecting him. What a night!

All the same, not counting the artist, my two elephants, and myself, there are nine cowboys in the room, and they're all revved up. You see nothing but mustaches, beards, and gaping mouths. They're all shouting and baring their teeth. I notice two or three who are built like weight lifters. The rest are just wimps: ninety-eight-pound weaklings, two feet tall. They yap, but if it was a matter of really getting down to business, they'd jump out the window. But the weight lifters—hang on a minute—that's a whole other story. And what's more, there are four of them.

So this is where things stand. I turn on all my charm: sweet looks and smooth talk. What a shame I'm not wearing my beautiful beard! At times like this it comes in handy. All the same, I'm making headway. Best of all, I land a clean punch on the little pest who keeps coming back on the attack. Now he's had it. Even his buddies are giving him a hard time. He slumps down on the bench. (They didn't suspect it, but I dealt him a real humdinger below the belt; it'll take him a quarter of an hour just to get his breath back. And it won't start to really hurt until tomorrow morning.) We have a moment to take stock. In total, there are only eight of them left.

What's this all about? Now's the time to find out. You don't gang up, nine or ten to one, on one poor devil. It just doesn't happen. Especially when he's my buddy. If you have something to say, go ahead and say it. We're here now to clear things up. So go on.

It's a regular brouhaha. Every one of them has a grievance against him.

From the conversation (if you can call it that), it turns out he's a cheat. Do they have evidence? Evidence! They're choking on their words. Evidence! They don't know to what to do with their drool anymore. They're spitting like seals. Evidence! Yeah ... I know.

He turned up here this morning, they say, and didn't let up playing poker all day. (This is music to my ears. Poker is about as low as you can go.) Just ask him how much he's raked in. People were leaving this room fleeced. Now enough is enough! He rigged the deck. We caught him. Either he's going to cough it up or he's done for. They tell me to get out. No way in the world! I brush off another wimp—he's eyeing my jacket from a little too close—and I warn him, "Easy now!"

Then one of the musclemen takes matters into his own hands. He asks who I am, and he adds he doesn't give a fuck. If this guy here is my buddy, he's a chicken, and again he doesn't give a fuck. And he's so far from giving a fuck that he himself—as I see him standing there—and these two others (they're burly) have come down on purpose from Saint-Crépin to teach the chicken who's hiding behind me a fucking lesson. Because, he says, forty-eight hours ago he bilked them out of thousands of francs, not to mention the assortment of other dirty tricks he left behind as bonuses. And if I have anything to say, I should say it.

Of course I have something to say, but as usual it has nothing to do with the business at hand. While this is going on, my artist is pressing against me. He might as well be stuffing his head under my jacket. His teeth are chattering. He says, "Smash their faces in." This sounds like the ideal solution. As if anybody would have the balls to pull it off! Apart from the fact that, from my point of view, it's not really the best course of action.

I ask some questions and they answer. Well, at least we're getting somewhere. Our talk bogs down. We get sidetracked. This is exactly what I want. But little by little I'm convinced it wasn't just a matter of a game of cards. Something sensational took place at Saint-Crépin, but it isn't very clear. These guys don't have much power of expression. What comes across best is that they're lumberjacks.

They make this clear in all sorts of ways while they're pounding their chests like gorillas. This doesn't make my two carpenters happy in the least. And they take the initiative. Like brutes. I hear a sort of sledgehammer sail by, close to my ears. It lands flush in the face of the muscleman across from me. I get sprayed with his blood. This is fucked up.

The artist pulls me backward. I sit down on a table. I get rid of two wimps. I grab a third one by the collar. He was taking off anyway. The rest of the scene looks really hideous.

All of a sudden, I think about the switchblade and it scares me. I shove the artist through the door and we take off. I hear windowpanes breaking and slaughterhouse shrieks. We cover a hundred yards at full tilt, hugging the bends through alleyways blocked with all sorts of garbage, until we run out of breath.

Silence.

We push on straight ahead and reach a nice boulevard— soft underfoot and deserted—that's playing in the wind, like a cat, with what's left of the leaves in its trees.

We leave the center of town, walking at full speed. I've definitely sobered up. We screwed up and I wish we hadn't, but it's too late. The artist is striding ahead of me, fast, not breathing hard. I notice he's carrying his guitar. The fact that a guitar could have escaped such an orgy of head-bashing in one piece is something to wonder at. So is the nerve it took just to think of getting it out of there.

We take side roads. It looks to me like we're already far enough away. He tells me no, we have to put a whole lot of distance between ourselves and the boys from Saint-Crépin.

I don't see why we need to go any farther. It's not the first time a bunch of guys have beaten each other up.

We go into a wood. When we come out the other side, we're overlooking the country from way up high. There's no moon, but thanks to the wind, lots of stars. We can make out the valley and the highway below us. The mountainside hides the town, but over in that direction there's a glow of streetlights. Given all this, it should be pretty safe here.

I hear some motorbikes. I can see the headlights down on the highway. He says, "That's them. They're after me. They'll never catch up with us."

We keep on climbing. I say to myself: If it's true that he did some dirty work at Saint-Crépin, it couldn't have been that terrible. I don't have any reason to feel so certain except for the fact that he didn't try to get farther away. And that he did stop at the fair, where he could easily have expected the others would be coming. When all is said and done, it's a point in his favor.

He's nothing more than a guy who's scared shitless. I tell him nicely: In my opinion, we've come far enough. And where will we get by trudging blindly along these roads? Does he plan on running around all night? He answers, "You bet I do! You want to freeze to death under a tree?"

"No, but there's no reason to push ourselves either. Those guys took a beating. So what? It can't be their first time. They'll get over it. The easiest thing now would be to head home, nice and slow." No way. He won't do it. So on we go.

When day breaks, my feet are starting to feel like lead. We're on the edge of some beech woods. It's not that warm out. We come across a covered sheepfold entirely made of stones. It's empty. I don't care how bad things are, I have to have a little snooze.

Afterward, I'm more fit for action, even if I'm as hungry as a wolf. I try to do a bit of stocktaking.

I've already been taking stock—of myself—for a minute or two when I wake up with a start and I see my artist standing in the doorway. He's looking out at the little patch of open pasture and the trees gleaming in the sunlight. I close my eyes again. I pass myself in review, and what I see is rotten. What I did to the waitress at the inn—it's rotten. Whether she's the owner or the waitress, what I did is rotten. I left without paying, and she'd put her trust in me. I hate doing that. Only yesterday morning I was warming myself in front of her stove while she was making coffee. I swear, she couldn't have had the slightest idea I was a bastard. I couldn't have had the slightest idea either. She must be regretting it. And I'm regretting it. But what can we do about it? That's the way it goes.

No matter how long I keep asking him about Saint-Crépin, the artist stays mum in impressive fashion. Believe me, when it comes to this kind of interrogation, I'm usually pretty skillful. But he's way stronger than I am. To find out what he really got up to, I would have to go on asking forever. It's not that he refuses to answer. On the contrary, he does answer. He lies. He sticks firmly to his lie. He dresses up his lie. I'm used to this sort of thing, and I'm still astounded. He lies honestly, if you can put it that way. I know he's lying. He doesn't hide the fact. And I know once I've heard his lie, I'll never know the truth. Even if somebody else tells me, even if a hundred people tell me. Even if I have the proof in my hands. *I have too much at stake in believing what he says.* And what he says fits so neatly together.

This, my dears, requires a hell of a lot of practice. And look what a shitty hand I've been dealt!

He tells me how when I came into the back room of the bistro with my two elephants, the lumberjacks had only just turned up and taken him by surprise. He'd spotted them at the fairground, so he'd been hiding out all day. He didn't think things would flare up so quickly. Yes, he had played a few rounds of poker. To shake off his boredom. But nothing serious. His idea was to meet up with me again in the middle of the night. He has nobody, he says, but me. He would have told me everything, like he's doing now, and we would have come up with some plans. Like we're about to.

So far, it's perfect. It's a perfect lie, a lie you can believe in. And I'm not asking for anything better.

Being reasonable like this leaves me feeling hopeless—a bad recipe for happiness. I can't hold back from saying idiotic things. "So what? In the end, when you come down to it, it was just a bit of slapping around. Which has never hurt anybody. It's like what you do with rugs—it gets rid of the moths. It's no big deal. Let's think about how much worse it could have been. If I hadn't turned up, your nose might have gotten busted. And so what? You can live just fine with a busted nose. Anyway, there's no need to turn it into a national crisis and go into hiding."

"If you hadn't turned up," he says, "it wouldn't have been my nose they were busting, it would've been my back. And whatever was left of me, they would have handed over to the gendarmes. Is that what you want to hear? I had it coming to me."

Gendarmes—that obviously changes everything. But for God's sake, what *did* you get up to in Saint-Crépin?

No one will ever know. I listen while he tells me the life story of a saint. Minor transgressions, all of them more than justified. Nothing worth shaking a stick at. And so . . . ? The gendarmes—why would they be interested in this incident? They're on call for the really nasty stuff. I console myself with this undeniable truth.

Good. We're going to proceed on this basis: We're two little daisies, white as snow; it's other people who are nasty. This fits perfectly with his lies. I decide to go along with them.

We keep climbing up the mountain. We cross to the other side and walk down through some meadows. We arrive at a pretty hamlet. It's surrounded by groves of chestnuts. All the houses have carpets of flowers in front of their doors and windows.

I knock on a windowpane and I ask politely if I can buy a little grub. The artist doesn't seem to realize that it's almost a miracle (I've put all of my know-how into my tone to ask) that they sell us some bread, pork fat, and cheese. There's something missing from this boy. He really ought to understand the ABCs of the trade. When you ask to buy something to eat, especially in villages like this one where they have more than enough of everything, you're always suspect. Often—this is the cruel joke—you'd be better off begging. If you have nothing, people understand. You must be wretchedly poor. If you offer to pay, you must have money. But if you have money, why are you drifting around? Why don't you have a place of your own, a wife, children? What are you? Sometimes they let their dogs loose. Here, it turns out, they don't. But while I'm paying, I realize that after last night's blowout I have only three hundred and twelve francs left, no more, no less.

"You see, it's not so bad. They didn't try to eat you. And they're just as mean here as anywhere else."

"At this time of day, only the women are at home. I'm not afraid of women."

We roam around the outskirts of the hamlet. The surrounding chestnut forest is vast. The sun slants down through the thinned-out leaves and lights up long avenues. We walk ahead in the white noise of the wind. My heart feels lighter, and I imagine the artist's feels lighter too. We come to the edge of the groves. A wide view opens up in front of us, over new, unfamiliar valleys. Light, bluish fog flows along mountains piled one on top of the other. We plan to make our way across them.

We sit down in front of this scene. We're glad to have our snack. The bread from here is solid and it fills me up. After last night's binge, I can taste some salt in my spit again, and is it ever good. Down below us, a solitary man in a big, empty field is raking a late crop of hay.

We watch the clouds pass by. We're taking a good breather.

The artist is leaning against the slope. He's idly strumming the guitar lying beside him. He's saying, unbeknownst to himself, that he's having a moment of peace and quiet. Finally, he lifts the instrument onto his knees and plays a little tune.

A tune that bears no resemblance to the one he played for me yesterday, when I first met him. It's confidential . . . friendly. I think about friendship. I make the grandest declarations to myself.

Underneath what's left of their golden leaves, the beech woods raise white boughs that glisten in the sun. At noon, the bullfinches think it's summer. They puff out their throats and strut over the top of the hawthorns. But on the north-facing slopes, winter shade has already settled in, and it disturbs the birds. They go look at it from close up, come back, consider the situation, and try some short, upward flights—like larks— to reassure themselves the sun's still there. Crows flock together, come and go in big waves. In the meadows, the grass is already russet at its tips. It mats together and lies flat. The man who was raking his late-mown hay—he's gone off now for his midday meal—is lucky to have scraped a little more together. I'm on the best of terms with everything around me.

A little boy, who must go to school in a village farther down, crosses the meadow. He too is interested in the sound of the guitar. He stops to look at us. Then a second later, he's not looking at us anymore; he's stroking his cheek with a hen feather. Finally, he takes off on the run, his satchel flapping against his rear.

At this time of year, the chestnut sap flows earthward and settles underground. It oozes from all the nicks in the bark that summer has opened wider. It has that hard-to-describe smell of bread dough, of flour mixed with water. A falcon, chased by a cloud of titmice, swoops by low over the trees. The midday warmth spreads like a quilt from my knees to my feet. I'm letting my beard grow, to contend with coldness in general. To live in love or to live in fear: it all comes down to memory.

We spend the whole day as happy as hares, the artist and me, on this sun-drenched mountainside. It's good for the blood. He plays the guitar. I listen. Finally, we stroll down as far as a fairly big village that's nestled below. And that's it for today. We head to the bistro. They give us a place to sleep in a storage room. By eight o'clock I'm snoring.

I manage to get myself hired, a mile and a half farther down the valley, at the mill where they press walnuts. This comes in the nick of time. Any longer and I was well on my way from poverty to destitution. Plus, I need to replace the gear I abandoned at the inn. I didn't have much to speak of, but I miss it. For example, nothing disgusts me more than having to blow my nose into my fingers. And this isn't just a question of bourgeois manners. I also need a couple of shirts. Small things, but important. I spend one Sunday sewing up a rucksack I've pieced together from an old tarpaulin, using shoemaker's thread.

I'm doing this out on the deck of the oil mill. I'm alone. The owners have shut down for the day and taken off in their car. They were all dressed up. The electrician was in his Sunday best too, and he got on his bicycle. The other two workers took off on foot.

I've taken shelter behind the big, cleaned-out barrels, and I'm sitting on top of some sacks, doing this bit of work for myself. I hear somebody coming from behind. I think it's the brats who show up asking for crushed walnuts, but no, it's a charming young woman. I ask if I can be of service. She's taken aback. She looks at my eyeglasses. Their style doesn't go along with my rucksack and my shoemaker's thread. Even so, they're proud enough of their electric presses here. In this day and age, a pair of glasses doesn't tell you much about somebody, one way or the other.

The young woman wants to see the owners.

"They left right after dinner."

"Do you know where they went?"

"They took their car. They were heading down the valley."

"So they must have gone to La Posterle."

"Could be."

"When will they be back?"

"I couldn't say for sure. Definitely tonight. They'll have to come home for supper."

"Unless they're eating at their sister-in-law's."

"That's possible too. Anyway, they'll be back."

"Yes, but that won't do me any good after dark. I need more than an hour to get home."

"I don't know what else to say."

"I get it, but I'm upset."

"Can I do anything?"

"No, I have to see Monsieur Edmond."

"Then I can't help much."

"No."

"That's a shame."

"Yes, it's a shame. Because if I have to go back in the dark, it means I'm not done yet."

"You're afraid to walk back on your own?"

"No way. Actually I run. But I'll have to come up with an excuse."

"You can say you had to wait."

"You think so...?"

"Because it's true."

"If only it was that easy!"

"They won't eat you."

"No, but if I get back after dark, you know... I'm going to see if there's anybody home at the Chauvins'."

(That's the farmhouse across the road. I pick up my sewing. She comes back a minute later.)

"There's nobody there either."

"It's Sunday."

"They used to have a dog. What have they done with it?"

"They still have it. It's out hunting."

"With their son?"

"No, on its own... Their son must have taken off on his motorbike. I think I heard him."

"What time is it?"

"Two thirty, three o'clock."

"Not later?"

"No. In this valley it always feels later. But it's barely three."

"What'll I do?"

"Come here and get out of the wind, with me. Wait a while. Unless you feel like climbing up to the village. Maybe you'll get to see Monsieur Edmond when you come back down."

"Not interested. There's nothing to do up there!"

"There's dancing."

"Thanks a lot. People just laugh at you!"

"They don't have to laugh at every girl who dances...!"

"When you come from somewhere else, they make fun of you."

"So, where's home?"

"Pont-de-l'Étoile."

"Don't they dance there too?"

"It's different."

"Anyway, don't stay on your feet. You'll get tired"

"What do you want me to do?"

"Sit."

"Where?"

"Here, on these sacks."

"Oh, all right, thanks. They're nice and thick."

(I arrange a place for her to sit, with some clean sacks and a piece of tarpaulin.)

"Have you been working here long?"

"Two weeks."

"Do you know if they've already done the Jourdans' walnuts?"

"They pressed them on Thursday."

"Have they come for their oil?"

"Not yet."

"Do you know if Monsieur Edmond will deliver it?"

"I don't know. He asked if I knew how to drive the van."

"Do you?"

"Yes."

"Anyway, when do you think it will happen?"

"Next week, I think."

"You don't know what day?"

"No, I don't."

"If you deliver it, could you do me a favor?"

"Glad to."

"On your way to the Jourdans', past Pont-de-l'Étoile, just after the roadside cross, there's an oak woods and a lane on your left. Any chance you could stop and honk three times?"

"Sure."

"It'd be good if it could be in the morning."

"I can't say if it would be morning or evening. After that, what do I do?"

"Could you wait there for a minute?"

"I'd be glad to, even ten."

"If I knew what day, I'd be out there waiting for you, but I can't do that all day all week."

"The people passing by wouldn't complain."

"Nobody passes by."

"If it's not going to be me, do you want me to mention it to Monsieur Edmond?"

"You could, maybe."

"Whatever you like."

"Yes, you could. But not in front of Madame Edmond."

"What should I tell him?"

"What I told you. To honk and wait for me. Please."

"Will he know who it's for?"

"When you tell him the lane on the left after the cross, yes, he will."

"All right."

"If you come, won't it be a lot of trouble?"

"What?"

"You'd have to take me all the way to the highway."

"That is a long way."

"To the highway, and then another two miles to the bus stop in the Châteauneuf woods. Eight miles total."

"It wouldn't be the end of the world. But what time's your bus?"

"There are four in my direction: two early and two late. It's on the main line. The last one comes at six."

"That's why I'm asking. Because if I come late in the afternoon, would we make it there on time? If not, I'd better arrange to get to your place early enough. What would you do in the Châteauneuf woods if the bus had already left? You could always come back with me, right?"

"Let's not talk about bad luck!"

"That's not very nice."

"Why?"

"If you think going back with me would be bad luck!"

"I don't mean going back with you. Going back, period."

"You can count on me."

"That's kind."

"Who wouldn't do anything to be nice to a pretty girl?"

"Oh! 'Pretty'!"

"No one's ever told you that?"

"Yes."

"So?"

"Where does it get you?"

"Anyway, it makes you feel good, doesn't it?"

"It's not hard to take. That's not what I meant."

"Better to be pretty than ugly."

"Men are all the same."

"Don't believe that."

"Why? Because you're just another one who's stronger than the rest?"

"Somebody has to be."

"What for?"

"To keep the world turning. It doesn't need men for that, but let's suppose there weren't any? You'd be in a real bind! What would you do?"

"All right, let's suppose. But what good does it do to suppose? You still have to get by with what you've got."

"Are you from here?"

"No, I'm from Pont-de-l'Étoile. From here or Pont-de-l'Étoile, it doesn't make much of a difference."

"I asked because you seem to know a lot about what goes on here."

"I know my own business, period."

"You think other people know more?"

"They might. It's possible."

"Yes, it's possible. Anyway, I don't know any more than that."

"You're not from here?"

"What makes you say so?"

"I've never seen you before."

"Maybe I was in hiding."

"Don't joke around."

"What would be so unusual about it?"

"The days of the Resistance are over."

"What if I started one all on my own?"

"Sure, come and hunt down the bastards. People will welcome you."

"Maybe I was being held in reserve in the woods so you'd have somebody close at hand, at any moment."

"I could always ask Monsieur Edmond."

"Maybe he wouldn't do the job as well as me."

"You flatter yourself."

"I'm not flattering myself."

"Maybe I would be happier if it was you. If you won't say anything afterward."

She asks me the time. I'd say by now it's getting close to four o'clock. She makes me promise to remember to honk three times. I swear I will, cross my heart. If it looks like Monsieur Edmond's going to make the delivery, I'll have to fill him in, on the quiet. I swear to that too. But I'm sure it'll be me. I tell her, "Maybe Thursday." She'll be on the lookout starting tomorrow. She leaves. She's wearing high heels that must be a pain in the meadows. They make a lot of noise when she walks across the deck and then on the road.

Once I've finished sewing my rucksack, I pack my things and head back up to the village. By the time I get there, it's dark. I've dawdled along the way, poking around underneath the hedgerows, looking for mushrooms. But the nights are too cold now. I've even come across a patch of frost on top of some moss on a north-facing slope.

The artist's keeping quietly to himself in a corner of the bistro. He won't lower himself to bring out his guitar, because earlier they were dancing to an electric cello. Near him are four or five belote tables, but he's fed up. He's looking at the cardplayers with scorn. Once in a while, there's an alarming glint in his eyes. I've seen the same thing in the eyes of circus animals when you go by their cages. It's hard to believe, but I think this guy will always have a strange effect on me. I feel like I'm constantly catching him red-handed.

I tell him it's chilly out. I sit down next to him on the bench, and the warmth relaxes me. He asks what me I'm having. An anise. What was I busy with all afternoon? I was putting this thing together.

"You like being on your own, don't you?"

"I like being alone and I like company."

He fools around with his deck of cards. To keep his hands in shape, he says. My jaw drops at every trick. Again, right before my eyes, it's the dance of hearts, diamonds, spades, and clubs. He fumbles certain moves, but he never gets flustered; he's sure he can pull them off, and in the end, he does pull them off. You can never say he doesn't know what he's doing, because he always knows. A guy like the artist never makes excuses.

After a while, this show of skills gets on my nerves, and I go to find the owner in her kitchen. I love being in kitchens. I like houses, but it's here, in their heart, that I feel my best. Nothing's as good as the scent of burning wood while I'm standing beside a kitchen stove with a plump woman who's stirring a pot of stew.

She asks me what I did this afternoon. I went to the mill.

"You don't spend enough time there all week?"

"Force of habit."

We're the same breed, the two of us. And I'm the same breed as the men here who are playing belote. When I'm around, she's always asking me questions because you can never know enough. The guy I'm with, do I know him very well? I lie; I say yes. When you come down to it, is it really such a lie? Maybe I don't need excuses either. Neither does the owner, neither do the belote players. Everything's going well. The stove is roaring. It's a good Sunday night stove.

In the morning, the weather is taking a turn for the worse. It's not fooling around anymore. It's moving on to a different sort of drill. There's still some autumn lingering at the tips of the poplars, but you can bid that season farewell. So, old pal, we're parting ways? You've been good to me up until now.

Life is drifting away on the winds.

One night, I'm even forced to sleep at the mill. You wouldn't let a dog outside in the gale that's blowing. My fellow workers try to leave, but they come back. Monsieur Edmond gets us to come upstairs for supper. By eight or nine o'clock, after we've stuck our noses out the door again, we decide it makes more sense to stay in here than it does to catch our death of cold. We stay down below, on sacks, in the glow of the burners that warm the oil vats.

There's not much left of last night's snow, but it's icy and the sky's the color of pea soup. We can tell: one way or another, we're in for a beating.

"Maybe we'd better take care of a few things while there's a break in the weather," Monsieur Edmond says. "Make a run up to the Jourdans'. They could get snowed-in any minute now."

He loans me his fur-lined jacket, and I set out driving along roads that are barely passable. He warned me to take it easy till I got to the bottom of the valley, but I'm taking it even easier than that. The north-facing bends are like skating rinks.

Lower down, it's better. But nothing to get excited about. I climb back up, following the fast stream, as far as Pont-de-l'Étoile. People give me curious looks when they see I'm heading out to the farthest hamlets. They think I'm cocky. And after I've had a look around, I have to agree. If I'd known what I was getting into, I would have thought twice.

Of course, the light in the sky today—if you can call it light—doesn't bring out the best in this district. Even at its best, it would still look pretty bad. It's high in the valley, almost at the top. There's barely enough room for the stream and the road that runs along beside it. On my left, I see nothing but gray lava fields, heaps of stones, and stands of stunted trees clinging to drab, bare soil full of razor-sharp schist. This road is just one gully after another, with water streaming across at the bottoms. When I get to each one, I have to plunge ahead blindly. If I had the bad luck to get stuck in a place like this in weather like we had last night, I don't know how I'd ever get out.

I see the roadside cross the girl told me about. It feels completely out of place in this stretch of back country. Right afterward, I spot the oak woods and the lane on my left. I honk three times and I wait.

I have the look of a magician who's messing up his act. I snap my fingers, and nothing comes out of my hat. What did I expect? To the right, to the left, ahead, behind . . . it's all a disaster. The only actors who belong in this show are the oaks. I have plenty of time to stare at them. They're solid and determined. They don't give a tinker's damn about our petty affairs.

I wait around like this for a little longer than I need to, and I start up again in the direction of the Jourdans'. I'll honk my horn again on the way back, to set my mind at rest, but I get the idea the young lady has decided to stay put. For this season at least.

The Jourdans are so glad to receive their last-minute anointment of oil, they set to work as soon as I arrive: the women, the children, and the old folks. In the time it takes me to get out of the van and slam the door shut, they've unloaded the canisters and are bearing them in triumphal procession to their earthenware jars. While they're passing back and forth, they bring me a glass of wine. This is one strange shack. It's as dark as an oven in here. All the light comes from the glowing front of the woodstove. Once you've adjusted your eyes, you get some idea of what's going on. Everything—alive or not—is red and black. Period. I've seen prettier pictures. I admire these people for being able to hold their heads high in such lurid surroundings.

I'm in a hurry to get away from this bewitching place. There's something foul in the air, as they say. Over by the mountain, mounds of mist and cloud are racing downhill.

When I come to the oaks, I stop and honk the horn again, three times. And—again—three more times so I can feel I've kept my promise. But there's still no rabbit in the hat. I head home.

None of this really surprises me. In this kind of weather, it would take as much guts to get out of here as it would to stay. But if the charming young woman who chatted with me on Sunday lives in a pit like the Jourdans', she must have resigned herself to being smeared all over with red and black for yet another whole season.

It's hardly a walk in the park for us here at the mill either. Every morning as I'm going down, I hear ice pellets whistling in the branches of the beech trees. I take advantage of an old knitted sweater Madame Edmond gave me and an American Army raincoat I bought for six hundred and fifty francs from Chopart Alfonse, the postman. He'd picked it up secondhand too. It's extremely useful.

I've told the artist he should buy one for himself. But he's set his sights higher. He's heard there are some excellent English navy coats. But they cost thousands of francs. Which puts them beyond my reach. What's more, you have to go hunting for them at the fairs. The artist claims he knows how to get hold of them. I tell him given the state of my wallet, I'm in no rush. My American outfit fits the bill perfectly. The artist says I settle for too little. I ask if he knows any other way. He answers yes.

"With a face like yours, I'd strike it rich," he says.

"What's so special about my face?"

The way he sees it, I have the face of a decent sort of guy. And after that? True enough, I do now have three full inches of frizzy blond beard.

"You inspire confidence. You might be the biggest bastard on earth, but when somebody sees your eyes, they're bowled over."

I'm happy enough to see it this way.

"But I'm not the biggest bastard on earth."

"Exactly," he says. "So I'm wondering what good that does you. Seeing as you'd like to have an English navy coat."

I tell him I couldn't care less about the English navy.

He tells me I'm a hick and I'll always be a hick, and he shows me a new trick he learned last night. Now this one is really different, and I challenge anybody to make heads or tails of it. You mix the cards; you knead them like dough; you form them into a loaf; you waste some time rearranging and rotating them. He picks up the deck . . .

"Obviously I have to pick them up to deal."

"Agreed."

He picks up the deck. He deals. He tells me exactly what cards he's given me. If I do the dealing, he tells me exactly what cards I've dealt to myself. I ask him how he does it. He tells me I'm not smart enough to understand. He gets me to put the aces on the bottom of the deck. He cuts. I deal. He has the four aces. I stick them into different parts of the deck. He cuts. I deal. He still has the four aces. I tuck them away, at random, while he's not looking. I cut. He deals. He still has the four aces. I'm convinced: Even if I put them all in my pocket, and no matter which one of us did the cutting and dealing, he'd still end up with the aces in his hand. Same thing for the king, the queen, the jack. Same thing for dealing me hands that are ridiculously bad but at the same time always within the realm of possibility (that's what amazes me the most). I'm telling you: Who wouldn't be taken in by his moves?

"You see," he says, "I'm not wasting *my* time."

But aside from this, he doesn't lift a finger. And now that the days are short, I hear he barely makes it out of bed before noon. Because at noon I eat down at the mill. I wonder if he thinks his cash will last all winter. It's true, he can call on me if the going gets rough, and I won't let him down. In all honesty, I'm expecting it.

"What the hell can you be doing in bed until midday?"

"Cooking up crazy ideas."

One evening at six o'clock, I leave the mill, getting ready to head back up to the bistro. But before I start out, I find the road's covered in ice and the night's as black as ink. There's a north wind blowing that could tear your face off. I hear somebody calling "Monsieur!" It's the girl.

I say to her, "What in hell are you doing out here? It's enough to kill you."

"Come over here, out of the wind."

She pulls me by the arm, right up against the door of the Chauvins' barn. It's half open, and we go into the cowshed, where it's warm.

"What's going on? This time it's pitch-dark. How will you manage to get home?"

I think of that godforsaken cross casting a chill, in a

manner of speaking, on the stony ground a hundred yards from the oak woods.

"I have an arrangement with Ernest, the Chauvins' son. He'll take me back on his motorbike. I'm supposed to be at my cousin's. I have until eight o'clock."

I tell her on Thursday I honked as loud as I could—on the way there and on the way back. She says thanks. She heard me. But on that day, there was nothing doing. She even claims her situation was grim. I understand. But she assures me I can't. If I understood, she says—if I knew everything—I'd see she wasn't exaggerating.

I tell her since she's made me promise to keep it secret, it's best for me not to know everything.

Can I manage to come and pick her up tomorrow?

"That, my dear, that's a lot more difficult. What reason could I give Monsieur Edmond for taking the van? There's nothing left to deliver to the Jourdans. Unless I tell him it's to go and pick you up...since you'd like to see him on a Sunday!"

She tells me, for the love of God, not to say anything to Monsieur Edmond. Until recently, she thought she could trust him. But now she knows she can't. Most of all, not a word to the Edmonds, husband or wife.

"Then I guess we're up against it."

What can I do? If she's on good terms with the Chauvins' son, and he's taking her back tonight to her famous cross, why can't he pick her up tomorrow and make the drive? Or even do it this evening—it wouldn't take any longer.

She answers no, and then there's a pause. I hear mice squeaking, and then all of a sudden I realize it's her—she's crying. This makes me extremely uncomfortable.

I tell her I'll do whatever I can. And I mean it. For sure,

I'll find a way. I'm going to figure it out. Finally, I cheer her up: I tell her to be patient. She should wait for me, I'll come for sure, she shouldn't worry. Unless we all happen to drop dead, or there's an earthquake. The sort of things you have to say to women.

There are no more mice in the cowshed. She thanks me. I feel her coming toward me. I touch her shoulder and I say, "Don't get yourself all worked up like this."

While I'm walking back up to the village, I'm thinking so hard about what I've promised, I don't even feel the wind. But I can't come up with anything. And again this morning, nothing. It isn't until late this afternoon that I have an idea.

I tell Monsieur Edmond I'm pretty sure I left a fifty-liter canister behind at the Jourdans'. This amazes him, seeing as he did the count himself when I got back (they're his prized possessions). "Still, come and take a look." And yes, one of them is missing (the one I've stowed away in the van, under some sacks). Now this . . . this really gets him upset. But the timing is just right: By chance, the weather is holding steady.

"Make a run up there," he says.

Now you're talking!

I even get a little reckless on the way down. It's only when I go into a serious skid that I come slightly back to my senses. There's still black ice and all its accomplices. I tell myself it's ridiculous to be so impatient at my age. It's fine not to want to disappoint this girl, but somebody has to get started. If nobody has already!

I reach the cross at nightfall. It's still not a very cheerful sight. At the oaks, I pull over and honk on the horn three times. I lean back to wait, but almost right away I see my lady passenger come out.

She's dressed to the nines. She even has on a rabbitskin

jacket that leaves me speechless. And naturally she's wearing high heels. She's dragging a suitcase that's fit to burst, in spite of its straps.

"You see, it worked out."

She barely answers. And I get it, we have to leave on the double. Which I do.

She's loaded herself up with rings, bracelets, and copper necklaces galore. When it comes to arms, she's well defended.

We're a little slow passing through Pont-de-l'Étoile because a lumber truck squeezes us to one side, and I have to maneuver in reverse into a little square. Finally, we get going again, and the road is better, as far as black ice is concerned. I pick up speed, and I can tell it's the best remedy I could give her.

But after a few minutes, I'm forced to slow down. I never imagined the road could drop so steeply. It's wide and well graveled. But I can still feel those skids from a few minutes ago in my rear end. I can tell the eight miles she talked about will amount to twelve. And I'm not far off. By the time I can make out the traffic lights at the highway, we've done fourteen. And it's dark.

I turn on the headlights. At the intersection, I ask, "Which way?" "Left." We haven't breathed a word the whole way. Does she know what time it is? No. Me neither. It's hit-and-miss.

We're overtaking autumn in retreat. It's camped out along the highway—in poplars, willows, aspens, and fruit trees. In my headlights the country seems enchanted, unreal... to the point where it's completely believable. Anything could happen to us. With every turn, I light up sensational backdrops.

The Châteauneuf bus stop is in the woods. It's up against a long wall, next to a park gate. It's only a concrete canopy.

What time is it? Has the bus gone by already or not? It's a matter of conscience. I can't risk letting my passenger get out. First of all, she'd freeze. And then it's only because I'm lighting up the area around us that it has any substance at all. If I left the scene, what would it amount to? I turn my headlights off to see. The end of everything. And we have the sound of the motor as well to remind us we're alive. But just imagine this place with only the sound of the wind in the trees. I turn the lights back on.

In the same instant, I light up a person coming toward us. I say "person" because of their trousers, but in fact it's a woman. "Here's someone else coming to wait. Your bus hasn't gone by yet."

I lower my window and ask what time it is. Five before six. Has the bus gone by yet? No. Anyway look, here it comes. It's honking full blast, lit up like a ship.

My little lady disappears on board. I hold the door open for the woman in trousers, but she's not getting on. She isn't even here anymore. She's made herself scarce.

Once the bus has left, I stay frozen in place for a second. I don't even know this girl's last name. Or her first. I'm such a strange character. Let's suppose I'd made her miss her bus. On purpose. That could have been an opportunity. But it would have to be summer too. And in summer it's still light out at six in the evening.

The park gate opens. A guy comes out. He offers me a cigarette. He asks if I've seen a woman. Yes, five minutes ago. Wearing trousers. Did she get on the bus? No.

I swing the van around. While I'm turning, my headlights shine past the gate and light up a stupendous drive and the guy walking back toward the house.

I get back to business. I make it to the mill on time. The

Edmonds are eating. I poke my head through the doorway. "I have the canister."

"Thanks. Would you like a drink?" I drink some wine. Then I go back downstairs.

I'm happy to be at this mill. It's too cold out to be roaming around. Every morning when I come down from the village, I consider myself lucky. The Edmonds treat me fairly. My job now is jack-of-all-trades. I make little repairs here and there. I take care of the heating. I keep an eye on things. I scrub down the equipment. I roll cigarettes. I stay nice and warm, and I collect my weekly wages.

One morning when I arrive, I find Monsieur Edmond talking with a skinny guy. I get a bad feeling from the boss.

"When you went to fetch the canister the other evening," Monsieur Edmond asks, "did you happen to pick up a young woman on your way back?"

"Yes, I did."

"Where did you take her?" the skinny guy asks.

"To Pont-de-l'Étoile."

They ask me for all sorts of details. Some of their questions I sidestep. To others, I hem and haw. I don't think it would be much fun to have the skinny guy's mug in your face all the time. It's not that he makes you feel melancholy. He makes you feel something harder-edged than that. And he makes me run the gauntlet. To listen to him, I don't even have the right to breathe. I tell him to get lost.

The next day, he's back again, without Monsieur Edmond, who's away this time. I can feel some big headaches coming on. And sure enough, they do.

"You didn't go to the Jourdans'," he says. "You came and honked your horn in the oak woods. I heard you. Somebody saw you in Pont-de-l'Étoile—you were backing up across from the Café des Sports. And somebody saw you on the other side of Pont-de-l'Étoile."

This last detail, he's making up. We didn't run across anybody there. He's getting on my nerves so much, I say to him, "And so? What the fuck does it matter to you?"

"You know she's a minor?"

"What does that have to do with me?"

"The law will stick it to you."

"The law? What does the law have to do with it? You think you ask people their age when they flag you down on the road? What about you? Would you have left her standing there?"

"She didn't flag you down. You gave her a signal. And what's more, this isn't the first time."

"You want a bit of advice? Mind your own business, and leave me the fuck alone."

"This is my business."

"All right then, if it is your business, mind your own and fuck off!"

I even feel I've been too polite so far. I throw in, "And stop breaking my balls!"

This doesn't impress him. He turns around and leaves.

Now I think I've made a fool of myself. There was no reason to go at him that hard. I made it sound like a capital crime.

When Monsieur Edmond gets back, I fill him in. He's not happy. He says, "So you had to go and get yourself mixed up in something like that!"

I tell him about my conversation with the girl last Sunday, how she came supposedly to see him, Monsieur Edmond himself. He seems shocked but not overly so. If he'd been there, he claims, he would have thrown her out. I suggest that if I did get involved, it was because I thought I was do-ing the right thing. He doesn't say I did anything wrong. He says the situation is far from rosy. Period. I'm getting the picture, from his looks.

I ask, "Who is that guy? Her father?"

"Her stepfather. Her mother's husband."

"Then why does he have to make such a big stink?"

"It would amaze me if he carried on like that," says Mon-sieur Edmond. "With a guy like him, it would be a bit dif-ferent."

The boss looks like he's swallowed a fish bone.

"How would it be, with a guy like him?"

"He'd be gentle. But you have no idea where that can lead."

It's wrong of me to want to laugh. I say, "Gentle—well, that tickles me."

No reply. He stares straight ahead like he's seeing all sorts of things only remotely connected with tickles. It's wrong of me to dwell on it, but how can you approach a situation like this delicately? I might as well just wade in.

"If he's not her real father, he has no reason to be worried."

"Unless he has better reasons," Monsieur Edmond says (with the shark bone still stuck in his throat).

This leaves everything up in the air. I think about the metal cross, all on its own out there, on a mission to bring joy to the mountain streams and the piles of schist.

"Looks like I've stepped into something that stinks."

"You could say so."

The next day and the day after that, I'm just as happy not to see any more of my skinny friend. I have no desire to see him show up, even with a box of candies. In the evening, when I get back to the café, the artist has a funny look on his face. He's over the moon. I'm relieved. He says, "You're one hell of a secret-keeper!"

Honestly, I have no idea what he's talking about.

"You're having trouble with women."

Even now, I don't get it.

"You're the best. You're worth your weight in gold. The day you want to team up with me, I'm ready to go all in. If you could see yourself, you'd see why. No questions asked."

He's sharp: He can tell I'm not just playing dumb. I really don't get it. So he dots the i's and crosses the t's.

People are saying that I abducted the girl. My first reaction is to laugh. Then on second thought, my laughter gets forced. I go into the kitchen to warm up by the stove. Tonight the owner isn't very welcoming. I say, "You of all people, you should have more common sense!"

She doesn't beat around the bush. The girl is a slut. Maybe I enjoy cleaning up other people's messes . . . Anyway, right now, I should back away. She needs to get at her stove.

She tells me: If somebody's out to make your life miserable, that changes everything. I tell her I didn't think it was that serious—I wasn't worried in the least. Anyone in my position would have done the same thing. She doesn't agree or disagree. I tell her the whole story. She replies, "And the Chauvins' cowshed—you were in there singing Mass?"

So that's it. Now I know who he is, the swine who squealed on me.

One morning, I lie in wait. And just as the Chauvins' son is getting on his motorbike, I stop him.

"All right," I say, "what story did you go around telling about the girl and me in your cowshed? What are you trying to prove?"

"I'm not trying to prove anything. Were you in there or not?"

"I was there. So what?"

Smashing his face in isn't going to solve the problem. On the contrary. He adds, "She came to me. She told me she wanted to see you, and I should leave the door open. So I did, right? What's your gripe? Is this how you say thanks?"

I let him take off. I've played the fool again. He's not going to stop acting big. I'm stirring things up, not calming them down. This whole business makes me sick.

The boss has let my two colleagues go. This was expected. The oil-making season is over. Now only the electrician comes once a week to check the machinery. We wondered who the boss would keep on for general maintenance. It's me. He cornered me. He paid me compliments. We agreed on a wintertime wage—a little reduced, naturally, since there's no more heavy work.

Basically, I have nothing to do aside from just being here. I stroll around the premises. I survey all the equipment. I fix things and I putter. I grease and I shine. I mend baskets and sacks. I put things in order. This makes me feel good.

It's so far from making me feel bad, you wouldn't believe it. This huge mill suits me to a T. We've made a marriage of convenience, and now we're on a strange sort of honeymoon.

Naturally, the snow has come to stay once and for all. I keep three big woodstoves fired up so that all this equipment and the vats of oil get the coddling they require. Inside here, frost would wreak havoc. With me around, it doesn't stand a chance. I'm keeping the windowpanes clean. If a snowflake lands on one of them, it's had it; the surface is warm, human. Early on, birds came to rub themselves up against the glass, the way they would against a cheek. I got a few of them to come inside—the least timid ones, who didn't take off when I opened the window. They're still up on the roof beams. I give them seeds and bits of soft bread.

But I'm not much of a tamer. You won't see me with birds on my shoulders or in my beard. (Speaking of beards, mine couldn't have turned out any better. Every once in a while, I even have to give it a trim.) I'm not one of those people you admire because they can make animals obey their commands. Or who seem like they can. To tame any sort of creature, you need to take care of it for too long. And work up a whole lovey-dovey routine—pecking each other's lips, that sort of nonsense—be too devoted, too kind, and so on . . . Anyway, it's the same with cats and dogs. I don't take the lead. The same with people. Rarely, anyway.

Of course, I'm sleeping at the mill. I have to feed the fires at night. The artist came to see me two or three times at the start. But he's been holed up in his room for a while now. It's true—the weather's awful. I went to see him the other day. I took advantage of the Edmonds being out for the afternoon, and I slipped away for a couple of hours. I nearly cracked my head open on the way back. A skating rink on a hillside has never been anybody's idea of fun. You'd have to be a bit twisted to enjoy it.

I've set myself up a perfectly lovely encampment between two piles of sacks, right across from the big, central wood-stove. Monsieur Edmond has given me a folding cot. I've organized a cozy den around it. The electrician has brought me down a length of wire, and I've hung the work lamp from a hook. I have light at the head of the bed. Fit for a prince!

The only thing I'm short of is reading material. This is a place where I'd be happy to have a book or two. I did ask

Madame Edmond (who, by the way, gives me the cold shoulder most of the time). She gave me nothing but trash: tales of the Virgin Mary, orphans, legionnaires. That kind of stuff really gets me down!

I'd rather smoke my pipe. I've bought myself a clay one with a bowl shaped like a bearded prophet. I'm breaking it in, and I have the perfect place to sit while I do it. There are two things I have to watch out for: frost and fire. I can't let it freeze, but I can't burn the whole place down to the ground. This is what my job is all about. So I can't smoke my pipe on top of a bunch of sacks. The tiniest ember could cause a huge problem.

But I have the perfect spot, worry-free: Over on the side that leads to the boss's private apartment, there's the bottom half of a staircase. Four steps up, it's blocked by the door. This is where I settle in, with my back against solid oak and my rear end on the seat cushions from the van. They sit just right on the treads. The first woodstove is straight in front of me. I can fire it up red-hot, if I want to. And past the stove, as far as the eye can see, there's all the stuff I keep watch over, all the way to the windows at the far end. So these steps are where I'm gradually blackening the face of my bearded pipe while I keep an eye on everything, without having to lift a finger. I spend an hour or two at this, especially after my noon meal. I listen to the radio they have playing in the apartment upstairs until the boss yells out, "Oh my, my! Josette, that radio! Can't you turn it down?" Then the sound gets softer, and I really enjoy it.

Once in a while, Monsieur Edmond comes down to see how things are going. He's so nice to me, I wonder what he's after. Either he brings wine or tobacco, or makes friendly comments about the breaking-in of my bearded pipe. It bothers me a little every time. I'd be happier if he bawled me out. But he doesn't.

One morning, in spite of the biting wind, he pulls the car out. Madame Edmond is bundled up to her eyes. She gets in beside him. But at the last moment, he comes down to see me. "Listen. This is between you and me. Sometime today, a guy will come to pick up five hundred liters. Keep an eye on him for me and make sure he's satisfied. He'll have his own containers. Don't use any of ours. Help him fill them. But if he's held up because of the weather and he doesn't get here till it's almost dark—we won't be home until nearly six—and if you see you won't be done before I get back, go up to the village and call 3 on the telephone, for La Posterle. Say to them, "Tell Monsieur Edmond to wait."

"Right."

He scratches a 3 on the floor with a bit of plaster. He has nothing to worry about. Madame Edmond is getting impatient and honks the horn. He had nothing more to say to me anyway.

Toward one in the afternoon, the guy in question arrives in a little truck. He's frozen stiff. While he's warming himself up, I try to see if there's any name on the vehicle, but there isn't. We get down to work and we fill, load, and tie down his five hundred liters by four o'clock. He takes off. All the best to you! I was in no mood to climb up to the village, and I don't envy him having to make the downhill turns while it's getting dark. To me, it all seems like fishy business.

The Edmonds get back at a quarter to seven. The boss comes to see me straightaway, in no more time than it takes him to get in upstairs and come down. I give him the nod that everything's in good shape. He looks at the tile where he'd scratched the telephone number. That too has been taken care of. He doesn't ask for any more details.

We have three or four days of foul weather. No matter what the season has dealt us so far, you'd have to say it had just been fooling around. But now it's really getting serious. Like a good workman, it doesn't make a fuss and it gets a lot done. Thick snow is falling day and night. I have to shovel out a trench to get to the road.

In my little encampment between the piles of sacks, I'm like a cow in clover. Mainly because of the steady warmth, and the fact that I'm snug in my blankets in this solid mill, in this heavy snowfall that's brought down the telephone lines and blocked the roads for miles in every direction. I'm in my element.

I could hardly imagine in the midst of all this that the artist would come and visit me. Even so, he does. I can't get over it! It's a windfall. I make some coffee. He says, "I've brought you a packet of tobacco. Cough up your eighty-five francs." In any case, it's a nice gesture. He actually gave it some thought. I shouldn't expect too much.

He looks superb. He's wearing one of those damn fur-lined parkas that I drool over, rubber boots, wool socks half an inch thick, and pale green ski pants the color of anise.

"You lucky bastard! That outfit must keep you really warm."

"Yeah, it's amazing."

What's he come up with? An inheritance or something? Where did he go to get hold of all this gear?

"Don't worry," he says. "Watch and learn."

That's no answer. He's like a kid. I say, "You can't pull the wool over the eyes of an old monkey like me. You have at least fifty thousand francs' worth of gear covering your ass. They must have come from somewhere."

"Fifty big ones? You're a little shy of the mark," he says. "It's Neapolitan lambswool." He's making me sick to my stomach! "Golden Neapolitan lambswool." He says it again, proud as a peacock. He wants to dazzle me. I'm a lot happier when he has a deck of cards in his hands, or a guitar. I also notice he's wearing a wristwatch. I say, "Well, kid, your Neapolitan lambswool doesn't grow on trees. The same goes for your watch, your ski pants, and the rest of your getup." (I keep coming back to my first thought. Where's it all coming from?) And I add, "What's the point? I can almost see why you might want to dress up in a place where it would make a difference. But here! I have no Neapolitan lambswool, and I guarantee you I'm not cold. If you go on like this, you'll be flat broke before winter's over. Don't you realize it's barely gotten started! If you were a Rothschild, it would be different. And even then..."

He laughs and lets me go on. He's smoking a cigarette—it's always an American one, of course.

"And what about those—do you get them at the tobacco shop?"

"No," he says. "At the tobacco shop I buy cheap shag for fools who dress in sackcloth."

"Have it your way! But what if I like it!"

"All right," he says. "I came here to talk shop. But if you're happy in this stinking hole, I don't see why I should bother to spring you loose. You're not the kind of guy who shows any gratitude."

Now he's really getting to me. Worst of all, he's actually causing me pain. I can't laugh this guy off. I see what other people see: He's completely worthless. But I have to ignore it. I try to make him see he's setting himself up for a fall. He tells me I should mind my own business. If he'd known what to expect, he could have saved himself the mile-and-a-half trek. He suspected it would be this way. It was pure friendship that brought him out in this kind of weather. Because he doesn't like seeing me living like a marmot in a burrow. Till now, he's managed on his own. All he has to do is carry on. He tells me I care only about myself.

As though I really needed this! Everything's back on the table again. I pictured him worry-free up there at the bistro. Everything was working out. And now nothing's going smoothly. I say, "All right then. Enough of that. Out with it!"

It's child's play. He's struck it rich. He has them playing poker up there at the bistro. What's so unusual about that? Nothing that I can see. They were already playing belote. One game or another, what difference does it make? I don't care either way. I'm not a member of the Salvation Army. What I'm saying is that, as a rule, the ups and downs of poker can be gut-wrenching for guys who are used to playing belote. And as a rule, when guys like that get their guts wrenched, they make other people pay for it. In other words, it ends up with people's faces getting smashed in.

"That's where you're wrong." he says. "Because I knew from the start I had to go easy and be satisfied with a pot of any size, big or small. Like a regular old family man. And on top of that, because this time I've found a bunch of rascals who are really loaded. They don't give a fuck about tossing ten thousand francs on the table, any more than you do about knocking the ashes out of your pipe. Fleecing them the way I'm fleecing them—calm as can be, business as usual, night after night, all winter long—it's a land of plenty. And they're over the moon. They're the ones who keep asking for more. I've never seen the likes of it before, pal. They whoop it up every night: blood sausage, rabbit stew, store-bought wines. You've never seen anything close, no way. They invite me into their houses. And do you think their wives go sulking around? You won't believe it: They're all smiles! And they come to play too. Harder than the men. You have no idea how much scratch there is to be had around that table. I'm telling you, it beats everything. When it comes to cash and broads and whooping it up, we're kings. I don't know where their dough comes from, but take it from me, they don't mind kissing it goodbye. Another guy had already told me about what goes on here in the winter, but I'm seeing it for the first time with my own eyes.

"Ah! And then ... Don't butt in! It's never small potatoes. Talk about ups and downs! It takes a lot to rattle me, but when there's real money right under your nose, it's real money. Don't worry about heads getting busted—they're in it for a completely different reason. There were some guys who couldn't keep up the pace, but they've crawled back into their shells. Now there are six or seven, at the most—all of them hard-core. I have dinner with them every night, sometimes at one guy's place, sometimes at another's. If I don't show up, they come and find me."

I let him go on talking. What a life he leads! There are times when I've had it up to here with living my own way. I'd be glad if somebody else took over. And let come what may!

Tonight I sleep badly at first. Then finally I sleep well.

I'd be happy to spend a few days with my pal, dining on pork and stewed hare. Obviously, here at the mill I have everything I need: heat, coffee, and grub. But winter is the season of longing. I build up some strange desires. From the time I've had my morning coffee until dark, I imagine things I can't make head or tail of. Inside here, you can't see much. Without the light reflecting off the snow, you wouldn't even see at all. I reach the point where I think the oil presses look like hulking men in armor. When I warm myself in the red glow of the woodstove, I can see the tip of my nose, my hands, my knees, my legs, and my feet. The heavy, crisscrossed beams on the ceiling look like the carcass of an ox. Gusts of wind beat against the walls. The comfortable life only makes you want more, and there's no limit to what "more" can mean. I could get worked up about all kinds of things. I'm thinking about marmots, balled up in their burrows deep in the ground. Why can't the rest of us figure out how to completely stop our blood from circulating? Often, I resist going to lean against the door to listen to the radio, and then finally I do go, every time. The only relief I get comes from splitting wood. Heaving the ax over my head, swinging it down as hard as I can, and seeing the logs crack and splinter—it does me good. I could go on doing this forever. I don't feel any strain. I like the sounds of the ax striking and the logs splitting. The heartwood is beautiful when it's laid bare, and it's a pleasure to run my fingers over the sharp edge of the splinters. I have a crazy desire to hurl myself into action. There isn't much to work with. You invent all kinds of stuff. You try out even the most far-fetched things. It's crazy what you can dream up.

When the wind dies down, I go outside to smoke my pipe. The sky is as white as the ground. The snow's so thick, everything has disappeared. Little black lines, like shreds of tobacco, barely hint at the contours of the trees. Someone's rubbed an eraser over everything: The page has turned almost blank again. The tall chestnuts at the Chauvins' are blotted out. There's scarcely a trace of where they stood. The silence and whiteness leave such a void, you want to put some redness and noise into the picture, whatever it takes.

You don't want to lose your grip. You hatch a thousand schemes. This is where families come in. Women, at a time like this, are a blessing. For ten minutes. Then what? To make the world whole again, you need stuff to work with. Most of the time, you have meaningless little things within reach, that's all. But safety and security don't bring you joy. When it comes to happiness, you have to call everything into question.

To be happy means playing trump cards, waiting for them to turn up or chasing after them. Forcing someone else's hand is grand. Ask people around here what time of year they were born: They were all conceived in wintertime. There's no more daylight in the village houses or on the farms than there is here in my mill. The windowpanes are gray there just like they are here. The Jourdans' kitchen, where I drank the glass of wine after I delivered their oil, is warm and sheltered, but that's it. Otherwise, there's only the sound of the north wind beating against the walls. What's it signaling? What drama is about to begin? Over at their place, in front of the red-hot woodstove door, they too are seeing just the tips of their noses, their hands, their knees, their legs, and their feet. Granted, they can laugh among themselves for a few minutes at the noses, hands, knees, legs, and feet of the whole family lined up in front of that glowing door. But after a few minutes... then what? You can't go on loathing forever either. When crimes are committed around here, they're committed in the winter. Abusing elders, even nudging them closer to the brink, may make some people happy, but... distractions like these are short-lived! One way or another, it's all over too fast.

So where to find pleasure, in the end?

I don't know. After I've been outside staring at this blanked-out world for a while, I come back in to warm up. The Edmonds had gone out too, for a breath of fresh air, and now they're back inside as well. I'm going to listen to the radio a little; so are they. There's nothing interesting on. Why should I give a damn about Indochina or President Vincent Auriol? Well, after all, it's noise: a guy talking. If he was here, you could amuse yourself for a couple of minutes with seeing what his face would look like in front of the glowing stove door; but he's not here, so *of course* you hate him. This doesn't get us very far.

There was a radio at the Jourdans'. And I bet there's a radio at the end of the road on the left, beyond the oak woods, past the cross (it must be completely snowed under). There's the radio upstairs at the Edmonds'. These days, they've both taken to bickering on and off, when they're on their own and when they have company. Something's worrying Monsieur Edmond. Something's on his mind. There must be a shady side to the deal he's made to sell the oil, little by little, on the sly. Somebody must be raking it in; I'd swear to it under oath. Madame Edmond carries on for weeks pretending to be someone who loves all the white outside and is getting as much of it as she possibly can. She has a fake, idiotic smile on her lips all the time. Now at last she's noticed that her husband is twisting in the wind. There's something on his mind. So here she's worried too, even in this house that's warmer than the deepest burrows where marmots are sleeping. In this house surrounded by white on all sides.

I hear them squabbling with a vengeance. They're not pulling any punches. The quarrel has something to do with the "charming young lady, that tramp."

All of life's pleasures come from the marked cards. They know this upstairs on the first floor just like I know it down here on the ground floor, just like they know it in the fogged-in villages in the valley and in the fogged-in village higher up. At this point, we all have our backs to the wall. You can't put on airs anymore about what you learned in primary school. To get somebody to believe that two plus two equals five can tickle you, in a funny way; this lasts for a while. And then you realize you have all the numbers to play around with, and this game really can go on forever. For anyone who wants to be king of the castle (and who doesn't?), what a wonderful resource! If there ever was a time (and I doubt it) when you could run the business of happiness with *entries in a ledger*, that time has passed. It's winter. You have to take the bull by the horns. There's a yawning gulf between truth and life. Time-honored remedies won't help you enjoy what really counts. Cheating doesn't let you down. It pays off in this business where, above all, you need to have a bone to pick. There are people who think you have to be wearing a top hat and tails to be able to turn talk into action. I've known some of them. They were wild about hunting. All day long, over hill and dale, with expensive rifles. And they weren't bad shots, not at all. You'd think what they enjoyed was watching the quail fall out of the sky. And besides, it was written on their tomato-red faces. They had marble teeth, golden mustaches, and the guiltless eyes of skilled killers. But if you looked a bit closer, signs of other things were engraved here and there. Choices made long ago had carved out creases around their mouths. As far as I could tell, the only reason they shot quail was because they had too much of everything else. And none of them proved me wrong through their actions. When you're face-to-face with the problem of what we call living—which is, at bottom, simply the problem of *passing your time*—you soon realize that nothing's going to change unless you change the way you think about things. Father and mother, wife and child, male and female neighbors: If you deal with them the way you're expected to, you get nowhere. But if you don't, what a miracle! Then things really do start to move: Green turns red, trout build their nests in bushes, mountains march on the slightest command. It's the only way not to end up empty-handed.

And there's nothing unusual about this. Everybody goes on about what's right and what's wrong. Who actually puts it into practice? Nobody, I should hope! Anyway, if they do, I'm not aware of it. There always comes a point when I lie in wait for them and I find them out—the ones who claim otherwise. It's impossible to move forward when you're knee-deep in righteousness. They'll all tell you they've marked the trail. But . . . just try. With the first step, you'll sink up to your waist. And then, forward march! Climb mountains, cross over passes, try to make real headway. Simply try, if you live off the beaten track, to get as far as the tobacco shop to buy a packet of shag. It could cost you your life. They all have snowshoes or skis. While you're slaving away, they're flying like birds. And suppose you do actually make it to the shop, you'll only find it empty. They'll have made it there ahead of you. You'll be sucking on your pipe stem while they're smoking the tobacco. So tell me: What, in the long run, counts more than knowledge won by experience?

Like anywhere else, of course, nobody here claims to be a hero; there are no knights in shining armor. The people in the village are honest sinners. Do you think they would have forced those hunters I was talking about just now to confess, before letting them off the hook? To draw up testimonials for them would require a whole army of scribes. You must be joking if you think the authorities have nothing better to do than investigate people who've gradually learned to behave in ways you're not supposed to. In other words, nothing better to do than investigate everyone! That's the way it is, and that's justice. And there it is: the big word.

Gambling for high stakes, that's life, and cheating so you don't run any risk of losing big. Never show your hand. The king who controls everything you'll ever want—even if he's the lord of the flies—has to be deposed.

I have my mill, my woodstoves, and my den between the sacks to keep me warm and safe, but to *stack the deck* nonstop in your own favor is a lot safer. If you wait without guile for the curtain to rise, until the north wind starts pounding relentlessly against the walls, then the same play, *One Day of Joy, a Hundred Years of Sorrow*, will be performed for you year after year. And all the children around here will be born between the end of July and the beginning of October. I'm sure you can see: There's too much of a pattern for it not to be a scheme. The mischief stands out in bold relief.

To cheat: how reliable, how profitable! You get such rewards for your efforts! And even the efforts are a pleasure. What sure protection!

Monsieur Edmond comes downstairs to make his tour of inspection and have his chitchat. For the past few days, he's been dodging the question. We've already loaded oil three times for that same truck driver. And always according to the same ritual. Since I'm like a member of the family, I ask for a day off. To do what? I don't answer. I laugh. "All right," says Monsieur Edmond.

I trim my beard. It's a thing of splendor. Gilded. I look like a pope. I heat a basin of water. I scrub myself from head to foot.

I climb up to the village wearing my old duds, but I go to the thrift store and overhaul my wardrobe. I buy myself a shirt, pants, a velvet hunting jacket, plus two feet of black ribbed silk to make the kind of little necktie I like. I go by Anatole's and have my hair clipped at the nape of my neck and trimmed around my ears. In the mirror I see one hell of a bright-eyed, bushy-tailed customer. Anatole wants to plaster me with violet pomade or a lotion with the scent of new-mown hay. I stop him. I like how I smell. And I've often noticed that it doesn't make the ladies turn their noses up. I'm a blond and I'm all fired up. Usually, this makes a good impression. I have no desire for Anatole to stink up my charms with his spray bottle.

I think for a minute, and I go around first to Louis's place. He's in his kitchen unpacking boxes of lined slippers. I ask if he happens to have some lace-up boots I can afford. We go down to the stable where he keeps his market wares, and he finds what I'm after: a pair with tough rubber soles and cowhide uppers. "Try warming these up," he says. "They're as soft as a glove." And in fact, in less than five minutes, it's true. He also finds me what he calls an "English" cap, and why shouldn't it be? In any case, it has earflaps. If that's how they make them in England, they must know a thing or two!

It's a treat to stroll around in this outfit. I have a weakness for dressing up. But I haven't let go of my old knitted sweater.

I climb up to the inn at the stroke of ten in the morning, and Ma Machin can't believe her eyes. She asks if I'm on my way to a wedding. I say yes. My beard, my velvet, my innocent gaze, and my scent perform their number to perfection.

I go upstairs to the artist's room. Naturally, he's still in bed. Seeing me in my new gear leaves him speechless. He didn't see this coming. I couldn't be happier. I'm on top of the world.

We order some veal steaks and potatoes. Without asking, the owner throws in some fried blood sausage and a plate of *chouilles*—grilled morsels she carved from the throat of her own pig, slaughtered the day before yesterday. We drink wine from a store-bought bottle. This is the good life, pure and simple.

At three in the afternoon, Nestor and Daumas Jr. show up. A little later, Ovide Molinier and Ferréol, along with a character I can't place, somebody they call Ironwire. Next, it's the oldest of the Gauthiers and Arsène Giraud, who's already roaring drunk. And then the weather, which was already overcast, turns to driving snow. It blots out the houses across the way.

All the members of this select company have shaken the artist's hand and mine. We've settled down at a table close to the woodstove and started knocking back liters of white wine. It's grand. My velvet jacket smells new, and the scent of it goes to my head.

We play "Catherine": a game from these parts—a kind of poker crossed with bezique. Something your grandfather might have played. But vicious and very fast. It's full of little traps like the side pockets on a billiard table. Just when you think you're safe, a blackjack goes whistling past your ear. All the gang members are smoking like chimneys, and the game suits them to a T: Giraud with his nose like a shoe, Ovide with his goiter, Ironwire, who could pass through the eye of a needle, Nestor, who tips the scales at two hundred and sixty, and the younger Daumas with his movie-star looks—all of them gluttons for the sort of thing we've just launched into.

I take my place at the table. After my purchases this morning, I have seven thousand francs left. Fortunately, they bear some offspring right from the start. Otherwise, I wouldn't be able to keep up. These boys barely say a word, but they play for high stakes. Even after somebody wins a big jackpot in a clean sweep, the silence is profound. And then the next round begins.

Basically, they couldn't care less about the dough. I know it's easy for them to earn money from their timber, but I still like the casual way they treat the jackpot.

There's certainly something else involved in this game, for all of us. It's not the first time in my life I've indulged in this kind of fun. I even come across like a hardened customer. That's to say, by enjoying risk for risk's sake, the way you're supposed to. I never sit down at a card table with a bankbook in mind. I know how to work myself up into a state of undeniable superiority, whether I win or lose. I'm aiming for what really counts: being fully alive and being somebody. When I feel like that, my wallet doesn't matter at all.

Obviously, this is true for everybody (more or less), and it's especially true around our snowbound card table because we've all come here to prove this very point. But the artist has given the proceedings a bit of an unusual twist.

During the early rounds, I keep a sharp eye on him but not in any obvious way. If he noticed, it would put him on guard. I don't see the slightest sign. Which makes me wonder if I only dreamt those nimble fingers, those trump cards streaming from his hands, just like they streamed out of the machine that made them. He isn't winning; he doesn't seem to be losing. Neither do I. I'm making some gains (like I said—or else I'd already be out of the game), but I'm winning in the usual way, *in the natural order of things*. And it's the same for the rest of these characters. Any one of us can get lucky.

It's stupid of me to wonder if everything's going the way it's supposed to. I'm so taken with the smell of my velvet jacket and so happy to see the black tips of my ribbed silk necktie underneath my beard, that I'd prefer the artist not to be on a losing streak right now. My fears are short-lived. He couldn't care less about my velvet jacket or give a fig about any of us. There's a crust of dried spit forming around his mouth like it does when he's on a roll. I've seen that ugly look of triumph on his face lots of times before when everything's been going his way.

But it isn't the betting that's making him happy. Nestor wagers wads of banknotes, emptying his pockets, then half closes his eyes and leans back in his chair. He's holding a good hand. But he knows that every good hand can lead to ruin. He raises the stakes to force himself to stay clearheaded. Daumas Jr., with his little handlebar mustache, bets like a kid. It's dangerous for everyone: for him and for us. This is what he wants. Two or three times he drags us into tight spots where the rest of us, twenty years older, are at risk of ending up being given up for lost, like dregs. He enjoys watching us flounder when real inspiration is required. Sometimes we're the ones who have it, not him. Then his disappointment spurs him on. Ah, youth!

Ironwire's style of play comes closest to mine. He can't lose—he's gambling for gambling's sake. However much he has, he'll give it up gladly. His cash couldn't buy him anything better than this. Everybody's a sucker, except for him. Nobody else around the table is skilled enough to worry about. Molinier, Ferréol, the elder Gauthier, Giraud: They're perfect partners for a square dance, and they move to the music by more than just instinct. You can't deny it, when it comes to doing a jig, they're second to none. They're happy to take the woman's part. They all have deep pockets. Not just that, but out past the pure white windows, where there's no trace left of the village or of the rest of the world, they can see, without even having to look, all of the assets that life and the compromises they've made day after day have heaped up around them: the power they could throw down on the table in one fell swoop, even at the risk of losing everything. What joy! (And some people say this region is poverty-stricken!) Farms, households, cattle, sheep, haylofts, croplands, cars, trucks, tractors, horse teams, logging camps, sawmills, lumber, wool stockings, bank accounts, safe-deposit boxes, gold coins, deeds of sale . . . And surrounding them, snaking through the crusted earth, all the roads that belong to no one in particular: the channels where, by a stroke of bad luck, everything could drain away like water.

I see the artist's beady badger eyes delving around in every direction, digging up truffles, savoring them. There are daisy petals of spit at the corner of his mouth. He doesn't need to watch his hands for them to perform their secret operations. That's why he goes undetected. I think he's found something *better than gambling*: He cheats. He's never safe. His winnings can always be challenged. He constantly risks his stake and his own hide. But his stake doesn't matter, because he cheats and can draw on it at will. He can shift it over to anyone else around the table, as a setup for winning the jackpot himself. What counts is his own hide, and that's what he risks. Winning a big jackpot only serves to put his hide at even greater risk. He has no reserves to fall back on, except for his four or five liters of blood, and they could spill out, at any moment, into the sawdust . . . where we're all spitting, profusely. And this explains the switchblade (we're no saints), which, without having to look, I know he has in his pocket. Regardless of this dishonesty (and, like I said, he's under no *obligation* to be a saint), he's a much stronger player than we are. He's the one who's playing for real. Cheating *obliges* him to put his very existence at stake. He is a true somebody.

Suddenly, I feel a little down. He's lying to himself, lying with that ugly look in his eyes that comes from wanting things more passionately, more badly than everyone else.

Naturally, there's no limit on the betting.

By about seven o'clock, we've had enough. I've won close to fifteen thousand. The artist is down four. Nestor is up five. The rest are in the hole, except for Ovide, who's taken close to sixty grand.

I would have assumed it's over. But it seems there are better things in store. Somebody says we should go and eat at Ferréol's. We run over there. But only in a manner of speaking, because a good eight inches of fresh snow have fallen during the afternoon, on top of the old, packed stuff underneath. It's like we're going two steps forward, three steps back, all the way to the edge of the village. And here outside the shelter of the walls, everything's frozen stiff, like iron.

A razor-sharp wind usually sets in at this time of day. The clouds have lifted, and now and then a moonbeam drops down to see if anything here on earth has been left in one piece. Nothing. The few trees still standing have been stripped of their branches on one side or in their middle. They're wrecks—bare outlines, heaps of debris. Toward the north, it's as white as snow (as they say). Now and then toward the south, one or two twigs still show signs of life.

All nine of us are climbing our own, separate paths. No one breathes a word except occasionally something to do with the cold.

Ferréol lives higher up in the first hamlet we passed on our way down here, the artist and me. It's a house with roofs that go on forever.

Ferréol's wife is a little boozehound intent on making use, in every way she can, of each and every ounce of her hundred and twelve pounds. I was worried she'd kick us out or make us feel like she wanted to, which is what you'd expect. But . . . no, not at all. As we're coming into the house single file, she passes us under detailed inspection, one by one, for her own personal ends. She has an amazing feel for this. Something like the artist's touch—well honed, well practiced. You couldn't possibly mistake her for a strumpet. But she knows what she's after, and you couldn't possibly mistake that either. And she quickly makes it clear to me that as the rawest recruit of the lot, I have some forced labor in the offing. Well, it's not the kind of duty I'm in the habit of shirking. She knows exactly what lies behind my sheepish looks and my standoffishness.

She's slender but shapely, maybe forty-two, forty-three. She acts like she's above it all. But I don't believe she could last for five minutes with any man—on foot, on horseback, on a train, on a bus, on a sidewalk—without striking up a conversation, exposing a weakness, swooning over trifles. "Oh, what lovely trouser buttons you have!" And so on. The last man she's met is always her Rainmaker, her king of the gods. It's as plain as the nose on your face. You don't have to be a specialist. A six-month-old child would be able to tell: This lady is strong medicine, for external use only. She's already wondering what to use as an excuse: my beard or something else?

The house reeks of money. I knew Ferréol was logging his thousands of acres. But I was far from picturing everything that a good little woman in need of company could make of that.

We start by knocking back aperitifs. And what's clear, aside from what I've just been saying, is that we were expected. Ferréol has brought us here to feed like bread crumbs to his little dove.

There are delicious smells: a hare stew—maybe even wild boar—and there must be a roast tucked into an oven somewhere.

Daumas Jr. would love to use his mustache to flirt with one of the maids, but he's not as commanding as he is at cards. He'd be more likely to pick handfuls of flowers out of thin air, or so it seems. Strange guy.

I'm thinking: With these three or four women (and one of them in particular), all it would take is a chord or two on the guitar, and the artist would be the most sought-after houseguest in this whole neck of the woods. But no, he's looking serious, and this suits his ugly gaze to perfection. Madame Ferréol and her serving gals are bouncing off him like billiard balls off the side cushion.

So while I'm reflecting—in awe, after all, of the countless enticements of this land of Cockaigne (I'm indifferent only when I'm trying to stay calm)—we take off our jackets, even our sweaters, to be able to withstand all the different forms of heat that are coming at us. And now it's time to eat.

We sit down to a stupendous meal, conducting ourselves with honor and dignity, as the saying goes. In my opinion, there's only one way to eat: Never let your belly stand in the way. If it acts like it's full—who cares? Keep on going! You'll be amazed by how much you can still stuff in. What we most need—each and every one of us—is strong blood. As much of it as possible. A lot of the things we love can demand it of us at any moment. How stupid to miss out on these wonders for want of a few drops of blood. Eating sorts all of this out.

We're storing up a lot of strong blood in this place hemmed in by snow, by night, by boredom . . . We load our bellies with morsels of home-cooked wild boar, swigs of wine, slices of bread soaked in pepper sauce, the way you stuff the pockets of your hunting jacket with handfuls of cartridges. And we don't save anything up—we're not hoarders. We're not here to bottle our blood, but to scatter it to the winds. There are still heaps of food on the table when we already have cards back in our hands. One more mouthful, and we're *cutting* the deck. We're setting the wheels of fate in motion. We're in a hurry and we have every reason to be. You'd have to have spent your whole life with your ass stuck to a chair not to understand why.

And the hundred-twelve-pound lady, I admire her after all. She shows she's interested in playing with us and just as hard. But she's not losing sight of the other way she can use up her blood and squander her resources. If she knew what I'm thinking about her right now, she wouldn't be flattered. If she knew what all these other men she's had delivered to her were thinking about her a minute ago, she wouldn't be proud. But pride is one thing and loneliness is another. You don't fire shots into the air to slay the Beast. No, you fire them to scare the Beast and to make yourself feel better. Who can fend off the physical need to be somebody? The end justifies the means.

In no time flat, they sweep the table clear. Ferréol pulls down the counterweighted lamp and brings the electric bulb level with our heads. I wonder how the artist will be able to keep on cheating in this much light. Inside his narrow ribcage, the well-oiled machinery must already be hard at work.

Ovide has a charming way of adjusting his shirt collar to keep his goiter firmly in place. Nestor rubs his butt against the seat of the wicker chair until his cheeks are comfortably spread apart and settled in. The hundred-and-twelve-pound lady moistens a quarter inch of her lip with an ounce of her tongue. We all get as comfortable as we can, and someone says out loud what everybody already knows: There will be no limit. You bet there won't! What would be the point?

Silence. The dealer deals.

This time we play fast. This is no longer café gambling. This is timber baron's gambling. Here in his own home, he's in charge. The first jackpot takes my breath away. The second one doesn't give it back. The artist is sitting pretty like the bearded lady at the fair.

Already I've lost heart. I fold two hands in a row. Ferréol didn't need to lower the lamp. I get the picture: The more you have, the more you want. These mountain forest men will never stop wanting more. They'll never be godlike enough in each other's eyes (or in God's eyes). Now they're using cash and sets of rules. They'll never get there. I'd feel better if they *were* playing for the money. I don't feel better at all.

It makes me feel even worse when I sense, vaguely, that the artist is still gambling like he does at the café. What does he have in mind, I wonder, spreading his largesse around under this blinding light? But now I see he's succeeding where the others are failing. He's the only one who's playing with the blood he's just stored up, and just as boldly as the others are risking their cash.

What's stopping him from performing his sleights of hand if he wanted to, like he does at the café? He's as skillful as ever. I can see he's forcing himself not to be. Every once in a while, *he loses his self-control* and pulls off an unsuspected coup, in spectacular fashion, without meaning to. But right afterward, he gets it back. There's too much snow, too much darkness; we're too far away from everything. Then he lets his guard down, discusses the hands, cheats in slow motion. He comes close to giving himself away. The other boys around the table stay poker-faced, no matter what; this is how you're supposed to play; it means they're taking the game seriously. At every moment, the artist's belly comes within a hairbreadth of the horns of the bull. He's chewing on a whole bouquet of saliva.

I don't have the guts, or the dough, to stay in the game. I get up to stretch my legs.

Why don't you go and get some wine from the cellar? Ferréol says. The hundred-and-twelve-pound lady lights the oil lamp, and down we go.

When we come back up, everybody's laughing. Did we plan to spend the night down there? they ask. They couldn't be less concerned if we'd been playing marbles. They're at the same point themselves. They're no better off now than they were before they started playing. Whether the dough's stacked higher or lower, in front of one guy or another—that's not what gives them their kick. If it was, they'd have to go on playing forever. But wouldn't they get tired of it? Wouldn't they need to switch to some other form of exercise? The artist keeps on risking his own hide, and he's hardly interested anymore either. He must have wiped his mouth while I was in the cellar. His lips are clean. He's telling a joke. He's stuffing a wad of cash into his pocket. The other winners are doing the same. It's over for tonight.

Nestor still has a good hour to travel before he gets home. He has to climb all the way up to La Clarée. Luckily, the wind has broken up the clouds. The moon swims in big stretches of open sky. There are moments when you see into them like it was broad daylight. It's freezing cold, and the snow is packed hard. The glass-coated forests are tinkling like crystal.

Daumas Jr. takes off to the left. I head downhill with the elder Gauthier, Ironwire, and the artist. From time to time, we give a hand to Arsène Giraud, who's been bingeing non-stop. Nevertheless, he's not that unsteady on his legs. He's been getting drunk around here all his life: winter and summer, day and night, in wind, in hail. He knows the local watering holes here every bit as well as we do. Ovide Molinier has stopped to drop his pants and take a dump.

We pass through some groves, where our merry band shatters the frost off the shrubs. We're glistening like Santa Clauses sprinkled with sugar. The farther down we go, the closer the fog comes to meet us, like a crowd of faces. Soon we're surrounded by a whole swarm of weird-looking characters. Ovide Molinier hails us, and we wait for him.

I still have to make it to the mill, but I take a little detour to see the artist back to the bistro. After the two of us have left the rest of the group, we stick to the ring of pastureland. This way we can stay in the clear, away from the village streets. All day long, shopkeepers and tradesmen will have swept up mounds of trash and snow that you can break your neck on. We walk without saying a word across the grazed slope. This is a peaceful moment. I feel completely at ease and very happy.

"So are you interested?" asks the artist.

"It'd be hard."

"What about giving it another try?"

"I'm not saying no. But not right away. Let's face it, you don't need my pretty face that badly."

"No. But I'd like to see if you could really sink your teeth into it."

"You've already seen me with my mouth full of steak."

"That's not the same kind of meat."

"I think it is."

"In any case, you have what it takes."

"You bet! Why wouldn't I?"

"I don't know. You don't have the look."

"Maybe not the look, but I have the eye."

"You know the door is always open."

I can't resist telling him there's no place, ever, that doesn't have at least one closed door.

He mulls this over for a minute. Then he laughs and says, "You're nobody's fool."

It's three or four in the morning when I push open the back door of the mill. I stoke my woodstoves, then I stretch out in my den without bothering to take off my fancy new duds. I scold myself for this just before I fall asleep, but it's too late now even to lift my little finger.

The weather puts on a forced smile for two or three days. We'd lost sight of the thickly wooded face of the landscape, for quite a while. I enjoy watching it reappear while the wind and sun jostle the clouds and the fog. You still couldn't tell that anybody's living out there. Seeing the unbroken layer of thick snow that's covering everything, you wouldn't think so. But from one day to the next, I see some black chevrons appear—they're the crowns of fir plantations—and some dark circles where the ground around isolated houses has been trampled. Close to noon, when the sun's shining, some small, shadowy creatures show up in front of the sheepfolds: sheep that have been let out to stretch their legs and get some fresh air. Then darkness falls, and the blue frost makes the forests crackle. Then it's night, and everyone goes silent.

Of course, I've added up the tally of that grand day of bingeing. In all, I won thirteen thousand francs. And, let's say, some perks on the side.

The Edmonds aren't getting along much better. On the contrary. Every day, the two of them are squawking louder than the radio. To make matters worse, when a row kicks up they turn the radio off. They only turn it back on once it's over. I hear scraps of bickering, a lot of it concerning the charming young lady. There are times when Monsieur Edmond doesn't hold back from being the one to hit the highest notes. To hear them go at it, you'd think they were both dirty bastards. Why not? It's all too likely. What difference does it make? Wouldn't it be better to agree to disagree? Instead, they spend all day trying to patch things up, only to find out that the patches don't stick. Why? Did they really think they would?

They've buried a young woman from the village. She died in labor. The baby was conceived in the spring.

You can try not to be ruled by circumstances. To be a hardheaded strongman is as good an act as any other. It takes all kinds to make the world go round. You'll find out soon enough about recoils and backfires.

Life (I'm reflecting) is made of a thousand nothings. Some people are happy to settle for this. But no: Maybe the first daffodil of the season really does count for something. And not necessarily because of its beauty.

An alarm goes up nearby. The Chauvins have a fire in their chimney. Everybody comes running. In the end, there's been a lot of commotion but not much damage.

The next day, Monsieur Edmond helps me clean our

stovepipes. We should sweep the chimney too. But with the amount of snow on the roof, there's no way. I come up with the idea that there might be an opening in the attic. We go and look. Yes, there is. We're able to do a proper scouring. Ten years' worth of soot. We've been sleeping on a volcano. Tonight as I'm going to bed, I give my den a funny look.

I think about Nestor, as big as an ox, climbing in the pitch-dark up to La Clarée . . . to return to what? To an endless succession of stages (as soon as we exit one, we enter another) where we perform our little number, every minute of every day, completely on our own. And then we go to sleep, with scenery and a full cast.

The weather has taken a turn for the worse. Monsieur Edmond comes downstairs and sits next to my stove.

"Would you do me a little favor?"

"I'd be happy to."

"Something's bothering me."

"Name it."

"I need you to go to that skinny guy's place."

"Okay, I get it. To do what?"

"Tomorrow at noon, come up while we're eating and ask me for two days off."

"That'll look pretty strange. It's not that long since I took one."

"I know. Couldn't you come up with an excuse?"

"I could run up there one afternoon with the delivery van."

"We won't use the van. You're going in secret. On foot. There are shortcuts, but you'll have to stay overnight at Pont-de-l'Étoile on the way back. There's no other way."

"You wouldn't want me to try and make it there and back in one day?"

"Out of the question."

"How many miles is it?"

"It's not about the distance. Even if you take the bridge, don't even think about it. The path I'm going to tell you about is rough at this time of year, especially coming back. I wouldn't want you to get stuck out there. You'd be in a real fix!"

"Will Madame Edmond believe us, no matter what we tell her? You know she always has to have her say."

"You're right, it's hard to get *her* to believe anything...!"

"Still, I guess the story would have to hold up!"

"You can say that again! It has to be ironclad. Most of all, we need to be sure she doesn't drive out in that direction."

"Then I don't know what to say. It's up to you."

He opens his mouth to give an answer (and I know what it'll be), when Madame Edmond calls me from upstairs. "Have you seen my husband?"

I give the boss a wink.

"He's in the cowshed," I shout back.

"I'm on my way," Monsieur Edmond whispers. And he leaves by the back door.

I spend the whole evening mulling over his plan of action. How can we keep the lady from poking her nose in? Now I have an idea, and it makes me laugh.

The next day at noon, when I figure they must have started to eat, I go upstairs. I'm going to try my best to sound like a complete idiot. Monsieur Edmond is hidden behind the daily paper; he has it propped up against the wine bottle. When he sees me, he chokes on some of his soup. "What do you want?" he barks. I ask straight-out for two days off. And at least (I insist) one night away.

"Again?" says Madame Edmond.

This is where sounding like an idiot works to my advantage. I open my eyes as wide as I can before I say inanely, "What? Yes!"

She's chewing on bitterness along with her soup.

"To do what?"

I look her straight in the eye. "I have a girlfriend in the area."

She's quick. She comes back without missing a beat. "You too?"

But I'd anticipated this move, and I carry right on. "Put yourself in my place." This leaves her tongue-tied. And while it's still tied, I add very nicely, "She has her needs."

She turns as red as a beet.

"Well then," says Monsieur Edmond, and for ten minutes he bawls me out. I'm subjected to all kinds of threats. He's not so bad at playacting either.

All in all, I was right: We had to be subtle and indirect. Words don't mean the same things for everybody. I head back into my burrow, with my two days off . . . and my one night. What was Ma Edmond really able to picture about my one night? In a flash, the vision must have held her spellbound . . . like one of those glass paperweights filled with snow, or balloons, or multicolored confetti raining down endlessly inside. Ah! The she-devil! I bet you can still squeeze a few glasses of heady red wine from even the driest of popes.

As usual, Monsieur Edmond comes downstairs early in the evening. At the same time, the lady of the house has the radio tuned to a jazz program I really enjoy listening to. She's busy doing a lavender stomach purge. She'd give every drop of oil in this mill to be sure of having sweet-smelling breath.

The boss starts off politely enough. We trade a few compliments. We waste a bit of time this way, but it doesn't matter. When he finally decides to tell me exactly what he's coming around to, it's more or less what I thought, and I'm hardly satisfied. He wants me to take two hundred grand, in cash, to the skinny guy. If one of us finds this jaw-dropping, it's me!

I raise an idiotic objection that rules itself out the moment I make it: "And what if I hang on to the dough?"

He's ready to fire back.

"First of all, you're not that kind of guy. Next, in this weather we'd catch up with you before you could ever make it to the highway. The telephone's working."

No reason to take offense—I had it coming. And he's right: The weather will work in his favor and keep me honest, as well. But two hundred thousand. That's too much.

"I'm not happy about this."

"And me?" he says. "Do you think I am?"

If he's coughing up two hundred grand, apparently not.

He reveals a bit more about the whole affair. It stinks of corruption like a basketful of rotting fowl in the rear compartment of a bus. I say, "Let's move on to the technical details." I'd be happier if they weren't fully spelled out. The less I know, the easier I can breathe. We should leave a lot of the particulars in the dark. We go over the directions.

By following his route, you reach the rapids at the bottom of the valley in two hours. He knows the path like the back of his hand. Tomorrow, if the weather's still messing around and rattling the windowpanes, it will take me at least three or four hours to cover the same distance—and even then only because I'm in good shape. First, I have to cross the stream. That's a piece of cake. And after that? After that, in fair weather, it's easy. And in foul? Harder. Just as I thought. There are three landmarks, supposedly: a couple of sheepfolds, which must look like molehills under the snow right now, and one farm, where I hope they'll have left a wide circle of footprints. I'll meet up with the road to Pont-de-l'Étoile, and from there I'll get to the cross. (It must be buried under ten feet of snow, that cross of hers. All the same, he doesn't think I'll have to root around too hard to find it.) Then the oak woods, then the lane to the left. Got it. I'll have to stay sharp and make it to the landmarks in broad daylight. Otherwise, I'll be up against it, maybe over my head. There's no question, nature doesn't clear the way for the march of progress.

"All right, boss, leaving aside your crack about the telephone, don't you think it would be better to try doing this on a day when the weather's good?"

He tells me he's not the one in charge, and it's urgent. He goes back to wallowing in his basketful of rotting fowl. He must know I have a sensitive nose. I give in to him in a minute.

He fills me in a little more. There'll be no receipt. The skinny guy will give me something in exchange for the cash. To my way of thinking, it better not be anything too heavy.

After this, he goes back upstairs. I have a bite and I hit the sack. No doubt he does too. Silent night, holy night, just like any other night: Jesus comes down to earth. I'd be curious to see the expressions on the faces of the guardian angels holding their feathered fans at the foot of the Edmonds' marriage bed.

Now the following morning, the weather's holding steady—neither fair nor foul. From what you can see of it, the valley floor's as black as ink; up at our height, a mass of clouds the color of whitewash is drifting past. But you can sense the weather's becoming unpredictable. Depending on its mood, it will do as it pleases. All you have to do is slide neatly between a rock and a hard place.

In a hurry, Monsieur Edmond comes down to give me the little package. It's tied up in newspaper. I stuff it into my rucksack along with a snack and a half liter of eau-de-vie.

The crust on the snow is firm enough to walk on. I start out to the right of the mill, like he said. Before I get to the edge of the woods, I head downhill. The lower I go, the more I run into balls of mist. They're flocking together like sheep stringing their lambs along the mountainside, nosing into clumps of trees, greeting me with their big, woolly heads. Some of them slide right across my body. They're smooth and unyielding.

An hour later, I'm lost. If I weren't, I'd be so surprised I'd actually be more concerned. I carry on downhill, watching my step. I'm in some woods, and I take care to grab on to the trees. The slope's not very steep. If Monsieur Edmond was right, down below there should be a scattering of farms, the village of Les Chauvettes. Sure enough, once I leave the woods I hear somebody whistle for a dog.

I head in that direction. A guy emerges from the fog. He looks amazed to find me here. Is this Les Chauvettes? I ask. No. Where is it? He doesn't know. Is he from around here? No, he's from Linganières. Where's he going? Well yes, that's where he's going. This amazes me. In my opinion, Linganières should be a long way to my left, and he's walking to my right. I tell him so. This doesn't seem to surprise him. I tell him I'm lost. He tells me he's lost too. On this note, we load our pipes. Was he whistling for a dog just now? Yes, he was whistling but not for a dog. Well then, for what? Well then ... for no reason. All right then, till we meet again. Where are you headed? I'm heading down. Safe trip home. You too.

I forgot to give him a shot of eau-de-vie. But it's not really that cold out—just cold enough—and it feels good to be walking. Truth is, I've been holed up in my den for so long, I've been close to prancing off to anywhere at all, in any direction. I couldn't care less about the boss's errand. I'm taking advantage of the chance to roam around. What makes it really worthwhile are these shafts of grayish light slanting through the mist. They're like the fog lamps of a car landing on a beech, a pine, a larch ... or hitting the blank surface of the snow, which suddenly takes on a hundred blended colors, like a seashell. I'm breathing so hard, it makes me wonder if you could possibly learn (with practice, obviously) to drown in air like you drown in water. You'd get to enjoy the classic sequence of events: a sharp knock in your ears, followed by a stream of all your memories, all the wild ideas you've ever had, but cleansed, enriched, and brightly polished.

This is the state I'm in when I suddenly wonder if the black patch I just happened to glimpse to my left could be the front of a wooden cabin. Yes it is, and there's even somebody inside. I say, "Hallo there!" Someone answers. I go in. It's a guy who's starting a blaze in the fireplace. We don't say any more than we need to. The fire burns bright. It's a fine moment, peaceful. This is the time when it's worth filling your pipe properly, tamping the tobacco down with your thumb. What am I up to in this neck of the woods? I'm on my way down. What brings him here? He's come to see his cabin. He was dying of boredom. He climbed up slowly, having nothing better to do. And what's he doing here? Nothing. Is he going back down? Yes. He'll warm himself by the fire, and then he'll head back down. That's good enough for me. Where's he going back to? Home. Where's home? His farm. Which one? Les Poulinières. This means nothing to me. I'm headed for the Pont-de-l'Étoile road. Am I going in the right direction? Yes and no. Oh, that's perfect! Let's enjoy ourselves while we can.

He fills me in about Pont de l'Étoile. If it was him, after Les Poulinières he'd head left and join up with the postman's trail. That's the way I'll do it.

What do I think about the latest events in the world? I ask which ones. Do I read the papers? No. I tell him a thing or two about my life at the mill. He knows my boss. He thinks Edmond's a good man. So do I. Here's something we agree on already. But he's amazed I don't read the papers. Do I listen to the radio? Yes. I tell him how I get to listen and what I listen to. This also amazes him. I tell him I'm just an ordinary guy, and it doesn't do me any good to have opinions on current events. I get by from day to day. That's my way. He shakes his head and tells me that's no way to be. Why? What's so unusual right now? All kinds of things. Indochina. They've put up a recruitment poster at the police station in Pont. And Russia, what do I think? Am I a communist? Well, if war breaks out, I'll be done for like everybody else in the long run. But what good is it not to be prepared? Things are getting worse every day. You have to get involved. Yesterday, there was a special meeting of the Council of Ministers. Basically, he's right: I don't keep up with anything, and it's a mistake. I tell him that, one way or another, I'm trying to stay out of trouble for as long as I can. What I'm saying is just plain dumb. I ask him for some pointers. He gives me some.

After this, we head out into the fog. It's gotten thicker. The bottom of the valley is turning a deeper and deeper shade of navy blue. He'd like me to come into his house. But when I ask him the time, I realize I need to get going. I push ahead blindly for an hour until I find the postman's trail, and I take it.

After a while, it brings me to some houses. I skirt around them while the dogs are barking. I get back on the trail, but it's the wrong one. It leads to a cistern and ends. I have to turn back toward the houses, and I make the dogs bark all over again. A woman comes out on her doorstep, shades her eyes with her hand, looks me over, goes back in, shuts the door. Now the dogs' concert is at its loudest. A black one with a sly look—he's as big as a donkey—comes at me step by step. His ears are straight up, but he's not growling. This I don't like. I back off, keeping an eye on him, and he keeps coming forward. In this fashion, he escorts me all the way to the edge of the beech woods. I slip into them as he comes to a stop and carefully sniffs my footprints. How trusting! But the dog and the woman were both right. This is how you have to do it.

By chance, I find my way back to the postman's trail. Now I have it easy for at least an hour. The slope gets steeper and steeper, and I'm dropping fast, deep into the navy blue of the valley. I'm going on blind faith. Everything's calm and dark. My tough rubber soles (I'm wearing my boots, of course) don't slip. They crunch in the snow. This is the only sound I hear when I stop, other than a light breeze as soft as velvet. It's such a light breath, I don't even feel it on my cheeks—they're stiff with cold—but it does make the glass frosting on the beech boughs click. Once in a while, the valley bottom (it can't be very far off now) lets out a deep, heavy sigh. It's probably around eleven o'clock.

I'm walking inside a film negative: the trees are white, the daylight's black. I'm strongly attracted to anything unnatural. If everything was how it was supposed to be—trees dark, sky light—I wouldn't enjoy it as much. Opposites arouse my curiosity. It's true: It only takes one sip, and you're hooked. I never stop wanting more.

I have the postman's trail right underfoot, and I don't stray an inch. I snack on some sausage and a crust of bread, and I drink a glass of eau-de-vie. Strange as it may seem, I reach a spot where I can see perfectly well ahead in spite of the inky darkness. So I figure I must be below the bank of mist. And yes, I can make out the bottom of the valley, shrouded in its own darkness, a few hundred yards lower down.

I cross the rushing stream. Half an hour later, I smell woodsmoke coming from Pont-de-l'Étoile. I stick to my right and steer clear of the settlement itself. It's around two in the afternoon when I recognize the oak woods. The lane that leads to the skinny guy's place shows up right away at the north edge. There are fresh track marks. But I walk for another twenty minutes before I see the house.

No dog. A lamp in one window. The snow hasn't stuck to the sheer banks of schist. In the midst of all the whiteness, they're as smooth and black as slate tablets: a stack of death announcement cards. I'm completely out of place here, carrying my two hundred grand. And once I've handed the dough over... then who will be out of place, surrounded by all this high-class mourning? Something's not right. I go up to the door, feeling a strong urge to laugh out loud.

I knock. A fine-looking little woman opens the door. She's as white as a turnip, pregnant, and cradling a one-year-old in her arms. Her husband's not here. She has the brightest blue eyes I've ever seen. What are you here for? It's private. Maybe for lavender oil? No. No? Come in anyway, don't freeze. A big woodstove takes up the whole middle of the room. Near the stove: a two-year-old in a high chair. Near the stove: an old, upholstered easy chair, the worse for wear. So why exactly are you here? Oh! Just a bit of business. Near the stove, on the floor: a blanket where a three-year-old is playing with bobbins. Are you from Pont-Neuf? No. No. I tell her where I'm from. Near the stove: a table, and behind the table, sticking his head out, a four-year-old (he must be), who's watching me. Will your husband be coming back? Yes, he hasn't gone far, just a few steps away, to check if there's any frost in the silo. If you want, I can shout out to him. Yes, I'd prefer not to stay too long, the weather's bad. She goes to the doorway and yells. You'd think she was a nanny goat. All the children have big heads and their mother's eyes. Since they haven't had enough time to learn much of anything, their gazes crudely express what hers must occasionally reveal: fear, spite, and the ecstasy of sucking on your thumb. She gets me to sit down. We talk. But it's her gaze (so bright, it amazes me) that makes the conversation the most interesting. When her eyes have done with wondering who I am, where I come from, and why I'm here, they take a lively interest in things more intimate than a woman in her situation should still be thinking about.

The skinny guy comes in. We settle our business in no time flat. There isn't a hitch until he absolutely insists on me having a glass of wine. While his wife's rummaging around in a cupboard for some glasses, I'm backing toward the door. I have no desire to drink, and the blue in her eyes would have to be of a different kind for me to be able to control myself and ignore it. He's given me a small package in exchange for mine. We're done. Good night.

Outside, the shadows are falling, but it feels like heaven on earth to me. I walk for an hour with a sense of purpose just as *special* as the famous Council of Ministers' meeting that guy was going on about this morning.

I reach Pont at night and head to the inn. I'm completely bushed. If I had to do the climb back up tonight, I'd be in big trouble! I toast myself with a glass of punch.

The local rich kids are playing table soccer. They're making an unholy racket. I'm going to smoke a pipe while I stand and watch a game of belote. Of course, belote's only distantly related to our "Catherine." Even so, it has the whiff of something familiar. If it weren't for the main road—almost a highway—that runs through the village, and the snowplow that clears it, people here would be just as pent-up as we are. An open road calms everybody's nerves.

I'm dying to go and warm my butt in the kitchen. In any bistro that's an inn as well, I can never settle down. Even when I'm worn out, the way I am now, I have to keep my legs moving. I'll go and join a game of cards or checkers, or I'll start chatting with the old folks sitting in a circle around the potbellied stove. But my final goal is the kitchen: the big cookstove, with the smells of meals being prepared. I have a soft spot for warming my rear while a woman, usually hefty and in the know, stirs her pots. The way I see it, this is what being human is all about.

So even though I've noticed some potted greenery on a marble table (always the mark of a certain class of roadhouse), I do what I usually do: I edge my way toward the kitchen. I can be extremely crafty when my own well-being's at stake. In no time at all, I arrive—like it was the most natural thing in the world—in the place of my dreams. Because of the greenery, I'd expected a fancier stove. I'd already gathered from the belote players that people in this village like to talk big. And even though I tell the owner a raft of tall tales guaranteed to appeal to housewives, in less than five minutes I get myself thrown out.

I take a seat on the "restaurant" side of the establishment and start making a ruckus to get some attention. It works. They give me the once-over, and they take my order with outward signs of respect. All in all, I have a decent meal, and I cap it off with a big dish of chestnuts. I wash them down with a liter or two of a more than acceptable local wine. I've reserved a room. But seeing as I'm out in the world, it's only right I should make the most of it, and I come back to the bistro side to spend the rest of the evening. People in Pont must have their hands full with their families. Here I am, all alone, twiddling my thumbs in front of the roaring wood-stove. Close to nine o'clock, the chambermaid comes to keep me company. She's mending a pair of socks. The two of us make one hell of a family too!

I make the kinds of gestures a young woman would expect, while taking care not to lay them on too thick. I know what women are capable of setting in motion, from one word to the next. You only have to act like an ordinary joe for them to leave you alone. This gets me just what I hoped for. She wriggles and coos but lets me know right away that she's "political." What does she mean by that? That she's thrilled to have the right to vote, and she takes her role seriously. I see it the same way. What do I think about all of the *cover-ups* going on around the world? Ah, now this is a subject of the utmost importance! I embrace it with plenty of loud muttering. But what particular *cover-ups* are upsetting her? What? What's that I'm asking? Where on earth have I been? There's that Russian schoolteacher who threw herself out a window in New York! If that isn't a *cover-up*, what more do I need? Well, there are lots more, and she paints me a complete picture of "where things stand with *the opposing forces in the world.*" I have to confess, I'm bowled over.

I'm not at all indifferent to the question. I don't treat these things lightly. I could be tempted to take an interest in them myself. But it's so damned hard to keep up-to-date. I don't think I've paid enough attention to the daily papers. Our petty goings-on and Madame Edmond's jazz that I listen to at the bottom of the stairs—they're important to us only because we aren't paying enough attention to what's happening in New York. Just speaking for myself. Life's a lot easier if you only let yourself get excited by things that really interest you. From a selfish point of view. Then you don't have to worry about things that could affect you whether you want them to or not. At least, I'd like to think so. If you can use your reflexes to manage the petty, dirty business close at hand, while allowing yourself to get excited about *the opposing forces,* you'll have as much fun as you would playing "Catherine." If fact, it's what you ought to do.

The two of us spend a really good evening together. She fills me in on loads of things. She's up-to-date with all the schemes and scandals in the world news; they're her bread and butter. Then she loans me a film magazine. I read two or three stories. And now I'm going to bed.

The next morning, I think I've made an effort to get up bright and early. But when I come downstairs for coffee, I see it's almost ten o'clock. The bed was good, but the sky's so heavy it doesn't warn you of the troubles it has in store for you. I think twice about following the postman's path in reverse. Instead, I stick to the main road. It's longer than I thought. It feels like it'll never end. It's so icy and slippery I have to hug the shoulders and take short steps. I could fall and break my neck at any moment. By the time I regret not having taken the postman's path after all, it's too late to go back. The end result: I wear myself out for the whole day, and I arrive at the mill toward dark in such a state that Madame Edmond has no trouble believing in my girlfriend. (Imagination always blows these things out of proportion.) I must look like I've done myself in!

The boss comes downstairs. I hand over his package. He's going to have a good Christmas. Me too. I spend it very happily in my den. I've had Chauvin Jr. bring me down a box of cigars; we've been on good terms since the chimney fire. I smoke two of them on Christmas Eve and three on Christmas Day, staying close to my stove. It's very cold out, which means it's clear. For the first time this winter I can see all the mountaintops overhead. They're like saw teeth, really jagged. The wind lifts long streamers of snow powder off the peaks. The floor of the valley is still blanketed in mist. Here, even though the sun's not out, the daylight is dazzling. Nothing's moving. You don't see a soul. At dusk, I hear quick footsteps on the frozen road.

Now a few days later, I'm smoking my evening pipe. In a minute or two, I'll have a snack and then I'll hit the hay. The weather's turned bad again, but this is normal—we're used to it. I hear somebody calling me from outside. I go to see who it is. The moment I open the door, one hell of a wind and a bunch of sharp icicles burst in. It takes me a second to realize that Ma Machin from the bistro is here too. And what a state she's in! I can tell she's talking, but her face doesn't look human. What she's saying doesn't sound human either. I pull her inside, without really knowing what to do, or what she wants, or if she's out of her mind. She's soaked to the skin. Suddenly, I realize she's talking about the artist: He's dead, they've killed him.

I shake her. What are you talking about? I'm screaming. But I realize she's rushed all the way down the icy slope into the teeth of the squall, and she's totally drained. She needs to catch her breath. But no, she doesn't want to. I understand: We have to get up there right away. And we leave.

She *did* say he's dead. But that means nothing. I can't make any sense of this news or of her. She's doing all she can just to keep up with me.

I expect to find him lying in the sawdust on the barroom floor. This is where I go looking for him when I open the door to the bistro. Not here. There's nobody at all. Only the kerosene lamp. Ma Machin waves. We go through the kitchen. He's in the scullery out back, laid out cold. For a moment I'm enraged. I think they've bled him into a chamber pot. But no, the pot's full of piss. Either he fell on it or they threw him onto it. I send it skittering away with a kick. This makes Ma Machin groan.

He's nothing but blood. Butchered so badly, I thought he was lying face down. But when I lift him in my arms, I can tell he's not dead. Fortunately, I figure this out before I see his eye—only one—open and staring from what I thought was the back of his neck. It's actually his face, caked with clotted blood.

We carry him into the kitchen, and I wash him off, or at least I try to. Where to start? Blood has frozen everywhere, in big patches. The hot water thaws it out and reopens all kinds of wounds. We have no idea what to do with all this blood. It might have been better to leave it frozen. This time, they really got him. Ma Machin has caught her breath. I ask, Who did this? She answers: For the love of God, don't get mixed up in it. I tell her it's my affair. No: They said if this didn't do the job, they'd come back to finish him off for good. I'd like to see them try. I go through the artist's pockets. I find the switchblade. It hasn't even been opened. Maybe he didn't have time. But it's just as well (and in fact I'm sure he didn't reach for it). In any case, I slip it into my pocket, with every intention of calling on it if the need arises. This is a disaster. What's showing up under my rag (I'm handling it very delicately) is a disaster. I'm pulling off strips of cheek and bits of nose. They've smashed his head in with their boot heels like they'd stomp down a molehill. But I'm more and more convinced he's alive. And at last he gives a sign: He's breathing.

This is as much as we could ask for. For sure, he's not coming back from wherever he is, not for the time being. But he is breathing. I try to get some eau-de-vie down his throat, and I finally succeed. He moans and shivers so hard he almost slips though my arms. But I grab on and hold tight.

"When did this happen?"

"I don't know."

"How?"

"I don't know. Not here."

"How did you get here?"

"They brought me."

"Who?"

"Three of them."

"You know them?"

"Yeah."

I've finished examining his head. It's in a sorry state. He's going to bear the scars for the rest of his life ... because he isn't going to die. I'm not a doctor, but I'm certain.

"I heard somebody fiddling with the latch," Ma Machin says. "I got up. They'd tied him to a sled. They dragged him across the garden. Blood all over the snow. They threw him in here. I opened my shutters. They didn't try to hide. They looked me straight in the face. They said: 'Don't get mixed up in this. Let him die. Whatever happens, he's a goner. If you ever stick your nose into it, we'll start all over again.'"

"Who was it?"

She doesn't answer. I don't give a fuck. I know who they are. There's no name for the likes of them, to tell the truth.

He's not injured in his chest or in his belly, except for a kick he took in the balls. That's how they dropped him to begin with. After that, they took their time.

"Were they here this afternoon?" I ask Ma Machin.

"No," she says. "He's been gone for two days. They started up at Christmas. It's been going on ever since. Sometimes for one day. Sometimes two. He hasn't been back to sleep for three nights in a row. He wasn't drunk, I swear. Not once. He's like you and me. The others started bingeing on Christmas Eve, and they haven't let up since. Almost none of it was happening at my place. I saw them coming over here. They came looking for him. They wouldn't take no for an answer. They were shouting on the staircase like fire had broken out somewhere. You can't say he resisted, no, not him! In truth, he never needed any coaxing. But me—I understand him a little. He didn't say a thing. But...you know what? He went off with them like he was their big brother."

I'm a bit taken aback.

"What are you talking about, 'big brother'?"

"You don't know what that means? You think it's about leading people by the hand to the Sisters of Mercy? You can be a ringleader for all sorts of things! Crude, disgusting things—a big brother can come in handy for them too. Why shouldn't he lead you into vice? With no ill intentions. Even if he's bored to death. And that's how he seemed. He was 'big': That says it all."

I say to her gently, "Pipe down, pipe down a little, please."

I carry on with the examination. I reach a part where they've caused unspeakable damage. It's his hands: They're crushed. It looks like they held them to one side and then the other, and smashed them with a hammer. He'll never be able to use his hands again. I'm not a doctor, but I know this too.

I dress it all in towels soaked with alcohol. The pain is getting to him. He's showing signs of losing strength. First, he closed that one eye, the one that must have been open for more than an hour in the scullery. And now he's unclenched his teeth. He's groaning through parched lips.

"We have to get him out of here," says Ma Machin. I agree. I'm just waiting for him to rally a little. I knock back a big glass of eau-de-vie; it sends a chill from my head to my feet and turns me inside out.

"Warm up your stove a little so we can keep treating him."

"It seems to me we've already treated him pretty well."

"We haven't done much. He's the one who has to do all the hard work, if he can."

"He's come too far to stop now," says Ma Machin.

Even though I do know some things—that's what matters right now, after all—I make a vague reference to the doctor.

"Out of the question," she says.

"Why not? He came the last time, for the woman in labor."

"This isn't a delivery."

"It can't be the first time there's been a beating in this part of the country. What are the people around here? Angels of the Lord?"

But I realize it's even more than that. They have money; that makes all the difference. To drive up here in a car, in weather like this, when you're a medical doctor...when you have every excuse not to, including the voice of reason... He won't get mixed up in it. But she has something more important to say. Since I've mentioned the angels of the Lord, she's going to dot the i's and cross the t's. She's owned the bistro for forty years, and before her, it was her mother's. She knows you have to run with the pack, and she asks me if I think there's any other way. Around here, there are certain things you mustn't touch, on pain of death.

"And what are they?"

"Belief."

"In what? The good Lord?"

"No. Belief in yourself."

This sets me back. I do understand her. But I explain: The artist and me—we also need to have a tiny bit of belief in ourselves. This is exactly what we've been working toward, with the means at our disposal. And what's more, the famous angels of the Lord haven't missed a chance to get the gambling going and to put their self-belief at risk (since gambling's the only way it gets confirmed). I say, "A full house with three kings is a full house with three kings. You have to agree, even if you're bending the rules." (And, it seems to me, this is just what we've done.)

"That's it exactly," she says. "He had a full house with three kings a little too often. The cards were a little too obedient."

I stupidly point out that this requires a gift, not to mention the dexterity that goes along with it. How to control your own luck isn't something everybody can pick up.

"Neither is knowing how to mend your ways."

Now I notice the artist has both eyes open. He's watching us. And probably listening.

I bend over and fill his ear with the sort of nonsense you say to kids and wounded soldiers. He tries to answer, probably to chew me out if he could, judging by his look. But we have more urgent things to attend to. Why the hell are we hanging around here debating our next move? Let's get moving! I'm taking him with me. How? That's the least of my worries—he only weighs a hundred and thirty pounds.

I sling him over my shoulders and I start on my way. Right this minute, I must say, I'm happy enough. Even very happy. The squall is still howling, but I don't give a damn. I'm taking him to my place. After that, we'll see.

At the mill, I lay him down on my bed. For the first time, I notice that my den isn't completely sealed off from the outside air. There's a draft coming from the direction of the door. I do what's necessary to deal with it, even though I have no intention of hanging around here much longer. Then I stoke the woodstoves—they were nearly empty.

I go up to rouse Monsieur Edmond. When I get to the second floor, the big clock says it's two in the morning. But this doesn't hold me back from doing what I have to do. Neither does the well-scrubbed hallway leading to the bosses' bedroom. I knock on the door and I talk. I need to be firm, convincing. In a flash, Monsieur Edmond is in the hallway, completely stunned, wondering what's going on. I'm just about to start explaining, and now here's Madame Edmond coming out in her nightgown. Seeing my two bosses in the hallway, bare-legged and shivering with cold, is pretty comical. But I don't give a damn about this either. In a second, I know the artist doesn't stand a chance in a thousand of surviving (what I mean by surviving, anyway) if he stays in this place. I'm not talking about his wounds. He'll get over his wounds in his own way; he's already started. I'm talking about something else: It's what I realized while I was bringing him down here over my shoulder. If someone cheats you and dupes you, they're your master forever. You have no other option: You either have to love them or kill them. It's your only choice. You can't go on living like you did before. Whether this is true or not, I don't give a damn. It's what I feel and it's what I think.

Of course, this has nothing to do with what I tell the Edmonds. They've had me come into their bedroom. It breathes a different sort of life (it takes all kinds). I break the news, with no extra details, and I keep looking Monsieur Edmond straight in the face. I always prefer to proceed by veiled allusions: I tell him he has to get dressed and bring out the van. I need it. He's barely caught his breath. He's not a two-o'clock-in-the-morning man. The lady, on the other hand, is in her element. I foresee complications. I don't have time to be polite. I confront her head-on. I've heard enough of their quarrels to make it seem like I know what they're all about.

Anyway, it's going like clockwork. While I'm talking, Monsieur Edmond is getting dressed as though it was completely natural (and it is, given the nature of the situation).

The lady goes back to bed, while he comes downstairs with me. I had the time and the good sense to give the mistress of the house a reassuring smile. It hit its mark.

The artist hasn't budged, but his eyes are open. He's breathing heavily, like somebody hard at work.

What do you really want? Monsieur Edmond asks. To get him out and away from here. Do you know where there's a doctor? There's Monsieur Martel at Pont. No, it can't be

Monsieur Martel at Pont. Someplace farther away. Then you'd have to go all the way to Sainte-Jeanne. Where's that? Five miles past Châteauneuf. On the highway? Yes. All right, perfect. That's where we're going. Another question: How big is it, this place? It's the main town of the canton. About fifteen hundred people. Excellent. Onward! Here's the plan: I'm going to drive, of course. The road's terrible on the way down. But you're coming with us—you'll have to bring the van back. As for me, no, I'm not coming back. I'll have to stick with that guy over there, who's in big trouble, as you can see. I'm really sorry (I mean it, from the bottom of my heart, I do!), I'm sorry to be leaving the mill and you, Monsieur Edmond. You're a decent man. No, I don't give a damn about the business with the skinny guy. Everybody has a skinny guy on their tail, more or less. No, I was happy to be here. You're a decent guy. The same for Madame Edmond, she's nice too. He agrees. He doesn't mind that he was startled awake. It's well worth it, at any hour of the day or night, to know that there's at least one person in the world (maybe lots—you can always hope!) who considers you to be a decent guy.

Ah! Another question. There's always one left hanging. Does he know any people at Sainte-Jeanne? Could he put in a word for us? We could use it right about now. He says yes and not to worry.

It would take only one more setback to get me completely down: if Madame Edmond gets out of bed, on the quiet, with the idea of making us some coffee. But I'm spared this ordeal, and I'm happy to imagine that selfish sourpuss in her nightdress, snoozing away up there with her ass stuffed under the quilt, while we're taking off.

We've put the chains on the tires. And because I'm driving

cautiously, we glide along problem-free to the bottom of the valley, through forests sleeping under masses of snow. It feels like we're on the planet Mars. My mind is a blank. I'll have time to fill it in again when I come back down to earth.

We're in Sainte-Jeanne before dawn, but there's already a bistro lit up, with its doors open. Monsieur Edmond tells us this where the bus stops at six in the morning. We could use something warm to drink. I go in and order some rum punch. I take a tumbler of it out to my artist, who needs no persuading. He knocks it back.

As for an inn, we'd better look into that right away. We can't leave the wounded man outside all night in the van. The bartender joins our conversation. I tell him just enough to get him interested but not too much. We're down in the valley now, on the road to the plains. People are going to be more and more curious, more and more talkative. We have to be careful. I'm an old hand at this.

The upshot: He gives us a tip worth its weight in gold. There's a convent here, the Little Sisters of the Poor. They're up and about at all hours. I say, "Hold on," and I go over there. It's two steps away.

I walk straight in. There's an old lady in a cornet head-dress, with the whitest hands I've ever seen. My beard makes a good impression, along with all my other masculine and virile qualities. I lay them on thick. Right away, she calls me "my dear." And I know things are going to work out.

Can the injured man afford to pay? Yes, but not too much because I'm the one who's paying. Is he a relative? Yes, he's my brother. How did he get hurt? I start with an apology. Then I tell a tale of jealousy, one she should be able to understand. By not saying the word "woman," I lighten up the story. And naturally she gets the idea. She could hardly imagine anything else. This is why she has her head wedged into a cornet. I'm forgetting to mention that she's treated me to a coffee. She's worldly to her very fingertips. It's amazing. I can rest easy.

She goes to see the Mother Superior, and when all is said and done, here's what we settle on: They have two rooms for the sick. Their community is small—there are only six members. If I think I can afford three hundred francs a day, they'll take my brother. I don't just think so, I know so.

I race back to the bistro, and I pick up Monsieur Edmond and the van. We transfer the invalid. Having the boss here— he's used to behaving like a townsman—does a lot to smooth the way.

Once my artist has been put to bed, with three black-robed women around him, I accompany Monsieur Edmond back to the van, filling my pipe on the way. I thank him. More to the point, I cut our ties. I tell him what this is really about: that the heavyweights—Nestor, Ovide, Ferréol, and the rest of them—are involved. So mum's the word: He mustn't have any idea where we are. He's scared enough and he'll keep his mouth shut. He even tells me he'll make it home before daylight with no one the wiser. He's only concerned about the Chauvins. They might have heard the sound of the van when we left. I tell him: If he thinks about the skinny guy, he'll have what he needs to keep the Chauvins from talking. I tell him about the conversation I had with the charming girl in the unlocked stable. And besides, the Chauvins couldn't have heard a thing.

In spite of the cold, the dark, and everything I've just been saying, we drag out our farewells. I give him loads of advice about how to use the chains on the way back up. At last, abruptly, with his fear to keep him company, he pulls away.

I watch his red taillights disappear. For a minute, I'm rooted to the spot. Who'll keep me company? Will the sun rise again?

They let me stay at the convent for the first night. I sleep on a couch in the waiting room. An irresistible smell of cabbage soup wakes me up. Broad daylight. I already know we're not going to stick around here. I knew this while I was sleeping. What I see when I wake up confirms it. It's not worth going into. I don't see anything upsetting. Everything's polished, quiet, peaceful . . . except: This isn't the right place at all.

During the afternoon, I go looking for what would be, and I find it. It's a Ma Lantifle's—the kind of place we're used to. This one has her digs at the edge of the village, on the forest road. Temperature-wise, you'd have to say it's perfect here. There's barely an inch of snow in the meadows. The village itself—pardon me, I should say "the town" (that's what they call it, and I have every reason to act like I see it that way too)—the town is a lot different than where we've come from. Here it's respectability and honor, right down the line. This is what I realized when I woke up in the waiting room this morning. This is what I notice, every step of the way, while I'm out looking for what we need. To the point where I lose hope. Just seeing the façades, you know you're in a part of the country where you have to hide if you want to have fun, with your eyes closed. Everybody has built their confessional box at right angles to the street. With façades as spotless as these, impossible to strip naked unless you're exercising the Rights of Man in the marriage bed. The same inscription you see on headstones at the cemetery— "Good Father and Husband"—is already etched with broom strokes in front of every door. Broom strokes that we . . . well, that *I'm* used to receiving on my butt when I'm in the buff.

In the midst of all this, I don't miss out on the chance to show off my curly (and blond) beard, my innocent eyes, and the manly, virile side that I got in motion so effectively with the Little Sister. It's only right to offer a few distractions to all these town ladies. They ogle me, and they go back home with something to whet their appetite.

I cover the burg from top to bottom, side to side, even slantwise like a Saint Andrew's cross, without risking to stick my nose into even the most modest doorways. I know what I'd find behind them. Finally, on the way out to the woods, I come across a roadhouse that looks promising. As soon as I come in, Ma Whatsit is absolutely to my liking. She's the ideal woman for nursing wounds. She has a mustache and a potbelly. I adore this. She talks and I'm in ecstasy. At first she's not polite, and then not in the least. What she tells me right off the top must have been banned everywhere, even among the apes. She has a way of guessing at my weight and the size of my chest that has me in tears.

As soon as I lay out the story of my buddy, she's in raptures. This is right up her alley. I knew it. We'll be here in five minutes, sweetheart. She doesn't hide from me that five minutes is too long. Are you still a Sister of Mercy? she roars, as I'm heading off. When I'm a hundred yards away, I can still hear her laughing and banging her pots and pans.

There's only one thing I'm afraid of: She might go overboard. In the straits we're in, we don't want too much attention or too little. This is the hard part. People never understand. It's always complicated.

My business at the Little Sisters' is complicated too. They've taken us under their wing. They've shown us love without question. A wounded man, and a blond, bearded man with broad shoulders and a rolling gait: In spite of their starched head cones, we're like candy floss for these women who live alone in what they call "self-sufficiency," at the edge of the woods.

As soon as I arrive, they start fussing around me. And I gather they've played an amazing trick on the artist. The instant he opened his eyes on this new day of suffering, they flashed a whole set of royal trump cards—cards he'd never seen before—right under his nose. He's lost too much blood not to be agog. And he is agog. I feel like saying to him, "You're not the only one!"

But I'm kind. I make light of the situation. I sit by the head of the bed. I look like I'm posing for an engraving. As soon as we're alone, I get straight to the point. "How do you feel?" "Good." This isn't much to go on.

I'm going to talk it over with the ladies. I know they're going to open my eyes to a whole world of troubles; they aren't in short supply. I'm with the Mother Superior. She's buxom and closely resembles the Ma Lantifle who's waiting for me. This Mother's spotless, of course, inside and out, but she's chasing the same ends and by almost the same means. If you measure them up, they're barely a hairbreadth apart. They're both mothers of big families.

She almost has the better of me. She's even caught me by the tail. She says my brother is *untransportable*. This word tickles me, and I can't hold back from laughing—it's so clear that she and I are poles apart. She has no idea what's going on in my head, and I have no idea what's going on in hers. She asks why I'm smiling. It's because I'm thinking about how I *transported* the artist last night from the bistro to the mill. But I tell her a story about my anxieties, my feelings, and the fact that I slept badly. She has them bring me a big bowl of linden tea.

The doctor has been around to see my brother. The head wounds aren't serious. They look alarming because "they're adjacent to and affect the seat of vanity" (her words). But all of this will get better, quickly enough. The same is not true of the noble parts (I have to admit when she talks about the *noble parts*, she takes me by surprise). And above all, this isn't true concerning the injuries to his hands. These, especially, are extremely grave. We don't know if he'll still be able to use his hands. Maybe for basic things, at best. What's more, he has a fever.

Now I'm in a real fix. She has a talent for raising obstacles. What should I do? (I'm the one doing the asking; for her, there's no question.) I don't know. She isn't telling me anything new about his *noble parts* and his hands. I saw all that clearly, right away. Plus, I tell her we absolutely can't have a doctor involved any longer.

She asks if my brother is on social security. Well now, this . . . this takes the cake.

In the end, I turn the whole story into a mush, and she gobbles it up. This is all that matters for now. And I go back to my cabin in the woods.

"So," the lady says, "this guy who's been hacked up, are you bringing him to me? Yes or no?"

Here I am debating with myself again. What do I really think? With her, though, I don't have to hold back. After a minute, it comes to me.

What would happen if I left the artist with the Sisters for, say, a week, while I stayed here?

"What would happen is they'll turn your brother into a little sheep," the lady says. "See, I'm not trying to line my pockets. You'll be here. That's enough of a payoff or me."

As for turning him into a sheep, shouldn't we wait and

see if it's all that serious? And when you come down to it, do I find the idea so distasteful? There are certain things he needs to get into his head, and the sooner the better. A little sunshine wouldn't harm the picture.

So I end up by going along with everybody. But all of a sudden it hits me: Something might be seriously screwed up. Are there any gendarmes staying in this house?

Yes.

And night falls.

There's nothing to be done. Ma Lantifle hovers around, not saying a word. I set myself next to the cookstove, warming my butt the way I like. The most delicious place in the world... And I feel empty. No appetite for anything. The better part of me is over there at the convent, in that orderly, modest room with my unruly, extravagant artist, who's at the mercy of the first comer. I imagine the scene a hundred times: The Little Sister of the Poor and the gendarme. The summoning of the established authorities. The explosive confrontation, where everything dear to my heart goes up in smoke. They'll want to know why his hands were crushed and why, since they were crushed, he doesn't sue for damages.

I have a vague thought. I put the question to Ma Lantifle. Do the people in this burg like to have fun? What do I mean by fun? I mean, do they like to sin? Sure, they like to sin, the same as people everywhere. Does she know of any examples? If she opened her mouth about what she knows—what everybody knows but doesn't say—plenty of men and women would go running for a hole to hide in. "So the rule around here is 'Whatever you do, don't say anything'?" "Like everywhere else, kid." She's amazed by my ignorance. And I'm amazed that I didn't think of this sooner.

I put on my nice rabbit-fur cap and get ready to go out. This hurts her feelings. She tells me she doesn't like rabbit.

"But isn't that what you're cooking?"

"Yes!" she admits. "And I was looking forward to doing a little hopping myself, to tell the honest truth."

I tell her I'll be gone for five minutes.

I go to the convent. I ask for the Mother Superior. She comes out. I get straight to the point. Her vestments, her position, oblige me to speak frankly. I fault myself for not having done so this morning. But the reputation of too many honorable people is at stake. I'd like to be relieved of this burden and entrust it to her. (I have lots of ways of talking, especially to *myself*. You might not have noticed this yet, because I use this kind of language mainly in spring and summer, when I'm surrounded by flowers, sunshine, and fair breezes, to remind myself of how lucky I am to be alive in their midst. So now I'm talking to my Lady Superior the same way I talk to such delightful, inanimate beings, and to the clouds.) She has the right to know the circumstances in which my brother was wounded in this way. Should I speak plainly? (She nods, gravely.) All right then: He tried to seduce a married woman.

"The devil," says the Lady Superior.

I agree, and I go on: A married woman who's very well established. And I get more specific. I toy briefly with the enjoyable sense of security that people in high places feel when they observe the trials and tribulations of the less protected. In her own position, she knows she's no longer exposed to this kind of scrutiny. When you come down to it, this is her cinema. And I give her a first-class screening until I'm able to say what really matters: If the gendarmes stick their noses into this business, God knows what kind of trouble the poor woman will be in! My words don't fall on deaf ears.

"God understands," she says, "and does not condemn. He has long since forgiven the adulterous woman."

On that matter, I have my own thoughts, but I don't breathe a word. The rest runs as smooth as silk. By the time we're finished, she herself is talking about a *professional secret*. I feel the urge to stand at attention and give a military salute (I tend to joke around when I'm happy). In any case, hats off! When it comes to certain things, society has foreseen it all in advance.

I go to see the artist. He's sleeping. I don't wake him up.

I assume "*professional secret*" carries some weight. What comforts me most is knowing I've set in motion the religious orders' *secret* system of automatic protection. I'm certain Madame Superior will keep her lips sealed. And even if things go wrong, she'll resort to a *white lie* (another form of protection not available to the dregs of society). She knows it's best to leave well enough alone. Is she wondering—for her own amusement and edification—where the sinner lives, what her name is? Maybe she isn't wondering about anything, because she's an authentic saint, carrying out her orders on the front lines—duty, duty!—and no questions asked?

Neither do Ma Lantifle and I try to get to the bottom of things on this first evening, now that the night is calmer, less black, less cold. We eat rabbit stew (no doubt it's really cat). We drink our liter each, then another, make some mulled wine, and have a little dessert wine. Then I get what I want; namely, that she's drunk as a skunk and feels so queasy she goes to bed early without asking for her final course. It's always best to break things to people slowly. I've never cut anybody off this hard.

When I wake up, I'm thinking about the gendarmes again. For five minutes I'm scared shitless. Then I remember the whole, tangled web of arrangements we have protecting us. I do a little stocktaking. It didn't occur to me to ask Monsieur Edmond for my last two weeks' pay, and he forgot about it too. I have seventeen thousand francs. I've been through the artist's pockets more than once: totally bare.

Ma Lantifle is making the coffee. There's a construction worker in the kitchen as well, warming his rear by the stove, right where I always stand and in the same way. This makes me like him. I get a bit closer, and we chat. I'd like to hear the news of the country—I mean the wider world—but he can't tell me any. He's from here and he's never left. All he knows is the bus schedule. So we talk about that, wherever it might lead. Strange kid. I thought he was a stonemason. So what is he? Nothing. That's perfectly all right. It's as good as it gets. But what does he do all day? He must need some dough. Chores. What kind of chores? Hundreds of things: hauling firewood, unloading firewood, splitting firewood, delivering parcels, picking up parcels. He needs jobs that wrap up fast, he explains. What he likes best is to warm his butt. Oh boy, do I ever agree!

I pester Ma Lantifle for my cup of coffee.

"You have a few tricks up your sleeve, don't you," she says. "Well, I have a few of my own."

But this is pure flirtation, and she serves me my java scalding hot. I swallow it down straight. This staggers her. I tell her she missed her shot: I didn't feel a thing.

The door opens and in comes a midget, who shouts out to the kid, "Hey, André, come give me a hand?"

"With what?"

"Help me carry a folding cot to the eight o'clock bus."

"Can't you do it on your own?"

"Don't be a dunce. You want me to get wheel marks all over my back?"

"You wouldn't look any the worse for it. Who's it for, this folding cot?"

"For me. I'm sending it to my daughter."

"She's had the baby?"

"Just about to. She's fit to burst. Félix needs another place to sleep. Come on."

"The things I have to do! Helping with deliveries at this time of day."

He leaves the stove, and I take his place. Now that I'm alone with Ma Lantifle, I explain what I pulled off last night at the convent. She's clear-sighted.

"You're like a mother cat who's run out of places to hide her kitten," she says.

Yes, I am, a bit. First off, from her point of view, I was wrong to worry. But even so, I did a good job. The doctor's soft in the head, she says. He chases after hookers. What's more, he needs them to be young. He'll be careful not to stick his nose where he shouldn't. As for the Sisters, they're on the level. Have I ever heard of Sisters who weren't on the level? Well, I've never spent a lot of time around orphanages. She tells me that gendarmes would be completely out of place at the Good Sisters'. It would be unforgivable. Do I have any idea what gendarmes do here, like they do everywhere? I claim I know. No, she says, I don't. The gendarmes are sitting by the main road, waiting to hand out speeding tickets. Cars are what they're interested in. It all makes good sense.

Another question: If we stick around for a while, would there be a job for yours truly, anywhere nearby?

"If?"

"A manner of speaking."

"You're at home here. You don't have to worry about a thing."

That's not the point. I spend all my time trying to get other people to understand my motives. It's a mug's game. Money aside, I have to keep busy. Let's say that work's good for my health. Like Swedish gymnastics! Understand?

"All right, listen: You should go to Robertet's. Hides and skins. Of course, at this time of year you won't find steady work anywhere. But there might be something at his place."

"What sort of something?"

"I don't know for sure, but it wouldn't surprise me if it was just rolling untanned hides around."

In fact, that's just what it is. It's not the most fun in the world, but there are no hassles. I last for two days. Then the stink's too much to take, and I quit. Because I've found another job, much more to my liking, at the local garage.

It felt rotten going straight to the Sisters' from the tannery. The artist asked, "Is it you who stinks to high heaven or is it me?"

"Don't worry, it's me."

So I took a little detour out toward the garage, and I found a much better setup.

I say to Ma Lantifle, "You didn't mention the garage."

"I hadn't thought of it."

She had, but ... oh, the rascal! The tannery served her purposes better: Because of the smell, she kept a tighter hold on me. And she knows that I know. She's laughing up her sleeve.

The garage owner's all on his own. He's a lad who knows how to get along with people. Almost too well. He goes full bore all the time. Finicky little jobs don't bother him. He does them fast and well because he's skilled. But all he really wants to do is slide into his jalopy and race around on roads as slippery as skating rinks. He's replaced the body of a Daimler with soapboxes. And to have an excuse to take it out, he calls himself a taxi driver. Needless to say, it skids off the road. People get pulled out of his machine half-conscious. He's chomping on coffee beans nonstop to keep himself up to speed. I say to him, "All we need is for you to have heart problems."

He tells me I've hit the nail on the head—his heart is his problem. Life's good, all in all!

As for red tape, I say, "All those messy payments to the government on my account—insurance and the rest of it—I'm letting you off the hook. Just say I'm your cousin and I'm lending you a hand. We live in a republic, don't we, until further notice? It's nobody else's business. It makes me your accomplice, so we kill two birds with one stone."

I repair bicycles and motorbikes. There aren't many cars, aside from a little Simca owned by a girl and some guy who seems to be under her thumb and who knows less than nothing about mechanics. They come by three times a week, either to have their windshield washers unblocked or their wobbly headlights straightened out ... I ask, in all serious-ness, if they wouldn't like me to give their fancy plaid seat cushions a brush as well. They're so nutty, they take me at my word. And I'm such a nut, I go ahead and do it. Aside from this, I'm not that busy. Maybe the boss and I get the chance to work on a truck together. Every day, he takes off for a couple of hours. He has to have his dose of high-speed insanity.

Anyhow, it all falls into place. I don't mix much with the locals. I do what's required, but I don't go too far. For example, I go regularly to the hairdresser for a gentleman's trim, even though, personally, I much prefer leaving my hair long, like Tolstoy's. I'm keeping my head above water at last. More than above water. The money problem has been completely sorted out.

I'm covering the costs at the Sisters', and each time I pay them, I add a little extra for their chapel. Am I ever on top of things! The artist is putting on weight. He's actually getting chubby. This hadn't struck me at first, since I see him every day, morning and night. I bring him the daily paper and some Gauloises. In the beginning, he threw the cigarettes in my face. Then he got used to them. The doctor must be one hell of a joker, judging by the book he's brought to distract the artist: Montesquieu's *The Spirit of the Laws*. Perhaps this was the only book he had. He left it on the night table. I grabbed it. I'm reading it.

The artist holds his cigarette with his fingers sticking out from the bandages. He even wiggles them around to show me how he's getting on. I figured they were more damaged. It seems I was mistaken. Hard to say. Anyway, it's odd to see how proud the Good Sisters are of this success. If there ever was a time to say the ways of the Savior are mysterious, this would be it. I'm amazed by all my mixed emotions.

Apart from some deep scars, which don't improve the picture, his face hasn't changed. His look is still the same. But I wonder: How will his hands really be in the long run? And no matter how they end up, what will be left of his gaze, for better or for worse?

To get a clearer idea, I use *The Spirit of the Laws* as an excuse, and I go to return the book to the doctor. I've paid the Good Sisters for his services, but I'm keen to thank him in person and mark the occasion. Would he be partial to this leg of hare? (I bought it off the renowned André, who got it from...I don't know who.) Yes, he would. Ma Lantifle had told me he was every bit as crazy for food as he was for sex, but I get the impression I've really hit the target. Right away, we're pals, and he treats me to a glass of anise.

First of all, *The Spirit of the Laws*: It was a joke, as I suspected. The Good Sisters had been nagging the doctor to bring their patient something to read because the newspaper I dropped off each morning was being spirited away. It seems I'd managed to pick the one left-wing rag. Bad luck on my part.

He lights his pipe and I light mine. We have the kind of conversation I like. I tell him how I was the personal valet, so to speak, of Dr. Ch., a guy from Paris who dealt with loonies and sex addicts. He tells me the name for that is a psychiatrist, which I already knew. I tell him how the doctor had bought an estate in the woods near Marseille, how he lived there, all year round, in the nude. A little cracked. Maybe even a lot. And how I took off because that way of life made it impossible for me to breathe.

He's amazed that I'm reading *The Spirit of the Laws*. I quietly get him to understand (and to believe) that I'm familiar with a few other authors, like Balzac (him, I adore) and Alexandre Dumas, Victor Hugo, Lamartine, even some of the moderns. Dr. Ch. used to loan me books, even forced me to read them. I guess he thought it was an interesting experiment, because he would question me about them. It was as plain as the nose on your face that he wanted to see if they had a big effect on how I led my life. On this score, he had his head screwed on completely backward.

My new pal takes an interest in what I'm telling him. We return to the subject over another round of anise. He tries, indirectly, to draw me out. It's obvious what he's after, and I play along because it's making him happy. Even more so because now we're landing on exactly what interests me.

I tell him about how this doctor character would have his driver (a handsome kid) recruit women in Marseille. The doctor required them to be of a certain class. The kid was Czech, and stocky; he dabbled a little in oil painting. Dr. Ch. had rented him a studio next to a ladies' tailor. The kid picked up some bonuses, of course. As soon as he spotted a prospect, he'd give her the big come-on about art and the artist, and then he'd lift the curtain in the doorway. "This way, Madame." And presto, the deed was done. The Czech had his way with her, and then he'd send her our way. There was nothing improper going on at our place. The doctor was studying the motives behind prostitution. He'd discovered it wasn't at all a question of temperament or money, but something he called the explorer complex or the Livingstone complex. He never stopped filling my ears about this. On top of that, the Czech would disguise himself as a dazed student, a laborer, or a lecher, and pick up women on the streets . . . And my doctor had another recruiter who worked the dance halls: a fat, bald guy in his fifties under orders to make himself completely nondescript but well-mannered. And the broads he made it with were by no means the ugliest. They were all classy. And we sent them home unharmed after a pleasant weekend. In a word, it was done scientifically.

"Well," my new doctor pal says, "you know a lot, even some technical terms. I've never had such an interesting conversation."

So I ask him what he thinks is going to happen with the artist's hands.

In theory, he says, nothing out of the ordinary. Under

normal circumstances, he would have sent him to a hospital. But when he first saw him at the Sisters', it was impossible. No ambulance, a fever of 104 degrees, and below freezing outside. Nothing to be done. Plus, no insurance. "And they told me there was something—I don't know what—that we had to be careful about. So I made do with what we had at hand." To be completely open with me, he says he's proud of what he's done. The artist will end up with, let's say, a 10 percent loss of capacity, maybe only 5 percent. What does he do for a living?

I sidestep the question. I say it's not so much his *job* that matters. When it comes to a job, you can always find something. What matters most is what he loves. And what he loves is skill, finesse. He's used to doing nimble things with his fingers. Will he still be able to?

"I've rarely seen two brothers who care so much for each other," says my new pal. In his opinion, we have to wait and see. Nothing's for sure. It's a question of willpower. "I've seen willpower perform miracles." So have I, in every sense of the word. I come away from this get-together none the wiser. Except now I know that in three or four days my artist will probably be back on his feet with a discharge note in his hand. We'll be able to go and get into hot water someplace else. Which, when you come down to it, is what it's all about, whether you go by Livingstone or by whatever name they give to the insignificant thing that you are.

I go back to Ma Lantifle's. In no time flat, I wrap up our affairs, financial and familial. She can tell I have no time to waste. (And she definitely gets the picture: She's already fussing over André again. Besides, the highway runs right past her place. It will always bring her something new.) Next, I go to see the Little Sisters. I'm the picture of sweetness and light. I get them to explain what I need to do to take care of his hands. They undress them for me. I think they look good. But I insist he has to keep wearing the bandages. They fully agree.

I explain things to the artist in confidence. What I tell him is quite wonderful, quite complicated, and altogether untrue. I lay it on thick, and he believes me. Today is Wednesday. He needs to be ready by Friday morning. I come back an hour later. Change of plans: We're leaving Saturday, at three in the afternoon.

A guy named Barruol is taking us. I fixed his truck a week ago. He's driving south with freight for the fruit and vegetable truckers. What I like best is that he doesn't take the usual highway. He follows it only so far and then he cuts straight across Drôme on a route that saves him a hundred liters of fuel.

I'm prospecting. I'm exploring possibilities. In some people's lives, *not* to prostitute themselves would be a mortal sin.

By arrangement with Barruol, we leave on foot on Saturday at two o'clock. He'll pick us up along the way. The weather is hazy and bright. Not snowing and not too cold. The artist seems to be doing pretty well. But, good God, he has to lose some weight! You'd think he was an abbot! His jowls almost reach his collar.

We walk a mile or two, taking it easy, and then Barruol catches up with us. We pass around a liter, we each take a swig, and ... away we go.

Two hours later, we've left the snow and ice behind. The grass is reddish-brown. There are kitchen gardens, black as ink, surrounding the villages. The pavement is bare. We're already on to smaller side roads. They're taking us where I want to go.

I'm looking for a quiet, comfortable spot where I can find work and the artist can gradually get back into shape. I have no idea what to expect on this score. Sometimes I wonder what in the world he'll be able to do. Most of the time, I tell myself that we've made it out, after all, with our colors still flying. As for the rest, we'll see . . . when the time comes.

We spend our first night at Saint-Michel. The next day—Sunday—we enter a wilder part of the country. From the top of each rise, we see hills piled in every direction. The villages are sparse. In between them, we see hardly anyone. We stop at Entrepierre, where we have to unload part of the cargo—some framing lumber. But of course this will have to wait until Monday morning: On Sunday, there are no men around to help. They're all playing boules next to the bistro. Barruol must have planned all this in advance. We haven't been here five minutes before he's joined a team.

It's chilly out. We go into the bistro, the artist and me. We make some plans over our mulled wine. As far as he's concerned, we should split up with Barruol and wait and see what comes along. I'm glad he's showing some interest. The last thing he wants to do is head straight down south. I ask why. He still doesn't want to go anywhere too crowded. Because of what? Nothing definite, just a notion. He tells me I'm free to do as I please. Anyway, it's what he's going to do. Do what? Split. Split from what? From me? Of course.

I don't let this get to me. I lay out the facts, calmly, clearly, across the marble tabletop. Number one: He said I was a free man. Yes, that's true. So is he. I have no desire to hang on to him. If he wants to take off, the road's wide open. Who's holding him back? Not me. I'm too much of an old drifter not to understand perfectly well why he wants to clear the hell out. So, that's number one. Number two: He's broke. I divvy up my cash. I have twenty-three thousand francs. Here's thirteen thousand. He asks what happened to all the money he had on him. I answer: When I found him freezing in the scullery, lying beside the chamber pot, his pockets were empty. Except for this knife, which I'm now giving back.

"You stole it from me?"

"I didn't steal it from you. I borrowed it for good reasons."

I'm waiting for him to tell me I borrowed his dough, too, for good reasons. But he doesn't. I'm sure he doesn't even think so. But we never really know what's going on in other people's heads. We make it up. It's a place to start. So that's the whole story about the money. He says: Hand it over. I don't back out, I give him the thirteen thousand in cash.

Now will he let me explain my idea? Nobody's stopping you, he says. Splitting up with Barruol: I was thinking about that. Crowded places: I was thinking about that too. All I was looking for was somewhere warm. But not for me—for him. He's grown-up enough to go looking on his own. Here's my proposal: He should go looking for what he wants, and I should go looking for what I want. That being said, is anything preventing us from looking together? No, nothing. So let's split up with Barruol, since we're in agreement on that. Let's take off together, since there's nothing stopping us. If he finds something that suits him and it doesn't suit me, then he stays, and I carry on. If I find something I like that he doesn't like, I stay and he goes wherever. Sound good? Agreed.

To say I'm satisfied would be going too far, but maybe I understand what he's after: He needs to believe in himself, to believe he is somebody.

The following day, I let him choose the route, and we start

out on foot. We talk about one thing and another. After an hour, out of the blue, he says very nicely, "You old fool!" I'm thrilled. It's a great day. It's not cold at all, but the country has a mournful look.

Toward evening—it gets dark around four o'clock—we wait at a crossroads, and we're lucky enough to be picked up by a van carrying workers from a gypsum quarry. The van takes us to a village we never would have known was there. It's hidden in the middle of a holly oak forest—a dozen rat-infested houses. The residents give us a warm welcome. We eat supper with a guy named Arthur, and we sleep in his shed with his goats.

When we talk, I'm careful to keep the artist's plans separate from my own. I say, "When I get there, I'll do this or that," as if he didn't exist. And I ask, "How about you?" His answer never changes: "I'll see." It's obvious he'd enjoy staying with me, and he doesn't try to hide it. But he doesn't want to be tied down. We talk while we're walking along the road and when we stop for the night, and we're always on friendly terms. He often calls me "you old fool." I tell him stories, and the time passes pleasantly enough. I'm the one who always picks up things for the two of us to eat. He says, "If we go through a small town, buy me another guitar." I'd already thought of it. Moments like these are some of my happiest.

We don't run into many people out this way. Every once in a while, there's a farmer driving an old car who takes us three or four miles and then makes a sharp turn into one of those villages hidden in the oaks. But the country we're hiking through is amazing. Compared to the weather up in the mountains, down here it's a piece of cake. The sky is gray, but the cloud cover is high. It only freezes at night and early in the morning. During the day, once you're warmed up from a little walking, it feels good.

We don't need to treat his hands anymore. No more dressings. To me, they look fine. I see them working like normal hands—just as well as mine. But in spite of the miles we're putting in, he still looks a bit pudgy.

Life is good enough. We run across lots of old châteaus surrounded by pines, on the tops of the hills. I fret a little about finding a job. We shouldn't let ourselves be taken in by the mild weather. There's still a chill in the air, and real springtime won't start for at least another three months. I'm talking about spring without rain and wind. I've already done some drifting around at this time of the year in parts of the country more or less like this, and I know you still have to be ready for some fireworks.

Plus, I've made my mind up about something. He wants to be free, and he will be. I don't like hangers-on, and I'm not going to be one. I feel a bit resentful. We catch up with a guy who's out walking. He says, "Hi there!" We strike up a conversation. He's not a drifter. He's from around here. What's he up to, tramping around on the roads? He's out for a stroll. I ask about the area, and he tells us about every part of it. He sticks with us for a while longer. Then he turns onto a dirt track and heads home to his farm. We can see it from the road. The barn is broad and low-slung. It must be chock-full of pigs. It gives off a strong odor. It's almost buried in piles of yellow manure. He makes his way back there after his little ramble, looking like he's on top of the world.

Suddenly, one morning I've had enough. Of what, I wonder, when you come right down to it? A little friendship isn't worth getting so upset about. I think what's bothering me are the empty spaces we're passing through and the bad weather setting in. The artist's gaze is ugly: That's true. I've had plenty of time to notice it wandering over things and over me. I'm not asking him to be less revolting. I put up with it. What I'd like is ... I don't know what! If I tell myself I'd like some kindness, I'm forced to admit right away: He has the right to be unkind. And besides, he is kind, in his own way. If I tell myself I'd like some attention, I think: I'm a damned fool to attach any importance to his antics. He could be performing them without knowing it, and he'll perform them anyway. If I tell myself I'd like some friendship, I wonder: What is friendship? I do feel some for him, and where does it get me? I don't know what I want, but I've had it up to here with what I've got. I want him to figure out, on his own, what to do. I get the sense that if the right thing did come his way, the cow would jump over the moon.

And back on the road we go, without further ado.

At the first village we come to, I make my decision. I say straight-out: I have to work. It's a long, narrow village. The road opens wide where the houses end, and anybody can pass through. Which means there's mischief afoot. There are lots of cowsheds and lots of cows. Maybe some good shit will catch up with me here! I need something meaningful—for better or worse—to happen. I can't come up with anything at all anymore, inside myself or by myself. Instead, I want something to come along and give me a shove one way or another. If the artist is leaving, he'll leave. And that will be that, period.

While I'm thinking these fine thoughts and a few more like them, I feel as soft as down on the inside, even if I'm acting tough. I go over to three guys who're standing outside the entrance to the bistro. Needless to say, they don't have any work they can offer me. They're just three guys hanging around in front of their local bistro. They have their usual chair, the card table, sawdust to spit into, and a potbelly stove they can stoke to the brim when they're cold: all of it near at hand. Each of them has a good friend, on either side, who knows their true nature and habitual ways. They aren't working at the moment, so there's nothing they can do for me. They're amazed that I'm asking to share their job. They can handle it easily enough on their own. They tell me: In this whole open-ended village, there's nothing for me to do, not a thing.

I start to be moved by things you notice (I've learned this from experience) at significant times. For example, winter gardens: vegetable patches with frostbitten cabbages, bunches of celery banked up with earth, blackened stumps of greens, rotted hollyhock stalks. Or the footprints of a man who seeks happiness in one spot, with everything taken care of and easy to understand; in a world that following the seasons, seems to follow you; that loving the sun and the rain, seems to love you; that fulfilling its own destiny, fulfills you... And what's more, it does all this without making a fuss, faithfully. At the moment, I'm alive to anything that offers certainty in any form. And I envy those who've found certainty in the earth and the four seasons.

Whether I'm discussing the work question (ever so indirectly) with the good fellows from the bar or I'm planted in front of the kitchen gardens, talking about one thing or another, the artist stays quietly off to one side, waiting for me to finish. And when I've finished, when they've told me there's no work to be had or when I'm convinced that this rosebush isn't going to bloom again just for me, I come back to my artist. And we're back on the road again, without taking a single step: side by side, mortal enemies, and all the more inseparable.

In this same way, we go to take a look at a few more villages. In this sparsely inhabited country, this means covering a good thirty miles at least. The wind has gotten really strong. We decide to head back as fast as we can to a main road, no matter which, and jump on a truck going anywhere at all. The artist is one hundred percent in agreement. He says, "Yeah, anywhere at all." I answer, "Wipe your mouth." He's been drooling more and more. I enjoy his self-indulgence. And even when I've thought about it, when I've drunk in all his "no matter which's" and "anywhere at all's" to the full, I see in his one hundred percent acceptance a sort of affection. I'll never be one to complain about too much of a good thing.

We run into a postman making his rounds. I ask him how to get to the main road. Two miles ahead on the plateau, take the road on the left, go down through the village, and it's there at the bottom of the valley. He starts to tell us about shortcuts, but I tell him we aren't in a hurry.

Once we've covered the first two miles, we don't need any more directions. There's a big, open space ahead. At our feet, far below: the highway, running through a narrow valley. Beyond it: another huge plateau. Thanks to this wind, which has cleared away the clouds, we can see the whole expanse stretching into the distance where it butts up against the blue mountains.

Everything about this country is clear, dry, and light. White as a bone. We could take the slope straight down to the road, but we decide instead to go into the village. Before we go down, I have a bunch of things I want to sort out inside myself, with a liter of wine.

It's cold. We're rubbing our hands. We're arching our

backs into the wind. The village is half a mile of twists and turns away. We make it down.

We burst into the bistro like bombshells. The woman inside has olive skin, almost a navy blue because of the darkness around her bright eyes, even around her lips. She laughs when she sees us come in and bang the door shut, with the wind whipping our tails. I shiver with relief from head to toe when I stretch my hands over the roaring woodstove. I give a whistle and I say, "Shitty weather! What do you think, madame?" She thinks exactly the same as I do.

The artist is warming his hands too. They're ash-white, with green scars crisscrossing them in every direction. The lady asks how on earth he got hurt like this.

She's a well-built broad with generous curves. She warms herself alongside us. We're wriggling around in our jackets. Under the circumstances, the woman and the warmth are just what we need. Just like that, I banish a few more of those winter gardens I've been brooding over.

I'm glad I haven't neglected my beard. Maybe this lady will fix us something to eat?

I say we had a hell of a good idea, not to head straight down to the highway like a pair of idiots. We exchange playful looks over this idea, the woman and me. The artist is eyeing a green cloth spread across a marble table. He says to me, "You old fool, you have to buy me a deck of cards." "Yes, you're not kidding, it's been on my mind. It's our first priority. Do they have any here at the tobacco shop?" "But I have cards," says the lady. The artist explains that he wants a fresh deck. And besides, I owe it to him as a gift.

"You're a guy who gives gifts?" she asks.

I say it's exactly what I am, more than she could possibly imagine.

She calls her helper. She sends him to Ma François's to pick up a fifty-two-card deck. I pull out my wallet and give a thousand francs to the kid. (You can never rely solely on a beautiful beard. Thousand-franc banknotes always have a part to play in matters of the heart. I resign myself to laying out the five I have left.)

We share a coffee, and this is an opportunity for all manner of flirtations. I accuse someone of brewing barley coffee; this someone goes and fetches the coffee box and makes me stick my nose into it. "So you think that's barley?" We're in a mood where the words you say don't mean a thing. The kid comes back with the cards. The artist stuffs the sealed packet and the change into his pocket. I give the kid ten francs.

Would we like to eat some tripe in a few minutes? You better believe it! I go into raptures over tripe. I declare it's what I love most in the world (and the funniest part is, it's true). I say it's good to be here, and just how much. And I make a veiled allusion—a subtle, sensitive one—to how close this rotten life of ours came to letting us pass right on by.

I enjoy listening to the wind. It's blowing like hell. I can see the empty square through the windows, two or three stretches of empty streets: this empty, white stone village.

We chat away. I keep an eye on the artist. I'm expecting him to pull the new pack of cards out of his pocket, but he doesn't.

The table is set near the woodstove (you can hear the wind whistling in the pipes). Toward noon the lady's husband arrives. He's a short, sandy-haired guy. They don't do a lot of cuddling. He heads for his plate of food and stays put. The whole time he's here, she lists in a loud voice all the things she needs him to do for her this afternoon. He doesn't say yes and he doesn't say no. And as soon as he's finished eating, he takes off without having a smoke or a coffee. There are some guys who will never cease to amaze me. He has the vacant look of a person who doesn't give a damn.

While we're digesting and the woman's doing the dishes in the kitchen, I say to the artist, "All right, why don't you pull out your new deck? Let's see." "No, not now." I ask a foolish question: "How are your hands doing?" And he gives me a hard, unpleasant look. Then he turns away and gazes at the village beyond the windows, with the same hard, unpleasant look.

We don't say anything for a few minutes. The woman calls out from her kitchen and asks if we're dead. I tell her no, and we go quiet again.

When she's finished doing her dishes, she comes out. Women have always been coming at me wiping their hands on their aprons. She's no fool. She doesn't take our silence lightly. She goes and fetches the bottle of marc and three glasses. She serves us without saying a word, serves herself, sits down with us, and starts looking—just like we're doing—at the white, empty village. This style of doing things goes straight to my heart. It doesn't take much. With some people, this "not much" comes easily. With others, you can starve to death while you go on asking for it for eternity.

A minute later, she says, "What should I cook for you tonight?"

She isn't asking us at all; she's talking to herself. She's raised the question, that's all. She knows that, from here on, things will take care of themselves, if they're meant to.

"Tripe, if there are any left," answers the artist.

The lady looks at me to see if that's all right.

I give a little nod. All three of us are in a state where the less we talk, the better.

And besides, in this fashion, everything does get said. About what matters, anyway.

As always, there are still some practical issues to sort out: the fifth wheel.

Does she have any rooms? The adjoining house belongs to her mother-in-law. There are rooms. "Two steps away," she says.

Speaking of mothers-in-law, what's her husband up to? What's his job? What sort of work is there in the village? Does he always take off like that? We hardly got a glimpse of him. Does he help out in the bistro sometimes? No, not at all. He's away all the time. You never see any more of him than you did today. You could even say you've seen a lot of him today. He works with game. He works with what? He works with game. What do you mean? Are you familiar at all with the region? Not at all. You haven't seen the château? Not one turret. Where were you coming from? We tell her about the plateau we crossed and the wind. Exactly: Up there, in a protected spot you can't see from above, that's where it is, Monsieur Albert's château. Monsieur Albert raises game birds and animals for big hunts. Presidential hunts, even. It's an operation run by the Ministry of Lands and Forests. There are huge game parks in the hills, surrounded by wire netting. They raise pheasants, cocks, partridges, hares. Wild boar. Even deer.

I'm amazed to hear of such a business.

The afternoon has worn on. I expect evening here will be as colorless as the rest of the day. We haven't seen a single resident, aside from the wind.

We do see a fancy sports car go by, with its top completely

folded down. The driver's on her own: a cute little number with her chin held high, like one of those people who pretend to live on nothing but air.

"There goes Madame Albert."

While we're on that subject, I'm really looking for a job for myself. Couldn't I work with the game animals too? If you have special training, yes. No. A specialist is the only thing I can't claim to be, unless we're talking about mechanics. Obviously, there I hold my own, when I need to. Do you know how to drive? With the best of them. I rummage through my pockets and pull out my papers. I show her my trucker's license.

"You have a nice first name," she says.

"Oh! Well, it's pretty plain."

"I like it."

I draw special attention to what my license means. And I tell her and the artist a few anecdotes that put me in a good light, going back to the time when I was charging around the roads of Savoie with loads of cheese. The cheese doesn't add to my allure, but I lay on the charm.

She examines my photo and tells me I look just as good without a beard. I remark that identity photos always make you look like an ex-con. That's not how she sees this one.

In any case, she thinks I have a chance. They had a guy who was delivering supplies with the van and taking care of the cars. He left two days ago. If they haven't already replaced him, that could work. If I'd known that, I say, it would have been worth having a word with the girl who was driving by with her chin in the air. She must know her? She knows her, but she doesn't say anything more on the subject. Except that the girl in question doesn't get involved in that side of things.

"It would be best to wait for my husband to come back. He should be home tonight."

"You mean there are nights when he doesn't come home?"

"Lots."

He should be here by around seven.

For a while, we were the only customers, but now the evening regulars have started turning up, one after another. There are four or five guys about my age—all of them, it seems, wild about mustaches. Every one of them has those drooping, gray tresses! Wonders to behold. You can barely glimpse their chins behind these monstrosities. Once these characters are inside out of the wind, they wriggle around for a minute or two—like fish out of water—before they take a seat.

I keep an eye out for when the belote games are set to start. While I'm sidling toward the kitchen in pursuit of my famous, customary butt-warming, I see the artist moving closer to the players and getting ready to follow the game over their shoulders.

The kitchen is tiny. Instead of slipping into position without saying a word like I usually do, I politely ask for permission. Granted. She has to come close to me to go about her business, and she does. And I discover she has a lot of business to attend to. Which is far from disagreeable. I feel a lot of sympathy for this woman. I ask her to tell me her first name. Catherine. Very pretty. I spend an hour without thinking about the artist looking over the shoulders of the card-players. Then I do think of him, and I pull away on the double from my stove to go and see. He's still standing there, firmly planted. He hasn't gotten mixed up in anything.

So the little blond guy, who couldn't care less, does get back around seven. I don't budge from my spot by the kitchen stove. I'd like the question of butt-warming to be raised right from the start. I watch for his reaction. Zero. Clearly, to his mind there's no question at all. Do you know what I think? To really understand me, you need to know this: I think I envy him.

But you can't turn yourself into something you aren't; you have to make do with yourself the way you are. Which doesn't always fit the bill. And there's the rub.

When it comes to jobs like the one at the château, you usually have to wait around for ages, running in place. Here, they wrap things up and hand them to me in no time flat. Everything happens so fast, I'm the only one who raises any questions.

There's no problem at all. Do I want the job? It's mine for the taking. I just have to go over to the château right now. The little blond guy comes with me. It's half a mile away. If it was a hundred and fifty miles away, I'd still jump at the opportunity, I have such a strong feeling that things are going to run smoothly.

On my way out, I whisper a word or two into the artist's ear about the job. And I add, "Wipe your mouth." (He's drooling while he watches them play cards.)

The little fair-haired guy turns out to be a decent guy. Very decent, even. As we're walking through the darkness and the wind, he says five or six things that really hit home. Then he shuts up. He gives me plenty of time to think things over for myself. Then he starts up again. He lays out a different kind of problem: It's a job with no security, and there's no fooling around. To have the things that interest us in particular and everybody in general, he took this job. And he's sticking with it, come what may.

You can't take anything away from what he's saying. Right or wrong, I'm going to look at things his way. Just in case.

We go into a courtyard. He talks to the dogs, who calm right down. This place is impressive in the dark. There are even some watchtowers. (And definitely some surroundings to watch.) I, on the other hand, I don't feel calm at all.

He pulls on a handle shaped like a doe's foot. A bell rings in one of the corridors inside. A woman comes and opens up. He calls her Marthe. Is the boss here? He is. Come up-stairs.

We head down one of the passageways. It's barely lit, but I can see enough to realize we've come up a notch in the world. There are paintings, shields, whole suits of armor, that sort of thing. Tapestries and so on.

We climb the stairs. We hear music. There's some guy singing. He must be big and fat. He's dishing out racy lyrics in Italian. He says, "And in Spain he's made love to a thou-sand and three." But the music—well, I have to say—the music is really something! I have no idea what's going on, but I do enjoy it. I think it's playing on the radio.

We wait on the landing until the song is over, then we knock. We enter a hall the size of a railway station. There's only one tiny spark of light. And under the lampshade, a guy who's changing a disc on a turntable like the one at Dr. Ch.'s.

I'm not thinking much, one way or another. If this is the boss, he's pretty tall and strong, lithe and skinny-looking. Yes, this is the boss. The short blond guy does his number on my behalf with impressive ease. I say to myself: If this works out, in no time I'll be doing the same for somebody else. For the time being, I cast some glances around this inky cavern lined with walls of books. And at this man with clear eyes and a hard, bitter face (bitter enough to scare you shit-less) and pale temples. He's at least ten years older than me—around fifty-five or sixty. I find him appealing. He shakes my hand.

He's the sort of character you can't take your eyes off. The more you look, the more you like. Will it be the same once you get to know him? What does it matter? I like his hang-out, what he was up to in here, the way he has of not spreading his bitterness around. He talks to me, kindly and fairly, to help sort out my problems.

It's a while later. I've already been hired, but he's still giving me encouragement—sincere and unconditional. I feel like I've taken the golden calf by the tail. All you have to do is hold on tight and let it leap ahead.

Now this evening, back in the village, I have a family chat with the artist. For the moment, we're sleeping in a room with two beds. Tomorrow, we'll have rooms of our own. We hit the sack and kill the light, and I talk.

To begin with, I say a word or two about what went on at the château: how I was welcomed, the job, all of that. Then I start into the main course—gingerly—blowing carefully over the spoon. You tend to be diplomatic when you're in bed. What does he think of the village? Nothing. This bodes well. There's money to be made here. It's a piece of what's essential. How to make something out of this "nothing": It's right up our alley. And it looks like it will be child's play.

I listen to the wind roaring against the walls. And I give the artist plenty of time to listen to it too. It's part of my case.

What does he have to say about these sheets? They're unbelievably clean! I've never seen sheets so white. He has nothing to say about them. Perfect. Is he warm? He's good and warm, he's doing just fine. And he adds, "Shut up, I'm half asleep."

This is completely untrue. Both of us know it. We're not fooling anybody. I leave him to grill on one side for five minutes.

On the money question, I show my hand: It's as promising as it gets. We can treat ourselves to everything, live like lords of the manor until the weather takes a turn for the better. The highway's always there for us; no one's taking it away. If we want to go back on the road, it will always be there, one day after another; there's no need to fret or make any compromises about our way of life. If this is falling on deaf ears, it's a shame. But I hope it isn't.

I know he's listening to me. He knows he doesn't have to answer unless it's to say something nasty.

I explain how I've set things up for the two of us with Catherine and the little blond guy. One whole side of existence is completely sorted out.

Silence. A little wind. A lot of wind (tons of it are needed, more, even).

I'm extremely cozy in my bed. I've shoved my hands in between my thighs. I'm warm. While I'm lying like this and drifting off, I'm in no condition to stir up trouble, obviously. But I'd like to know if he's tried out his hands. Can he still play tricks? To my mind, this would be a kind of insurance.

I ask myself all sorts of questions, each one dumber than the rest. In this out-of-the-way village, will he find what he needs to be able to go for broke, apart from his hands? In case they won't serve that purpose anymore.

I'm comfortable under my quilt. Laid out flat on my back like this, I wouldn't trade places for all the money in the world. But it's not so great to be worrying when the warmth of my own body's forcing me to relax.

I imagine he's sleeping. What a fine thing friendship is!

I hear him breathing, and that's enough for me. He must be thinking similar thoughts because he says in a very clear voice, "You'll buy me a guitar."

I'm in a rush to answer yes. You're not kidding! But I'm already asleep. And I spend the whole night answering him. Nights like this are amazing!

I wake up at five o'clock. I get dressed quickly in the dark. I go down. The daily routine is already underway in the kitchen. Catherine is working the coffee grinder between her thighs. The stove is roaring. It's one of the most beautiful kitchens I've ever seen.

It looks like the little blond guy has already left.

I have a quick rinse at the sink. I also style my beard: in tune with Catherine, with this neck of the woods, with my new boss, the whole kit and kaboodle. I trim it closer to my chin, leaving just enough length for it to curl. I warm myself by the stove while Catherine puts on a whole theatrical performance. She plays the sensitive, tender sweetheart. It's like sugar candy. We talk about one thing and another—in other words, about her and me. And with this we make a little medicine to fight off the wind (still blowing) and all of those bone-white buildings and stones that are going to stride out of the darkness an hour from now, proud as can be.

She touches my beard. I pretend to bite her fingers. She's delighted to scream in fear like a little girl. Human beings have so much potential.

I get to the château at daybreak, and I stand and wait on this side of the dogs, who don't recognize me yet. A guy turns up. He's heard about me. He has me come into a sort of shack that serves as a guardhouse. There are already two foresters inside, warming themselves up. We talk about the district.

I find out I'll be going to pick up bird feed—sunflower seed, oil cakes, sesame seed—at D. It's ten miles away. They give me a list of the suppliers. Everything's written down: weights, specifications. Will I be able to handle it? I tell them I've done lots more than this plenty of times. The guy I replaced must have been the village idiot. They give me endless advice. They're veterans, and I'm a raw recruit. They're showing off. Fair enough. I'll be glad to let them pick up bonuses.

I check out the van. They didn't bother to cover the engine, and I have a hard time starting it up. The garage faces north.

In daylight, the château looks weird, incredibly ancient. I also notice something I hadn't suspected in the dark: There are stepped terraces with ornamental pools and white balustrades. You feel like you're wrapped up in lace.

On the highway, the wind grabs me full force. I can feel it in the steering wheel—it's no laughing matter.

When I arrive in D., the town is asleep. Because it sits in a bowl, the light of dawn hasn't reached the streets yet. All the stores are still closed. I find my way to an open bistro on a square where there's a bus depot. With a cast of pale-faced characters dressed to the nines, I drink a cup of coffee that tastes like dirty dishwater. The whole crowd is hung over. All these tarts (well, somebody might love them, somewhere else) and traveling salesmen are giving off a strong odor of bad teeth.

I go out for some fresh air (and it's nippy). While I'm waiting for the locals to decide to get out of bed, I stroll around the town. It's the capital of the region. I get my blood flowing in these deserted streets where the storefronts and windows are shuttered tight. I think about all the bedrooms filled with couples. This must make for quite a ruckus. A chorus of cash registers and hanky-panky. These ten thousand souls must support a hell of a lot of whoring and soliciting! Let's call it a continuous stream, to be polite.

I might sound bitter, but I'm not at all. On the contrary: I'm the very soul of indulgence and understanding. I'm the most *understanding* guy on earth. You have to assume they're innocent until proven guilty.

Men are leaving for the factories, with rucksacks on their backs. I ask where they're going. There's a cardboard mill in the vicinity, a little spinning mill, and a dairy where they make a low-grade camembert. I'm hitting all the high spots this morning! I'm starting to unwind.

In the end, the guys who were still in bed—the ones I was thinking the worst of just a few minutes ago—finally do get up. They half open the shop doors; then they open them all the way. The guys look all right, to tell the truth. And the women mounting displays of bedding in the shopwindows— sheets, blankets, quilts—they're far from shabby. Each and every one of them could tell me they're just doing their job. And if I know a better way, I should just say so. No, I don't.

I say a few polite words to a short, lame, brown-skinned woman who's bringing out crates of vegetables for her stand. She has velvety eyes. She's ill, and I give her a little help getting set up. I do this on account of her eyes; they're nice to look at, soft and submissive. I stay with her for as long as it takes to see her smile.

Next, farther along the street I spy a meat pie in the window of a cookshop. I go in and buy it. I get it wrapped up for the artist. This will give him a pleasant surprise. For myself, I pick up two stuffed turnovers, which slide down my throat like letters into a mailbox. After this, I fill up a first-class pipe.

My oil cakes, sunflower seeds, and sesame seeds are loaded

in the blink of an eye. At the same time, the château has telephoned to tell me to pick up the newspapers and then drop by the place of someone named Madame Anita. She'll give me a parcel for Madame Albert.

I go to Anita's. She's a private dressmaker. You have to climb up to the second floor in a house that smells like a bordello. The lady puts on unbelievable airs while she wraps tissue paper around a tartan jacket so tiny that I ask myself how any living creature could possibly feel comfortable inside it.

In spite of the early hour, Madame Anita is powdered, combed, made-up, smartly dressed, and as perfumed as a grove of lilacs. She's plump and she lets her flesh show a little. What you can see is the color known as Deputy Director's Delight. Her voice is husky. She matches her staircase in every way: shadowy, silent, and discreet, with doubled soundproof doors. All this takes me back twenty years, to when I still saw the world through rose-colored glasses. For sure, I'd have lost myself in this place; I can feel the illusions swarming back.

As soon as the pixie's jacket is wrapped, I take off.

I was expecting a "so long, good-looking," but Lady Anita just breathes, "Tell Madame Albert I need her for some fittings this week." Yes, madame, happy to be of service.

I put Anita's carton on the seat beside me. I start up and away I go.

I do this low-class chauffeur job for two or three days. It's not much of a challenge. Apart from the trip to D. every morning, I have time on my hands. I don't count as work the wipe with a rag that I give to the top of the lady's convertible or the kick to her tires to see if they might need a little air. I tidy every part of my garage. I give the boss's motorcycle a full inspection. I top up all the fuel. I grease. Nothing much for a guy like me, who'd rather keep busy.

No matter how hard I look for stuff to do, I still have too much time to think about the artist.

I'm very reserved when it comes to certain things. For example, I hate going through anybody else's pockets. I turn it into a really big deal. But one morning while the artist is snoozing, with his head facing the wall, I search his jacket. I can't get the thought of that new deck of cards out of my head. I want to see what he's done with it. He hasn't done anything with it. The packet's still unopened.

At the château, I can't help but notice a whole lot of things, seeing as I'm lounging around so much. The little number goes out in her car every day at the same time: around three in the afternoon. Monsieur Albert is always there when she leaves, whether he's standing on the steps outside or upstairs behind one of the windows. She backs the car out, gets set, and takes off like her ass is on fire. If it were me, I'd turn around and give an affectionate wave toward the steps or the windows. But she's not me, and she doesn't give a wave. I imagine she's going to D. In any case, that's the road she takes.

On Sunday afternoon, we head out—the artist and me— for a ramble. This isn't something we'd normally do. After all the legwork it took to get here, we look ridiculous wasting our free time wandering around. But it's still the best plan we can come up with.

We stroll along at a leisurely pace like well-heeled towns-people; in fact, we are feeling bourgeois. You might say I'm seeing the world for the first time in my life, and it's leaving me cold. We're forcing our legs to move, as if the doctor had recommended it, while our minds are on other things. You can't really call it a diversion. But what can it be called, when you come right down to it? I picture all the other people who are doing the same thing. I think to myself: There must be an awful lot of us in this predicament, across the surface of the globe.

Finally, we find a sheltered spot, and we lie down on the side of a slope. As usual, there's plenty of wind and a hazy sun. I do everything humanly possible: I try to sleep, I suck on a sprig of rosemary, I stare at part of the country I couldn't care less about. None of this gets me very fired up.

I ask the artist if money means a lot to him. He says it means a lot to everybody. I agree. But take me, for example—I'm not so attached to it. It's important to me only as far as I need it. "Far enough not to stop you from going through my pockets." I wish this was happening on a day when I felt up to getting angry. Even so, I calmly explain why I frisked him up there on the mountain: I wanted the knife. While I'm talking, I can see the scullery again and the blood. For a couple of minutes, I feel like I did when I was carrying him downhill on my back. This revives me. It feels nice. Then it fades away, and here I am again, trying to get it through his head that he didn't have a cent on him. He's stubborn. He doesn't believe it.

I ask him if he thinks I'm that kind of a guy. He answers: All guys are like that. Granted. I don't believe in fairy tales. I've seen too much. But what if our positions had been reversed? What if somebody had smashed my face in and he'd come to rescue me, would he take advantage and go through my pockets? First off, he says, I wouldn't come to rescue you. I don't care about other people's problems. But if I came across you by accident, it's possible I might go through your pockets. I don't see why I'd pass up the chance.

Granted once again. I know that money's a physical need (I want to add that it's even a *natural need*), but in some cases you're willing to part with it for the sake of a lot of other things. That, he says, that's just a load of crap. And crap is what they've been feeding him since the day he was born.

A load of crap? Not so much. Take family men, don't they hand their pay over to their wives for the kids and the rest of it? No. They hand over their pay because they have to. And when they don't have to, it's because they've made arrangements. What kind of arrangements? They make it work to their advantage.

All right then, take me, for example: I gave him thirteen thousand francs. Why did I do that? Because I'd robbed him of even more than that, he says. No other reason? No.

It's not worth getting angry. I try to make him understand. First, that I didn't rob him. Not at all. Next, that there are times when it feels a lot better to give than it does to keep; better to share than to hold on for your own sake. That sometimes giving feels good. That for the same amount of money, you couldn't buy yourself anything better. Then I realize this is all just grist for his mill, and I shut up for a while.

He's not that much of a fool. He knows I've been biting my tongue. He's wearing a nasty smile, and he gives me all the time in the world to consider things from every angle. The part of the country we're in is miserable beyond belief. Scrubbed bare. Wind ... and nothing else. Impossible to connect to anything whatsoever. No choice but to go looking inside yourself.

I've known plenty of places where it doesn't take much to change your state of mind: a bird, a grasshopper, even the wind. When I look closely, I can see that there would be grasshoppers here too. There's no lack of birds, and it might even be fun to watch them beating their way through this fierce wind. But I couldn't give a damn about what they're doing or what sort of birds they are. I'm in a strange mood. It's no laughing matter.

Basically, what I'm after has to come from the artist. And what is it I'm after? I haven't got a clue. I'm stuck. I want to be friends, not talk about anything anymore, not have any more doubts, be certain, not wonder all the time where things stand.

The story he believes—that I swiped his cash—doesn't bother me all that much. Besides, it's only because he really does believe it that it doesn't make me mad as hell. On the contrary, in a certain way it makes me glad. Because, he truly does believe it. *It's something that doesn't bore him.*

I have no desire, none at all, for him to start strutting around. I like him the way he is. And he's next to me now, just the way I like him. What am I after?

His look is more ugly than vicious. I know there are people who'd prefer—who do prefer—to keep their distance from him: Catherine, for example; the little blond guy, for example; the boss, for example—he's already asked me who he is, this character I drag around. I can't say I like his look. Nobody could. It doesn't bode well. It's out to take advantage of you. As for me, I know that the guy with that look on his face, who does want to take advantage of everybody else, is no longer capable of taking advantage of anyone.

At the start, in the early days when I was partial to that look—the one that disgusts other people—I realized that the man who wore it could get the better of other people— and of me—only by means of an incredibly elaborate system of trickery. When you come right down to it, I enjoyed smoothing the way for him (and, as far as I'm concerned, I'm still smoothing the way for him). Is that friendship?

When I'm done mulling this over, when I've had my fill of the bare hills around us, I ask the artist if he isn't going to decide, after all, to play cards again, even a little. He answers: Am I already fed up with paying for his room and board? I'm quick to tell him I haven't given it a single thought. It's the truth. I add (and this isn't true) that Catherine's giving it to us for free. "Are you paying her in kind?" he asks. It's painful to say yes, but I do say yes ... if that's what it takes to set his mind at rest. No, it's not about the money. His gambling interests me as an *artistic performance*. He answers that he doesn't play for his own amusement or for the amusement of others.

Even so, on the night when I helped run his con up there on the mountain, he seemed pretty excited.

He gives me a scornful look.

"I don't need to go down to the cellar with a broad to get excited."

I ignore the allusion.

So what's this story he's telling about not playing for his own amusement?

Now it's his whole face, and probably his whole body, that's heaping scorn on me from head to foot.

"Do you do everything for your own amusement?" he asks.

What I'm doing now isn't for my own amusement, that's for sure. But I have nothing better to do. I feel like he's seen right through me. He's trying to make me understand something serious and important, something a man never agrees with himself about, let alone anybody else.

What a strange Sunday!

I'm a bit scared by how much he understands. It's one hell

of a lot. But I understand a whole lot of things too: in particular, everything he's just said, everything he's said to me ever since I've known him. There's never been a single kind word. That's another way he cheats. I have only the illusion of being happy.

I say, "But you cheat!" (Am I talking about cards or about him and me?)

He answers, "Naturally I cheat. You want me to play like everybody else?"

I'd like to say no, but I don't.

Am I on the road because I have no other choice? Or—like him—because there's nothing else to do? (Like him, exactly like him. Even if there are times when I want something else.) Do I get involved in anybody else's schemes? He can see that I don't. Has he done anything, anything at all, to cling to me? No. Has he asked me for anything? I say, "Once." "When?" "The night of the fair." When I came in and they were beating him up, he hid behind me.

He's wearing his ugly smile.

He cheats because it's a scheme he can run on his own. Yes, he hid behind me. Agreed. But was he behind somebody when I got there?

I say as politely as I can, "No, old chum, you weren't behind anybody."

I look at him. He doesn't get it. He must be thinking about his scheme.

Why ask any more of him? Do I ask any more of myself?

We're back to where we started. This isn't something I'm used to. It's rare for me to go back over the same roads and return to the fold. The sky is white. I'm amazed to see some birds up there. As we're nearing the village, I hear the wind roaring through the vacant streets.

I realize it's been really cold out today. In the bistro, there are three belote games underway. The artist is standing at his post next to one of the tables. He's watching the game over the players' shoulders.

I'm going to warm myself in the kitchen. Catherine asks where I've been. It doesn't take long before I tire of that. I go back into the *beverage room* and sit down beside Papa Burle, the road repairman. He's puffing on his pipe. This reminds me that I haven't smoked mine. He's reading the newspaper. I ask if there's any good news. He says no. He has me read the headlines. I watch the artist out of the corner of my eye.

After this, we have a few cold and windy days of heavy, driving rain. Every morning, I make my run into D. for the bird feed. Every day at dawn, in the same bistro I went to on my first day, I see the same gang of shivering johns and molls. They're waiting for the first bus. They're all green around the gills, and the broads have put more rouge around their lips than they've managed to put on them. Everybody's huddling inside parkas and lambskin jackets. They're stamping their feet. They go countless times to press their noses against the window and wipe away the mist in order to see if the bus is in the square. Then they come back to the bar to suck back a little mug of coffee the color and taste of shoe polish. I don't know if it's because they were kicked out of bed early, but they look lousy and they smell bad. I don't know how many of them are good fathers or wives, or tight-knit couples, but what's clear is that every one of them would give up all the rest to feel a little stirring in their loins. Except one woman, who smells of bad teeth like everybody else but who's holding on tight to a little kid. She's opened her coat to cover him up. You won't tear her bone away from her!

It's for all this harmless sleaze that I come here. I need a dose of reality. I run the château's errands at the suppliers, and I love the ring of their cash registers too—it's my birdsong. We all rely on little tricks to make ourselves feel good from time to time. This is one of mine.

And nearly every time, I also go to Lady Anita's. There's always something to pick up or drop off. I've seen jackets and skirts, blouses and sweaters, even black silk panties. I wonder what particularly disgusting smell she keeps hidden behind her violet-scented lotion? She must spray herself with an atomic bomb as soon as she gets out of bed. You can smell it all the way from the landing. Actually, I don't really care. After she'd tried everything she could think of (which was more than a little), she must have decided I had no balls.

She wraps the items up, and I take them away. That's all there is to it, even if, on the pretext of taking the utmost care, she's shown me—down to the tiniest stitch—what she's putting in the packages. If I were the least bit interested, I could easily picture the boss's wife in the buff, seeing how much of her stuff Lady Anita passes right under my nose: slips, panties, brassieres; black, pink, even green (she explains that green goes well with a suntan), even blood-red. It's the first time in my life I've seen anything like this. I tell her it reminds me of a meat market. When all is said and done, I put the parcel on the seat beside me in the van, and I drive back to the château.

The rest of the time, I go about my business in the teeth of the wind, and lately of heavy freezing rain as well. I go into the guardhouse to unstiffen my fingers next to the stove. There are a few foresters in here. They're good guys. I exchange a couple of words with them.

I fill the *wind-drinker*'s gas tank. I polish her convertible top. She goes out every day with it folded down in spite of the rain. She'd go out in Noah's Flood with it folded down. She has a whole set of American raincoats and sou'westers she adds to her Scottish kilts, her Scottish jackets (either plaid, or snow-white wool), on top of her panty girdles and thingamaboobs in black, green, or red rat-a-tat. All of this ends up giving her a kind of figure. And away she goes. She goes to D., or the devil, or both.

Up above at his windowpane, Monsieur Albert watches as she takes off. At D., with some of my spare cash, I've bought four earthenware pots, and I've planted thirty crocus bulbs as a gift for the boss. They're already sprouting nicely. In a couple of weeks, there'll be some flowers to nibble on.

I don't know why I thought of the crocuses, but they're a good idea. They cheer me up too. I enjoy pampering them. I cultivate their soil with an old fork. I keep them moist. There's already a hint of green at the tips of the shoots.

One afternoon toward two o'clock, I'm tending to them in the lean-to behind the garage. The weather is still crappy. I hear the sound of people walking: two sets of footsteps, side by side; one of them a long stride, in boots; the other, a quick trot, in Louis XV heels. I don't have time to let them know I'm here. And besides, a bearded man drooling over sprouted bulbs isn't a pretty sight. I take a quick look, and I rest easy. It's the boss and his chick. She goes to her car. She gives her seat cushions a pat. She rummages around, opens her purse, looks for the ignition key. The boss is standing next to her, upright in his boots, legs apart. I feel for this guy. If I could speak right now, I'd say to him, "Give her a kick in the ass!" We're always so good at cleaning up other people's problems.

She settles into her seat and bangs the door shut. He puts the toe of his boot on the running board and leans forward.

I like this guy's gray hair and his self-contained ways. He says to the girl, "You hate me. You're finally going to be truthful to me. You can't deceive someone you hate, because you don't want to—it would be unpleasant." She pushes the starter button. I don't hear what he adds. I see her lips form around a few more words, then he stops talking. She backs out of the garage, but this time she's looking at him. She swings around and leaves. And so does he, with long strides, like a few minutes ago.

Once I'm left alone, I hurry to get back to a less unholy place. This weather is truly crappy. Without rain, this part of the country is good for nothing; when it rains, it's good for even less. But it's easier to deal with something, even with *shortcomings*, than with nothing.

One night before I hit the hay, I go the artist's door and listen. "You there?" "Where else would I be?" I go in. He's in bed.

What do I want? Nothing, and everything, as usual. He gives me a funny look. It's about the conversation we had the other day. What "conversation"—are you losing your mind? Or are you drunk? No, I'm not losing my mind and I'm not drunk. You backed down a little the other day. Backed down? You must be dreaming. How did I back down? If you really want to know, you were friendly—you talked to me in a friendly way about your cardplaying schemes. I'd be glad if you showed me a few tricks like you did that time when we ate our snack beside the fountain. Are you looking for somebody to get killed? he asks. No, I don't want anybody to get killed! Then why are you going on about it? Exactly, since there's nothing to go on about, why make it into such a big deal? He answers: This isn't the right time. And then he points out, very nicely, that I'm going to freeze my nuts off. I keep insisting anyway. He answers that he doesn't show anyone his tricks or how to use them. I tell him—and very nicely too—that I couldn't care less how he puts them to use, that I'm old enough to put them to use my own way, that all I want is for him to show me his tricks, the way he has lots of times before now, to amuse me. I feel like I've left him at a loss. I regret having the upper hand, and I ease off. I'm not cut out to be a winner.

I'm in my shirttails, with only a jacket thrown across my shoulders. He says if I'm out to deep-freeze myself, he has no objection—there's no accounting for taste. He learned his tricks in jail. To learn anything, no matter what, you have to be in a place where you have the time. Prison is perfect. The longer you're locked up, the more you withdraw into yourself. That's the way it is. What is there to look at? Nothing, just some walls. You're left to yourself to act out your little comedy, and you play it right to the end. Take the three-card trick, for example. It's unbeatable. How to make the right card turn up, when everyone would swear, on their mother's life, that it can't be there—you don't learn that in five minutes. He reminds me that I gambled three hundred francs on it and I lost them all; I could have bet a hundred thousand, and I still would have lost them all.

I say, "Show me another." "No, it's not the right time." And he adds, "It won't work on this bed, and I don't feel like getting up; it's freezing."

I couldn't care less that it's freezing. So according to him—and I'm taking his word for it ("Oh!" he says, "'you're taking my word'! I played the trick right under your nose, and you were completely taken in!"). So yes, I am taking him at his word: He can make the right card turn up in places nobody would expect. What more do you want? he asks. I've proven it—I've played the trick right in your face more than twenty times. To take three hundred francs off a guy like you, who makes only piddling bets, you have to have more than a few tricks up your sleeve. If that's not enough, what more do you want? I tell him he's missing the point. He makes the right card turn up... So does this mean that there *is* a right card? He asks if I'm a bit off my nut! Of course there's a right card! There's always a right card because it's the one you get your mark to bet on. It's all about putting it where nobody expects it.

I go to my room, and I come back after I've put on some pants. Tonight, finally, he's not too tired. He says, "You're freezing! I told you so." "Don't worry. I'm a guy who warms up fast. I have great circulation." In that case, he asks, how do I manage to keep my great circulation under control? How can I work for other people and still be so calm and collected? He could never understand, up there on the mountain, why I stayed on at the mill. And here at the château, what kind of game am I playing with my delivery van? If he was a mechanic or a driver like me, he wouldn't put up with it. I answer: I'm far from satisfied. And besides, everybody's in the same boat. If he hears anybody say they're satisfied with that sort of a job, he should tell them they're lying. In reality, we're all alike, chum. I've been kicking around long enough to know what talk amounts to. There aren't a hundred different ways of passing our time here on earth—two or three, that's the max. We're all going through the same daily grind. The only difference between us is the way we grind. Anyway, most guys take the easiest way out. They have their multiplication tables: Two times two makes four, two times six makes twelve. They do them over and over, one after another. Takes care of everything.

I tell him about the goings-on at D.: the strange creatures who wait for the morning bus, and Lady Anita. As far as I know, there are more than a hundred bordellos for a population of four or five thousand. "Believe me, I've never run across a setup remotely like it. You've seen cash registers that play tunes from operas, like *The Daughter of Madame Angot*, haven't you? In the inventor's hands, yes, they sing like the girl in the aria. But in the hands of the madams, they go *ding*! Period. And they're ringing all day. I wish I had a brass band in a corner, and each time one of the johns paid his bill, I'd get them to play *Ramona* or *Boléro* for him. What a look you'd see on his mug!"

He chuckles. He says, "You know shitloads of stuff." I answer, "You better believe it!" And we split our sides laughing.

"That Lady Anita, even if she pours a barrel of violet up her you-know-what, she only has one of them, like anybody else." He answers, "Two at the most. And she has to make do with what she's got." We let loose a volley of truly disgusting filth. This lightens things up. I think of my *wind-drinker* and her guy, who's pearly gray around his temples. If he were here, he'd see things for what they are.

But I *am* here, and I can't figure things out at all: It's the first time ever that the two of us aren't picking a fight.

He tells me, "They nailed me hard. But I swore I'd get my own back, and I keep my word. They fucked me in jail. And in jail I learned how to screw them. They had the better of me back then because I was a just a punk, a stinking little asshole. Now they're the ones who can fall into line!"

He's talking so fast, he runs out of breath. He was about to say more, but he clams up. He sucks the saliva from the corner of his mouth.

I tell myself: Let's talk about the past. I take him back to when he was king of the mountains. I recall that terrific night we spent with the guys up there. I know he couldn't care less that they gave him a beating (and even worse than that). It just shows there was no other way to put a stop to the likes of him. The fact that they dumped him, covered in blood, his hands crushed, beside Ma Lantifle's chamber pot, the fact that they had to go to such lengths: That was his victory. At least, that's what I think. And I'm not wrong, because he starts to drool while he's listening to me. He's going to turn cocky and mean again, it won't be long.

To put a stop to him? If they had to go that far—to kill him—to be able to put a stop to him, it was because God the Father couldn't have fucked them any harder than he did. He conned them to their very core. After that, who wouldn't have wanted to put a stop to him?

I talk to him about the night at Ferréol's, and there we are again, reliving it. I see he's also reliving those thousands and thousands of nights and days he's spent gambling since he got out of jail. He says he was the one who got the gang up there into the habit of betting without a ceiling. Before he came along, they were setting a limit on how much they could lose. He can't set a limit on his losses. Whenever he gambles—no matter who with, whatever the game—that's his only rule.

"And you never cheat against that rule?"

"You must be joking," he says. "It's my own rule. I don't cheat against myself. What do you take me for?"

I take him for a strange little boy. He lies like a huckster. Wouldn't that be rich, to cheat against yourself! I've barely finished the thought, when I notice his ugly look and the daisy petals of spit around his mouth.

No ceiling: Obviously, it gives you headroom. I know what's it's like to live without a ceiling, even without walls. But then there's always the horizon. And there you come to a halt.

It's made me laugh to find myself trapped inside. Whether my laughter's been forced, who's to say, if not me? I'm the one wrestling hard with this notion of cheating against yourself. Right away, it has me dazzled. But I get a glimpse of how you can carry on this way forever—straight ahead—with no risk of getting your feet tangled up in the stratosphere.

But up to now (and if so, good Lord, I swear, it was an oversight!), I've tried to limit my losses.

It's what comes of being born legitimate! You get in the habit of conducting yourself like a minister of finance, and this never satisfies the needs of a common foot soldier.

I've seen all the fine points, I tell him. Of what? Of the tricks he played at Ferréol's, of course. I'm not talking about anything else.

What could we tell from his hands? he asks. Nothing more than we could tell from Ferréol's, Ironwire's, Nestor's, and mine: hands going through the motion of picking up a card and throwing it down on the table. What his hands had done before and what they did during and after: the most important part was invisible. I'm over the moon.

He shows me how to play one trick after another. All the moves are stored in his head, and I realize how much of his life they add up to. The way the king popped out at just the right moment; the way the ace had slipped behind the ten of spades; the move he made to win the big jackpot; and how all of this was due to the secret agility of his index finger, exactly three seconds beforehand, while everybody's eyes were fixed on the cards hitting the table. Now it's clear as day. I realize there's no point worrying about that, any more than the fact that he's breathing, because it happens just as naturally, just as simply, just as inevitably.

There was no way you could tell he was cheating. He was alive. Once you'd seen that, you'd seen all there was to see. The rest flowed from a secret spring.

And who was going to mistrust such a spring? Even so, one night they caught him. "They were playing for the max," he says. Money, is that the max? If you decide so, it's as big a deal as anything else.

Was it after one of his "*reckless moves*"? (That's what I'm calling them, for want of a better word.) After one of his slow-motion cheats? When I witnessed one in person, it chilled me to the bone. He drools a big blossom of saliva from the corner of his mouth, in triumph. He's delighted that I saw what he was up to. I say, "You were playing with fire." He answers, "Naturally!" (A word I'll remember.) "What do you want me to play with?"

But no, it wasn't after anything, he says. That night, he was even more invisible than usual. So what happened? Too invisible. They had to come up with something. And once they'd run out of other possibilities, they accused him of cheating. On the off chance. And it was true. So they found him out.

Right away, he goes back to explaining his moves. There was a time when he wouldn't explain his moves. He was standing beside the fountain, more a king than any of the cardboard kings his hands were fluttering through. Now his hands are lying flat on the blanket and he's talking. He is, as they say, one of those people who amount to nothing: He's all talk.

"Tell the truth: Can you still use your hands?"

"No." (He says it nicely, without hesitation.)

"Have you tried?"

"Yes."

"You haven't unwrapped my deck of cards."

"I bought another one."

He pulls my deck out—untouched, sealed in its wrapper—from under his pillow, and the other one, which has been used.

I ask, "What can we do?"

"I'm looking into it."

With that, I go to bed and sleep like a log.

The next day, suddenly it's warm. The sky's so overcast, I misjudge the time; I have barely a second to give Catherine a little peck on the cheek. And I do it only because, for the first time, she insists. I'm late. I race off.

I needn't have worried. At the château, they still can't see a thing. I have to switch the headlights on to be able to back up and turn around on the terrace. I don't douse them until I get to the highway. And then after five minutes, to be on the safe side I turn them on again.

The clouds are so low, you could touch them with your hand. I've never seen clouds this black. The line of plane trees that accompanies me all the way to D. seems none too pleased.

It looks like midnight here in town. Not a soul stirring. And over the rooftops, these piles of coal-black clouds are ready to crash down at any moment.

I have just enough time to make it to my usual bistro. There's a blast of thunder that makes my ears crackle. I hurry inside to take shelter.

In here, you can barely see the end of your nose. They're using candlelight. The power's been cut off. My regulars are still waiting for the bus, and they're all saying it's not going to be much fun today. But unlike on other days, they seem to find this amusing. It's the first time they've been cheerful.

We all go and press our noses to the windows because it's raining buckets. It's a spectacle. Suddenly, the rain turns into heavy hail: hellfire and damnation. Everybody's yelling. The hailstones are the size of billiard balls. They're going to rip through the canvas cover on my van. What can I do? This is no time to go outside.

The thunder's rearing up again, throwing its whole stockpile of sheet metal into the fray. Rumbling like an express train. How can there be so many echoes out there? Where does the thunder go to find them? If the lads in the flophouses are still asleep, their consciences must be really clear! If they're awake, what a racket they're hearing in their beds!

We're in raptures because it keeps on roaring. It even builds. I've rarely seen weather this bad. But the air is mild, almost hot at times. We feel twice our normal size. The broads chat with everybody, including me. I'm thinking—I have no idea why—that I'll have to trim my beard a little. Nothing to do with the present situation, obviously, but that's how it is.

One last blast leaves us shaking in our boots, and the hail stops like it's been cut it off with a scythe. Has my van suffered any damage? I go to check. No, it hasn't. A miracle. You couldn't call these hailstones; they're big enough to fell an ox! I cover the hood and go back inside because what's rumbling over the rooftops looks really nasty. Huge raindrops are starting to pelt down again.

The thunder's no longer directly overhead. It's prowling around the district. Where can it be finding all these deep valleys! I never imagined there were so many out there.

The crowd in here wonders if the bus will leave in spite

of the bad weather. Opinions are divided, and everybody enjoys sharing them. There's a loud buzz.

We blow out the candles. As will happen in the normal course of events, the sun has risen. But it's not bright yet. We're in a sort of twilight. It's still raining heavily. One gust after another brings us within a hairbreadth of the fury of a few minutes ago.

Finally, here comes the bus. People run to get on board. I wonder if my oil cake guy has stuck his nose outside, if he's opened up his shed. I allow myself another five minutes of leisure. I spend them with the bar boy at his counter, where to honor the occasion I knock back a shot of rum. This dark weather, this thunder that's rattling cupboards and echoing through all the valleys, these sheets of lightning taking off from the roofs like flights of partridges, even the rain itself: all of this is like a celebration. In reality, I believe it's mostly the warmth that's lifting our spirits. And in my case, the rum I'm mixing in.

When I step outside, I come back down to earth. Rain tends to put a damper on things. Nevertheless, I get going on the double. I'm glad I don't have to run an errand at Lady Anita's this morning. This weather's too warm. It's crazy how suddenly it's changed. That's why we're so excited. Plus, we know that once this heat ends, the cold from before will come back. It hasn't put in its last word.

You can say that again! With the deluge coming down and what the sky overhead could have in store for us, there'll be hell to pay if it stays warm. It's still only the beginning of March.

I need all my concentration to be able to drive. The streets are rivers. Even with the wipers on, I don't see half the headaches in front of me.

The feed guy has opened his shop. He's all fired up too. He can't keep still. He tells me tales that are none of my business. Each time the thunder crashes, he laughs. He says this is the start of spring. It's packing one hell of a punch.

Just what one hell of a punch means I'm finding out on my way back. It's pitch-dark. I have my hands full. For the first time in months, my shirt's soaked with sweat. The windshield wipers—these famous cyclone sweepers roaming across my windshield, these so-called tornado tamers made of rubber and chrome—they're waving back and forth in front of my nose without making it one bit easier to see, no matter how much sweeping and taming they do. I'm looking at a rippling road from inside an aquarium. Every second, I have to ask myself if it's for real. I stop ten times to scrape ice off the windows. It's useless. The water's almost up to the hubcaps. I start to think if I stay out here, they'll have to rescue me with a boat. Finally, I piss on a bit of cloth. I use it to wipe the windshield, and I can see a little daylight. Enough to get to the turnoff.

But here, shit! It's a lake! I can't risk launching into it. I pull over next to a pile of gravel, and I tell myself I'm going to try and stick it out. The road up to our village looks like Niagara Falls. The whole country is topsy-turvy, and the lightning keeps on attacking it.

I fill a pipe, and I slide over to the middle of the seat because the seals around the windows are leaking like a sieve. I leave the motor running.

I stay in this spot for a good half hour. Then the squall moves off to deal with another district. It leaves a sentry behind: a light rain it had held in reserve. This we can handle. I wait for the lake to drain a little. I start in at a crawl. I drive through and I make it to the far slope.

Our local road has taken a real beating. Papa Burle has his work cut out for him. He'll never be done. The ruts are a foot deep. I get the feeling I'm on a navy gunboat in rough weather.

The rough weather is for real, in any case. In the direction of the château and the village, the sky's as black as ink. The rumblings aren't letting up, and every minute the sky splits open from one end to the other like a plate cracked with a hammer.

I get back to the château just as things are starting to turn bad again. They tell me they've been worrying. And for good reason. From the overlook here, you see miles and miles of disasters. They seem to be centered around us. People in other places must be feeling the same way too, but that doesn't help us out.

Toward midday, I take advantage of a bit of brightening. It's over before it begins, but I make a dash up to the village for a bite to eat. I change my mind ten times before I decide to go. Then I fly up the hill with the hail biting my ass, and I make quite an entrance into the bistro. I can't get my wind back for at least a minute. I see myself in the mirror: I'm as red as a rooster and my eyes are popping out of my head. Catherine's laughing and slapping me on the back.

The three of us—Catherine, the artist, and me—eat to-gether. For the first time, we sit away from the woodstove. We're having rice stew. Catherine pours me one glassful after another because, she says, "Rice comes to life in water and should die in wine." This makes me feel just fine. This weather's shaking things up, bringing us some variety. All in all, the world's as it should be.

As it turns out, between two downpours I manage to get back to the château without risking my neck. Once I reach the garage, I go to check my crocuses. They're sprouting, nice and firm.

The thunder doesn't stop. All day long, it goes roaring back and forth like a bull in a china shop. But toward evening, the sky suddenly opens from top to bottom. A big, blue expanse appears. Rainbows shoot up from the ground.

There are four or five of us out on the terrace enjoying this unexpected bounty. We don't know which way to turn to take it all in. You'd think we were watching a fireworks display. We cry out at the gorgeous blue, the gorgeous green, while the setting sun sprays light in every direction, like a pony shaking water from its back.

Then a bolt of lightning strikes an oak just a hundred yards in front of us. We sprint off, stunned, to the guardhouse, with our ears ringing. I'm deaf for five minutes. My mouth is full of phosphorus as though I'd been sucking on matchsticks. When we emerge from our stupor, the sky has clouded over to the point where it's impossible to imagine a sun of any sort whatsoever.

Night falls. With each flash of lightning, we see the core of the storm—denser and denser—circling overhead like a cloud of crows. What a drumbeat! And flashes of red are inciting arguments up there. With no end in sight. It doesn't look like they're getting things settled. Quite the opposite!

Nevertheless, I wait till the end of my workday before flying like an arrow to the village. The Prophet lights my way with beams from lighthouses he's forgotten to align. A hundred times, I risk falling flat on my face.

At this hour, the bistro is usually empty. This evening, it's full of people. And they all look like they're standing around at a picnic. Everything's been so electrifying, I've lost track of the fact that it's still mild out after dark, even hot.

Everybody's drinking anise. It feels so much like summer, I'm having trouble breathing. I knock back two shots, one after the other, with the artist.

I'm going to have a look around the kitchen. Catherine is doubled over with laughter. She's as fresh as a rose. She looks good when she's flushed. She gets tickled by the littlest things. I do a little soothing, then I go back to drink.

Outside the storm keeps getting louder, while inside the voices have risen to the point where you can't even hear the thunder anymore. I have a crazy desire to cut my beard off. I tell Catherine. She breaks up laughing. She brings me some scissors, and everybody joins in the fun. I start out by making comical shapes: I do Richelieu and Napoleon III. People are asking for hunks of it, and I hand them round. Finally, the artist goes to find some soap and a Gillette. I lather up. This is an excuse for everybody to stick suds to their noses and kick up a hullabaloo. It lifts our spirits.

I'm going to the kitchen to finish shaving. There's no safety razor that could live up to its name in this crowd. They wouldn't think twice about smashing the whole place to pieces. I rinse myself off at the sink and raise my face, smooth and fresh, from the basin. My firm chin and my thin, hard mouth are on display. I'm wearing my springtime face.

"Do I ever like you like this," Catherine says.

She gets the first taste of it, and she'd much rather stay here in the kitchen (me too) than in the bistro. Judging by the uproar, though, we need to go back out.

We have a quick bite to eat, even if we're not very interested in the food. What does interest us is the crowd: the people coming in and going out in time with claps of thunder and bolts of lightning. You can hear the din of the warm rain pounding on the roofs, in the downspouts, against the windows. It's hammering the panes so hard, you're afraid they'll burst.

The bistro isn't getting any less crowded. There are guys here I've never seen before. They must have stayed close to their home fires until now. Each one comes in, opens his change purse, buys himself an anise or two, and stares at his glass like it was the Messiah.

I ask Catherine where her husband's gone. He's nowhere to be seen. She answers: Don't count on him. So what's the story? She says he has something he loves doing, and it keeps him satisfied. He's gone off to check the pheasant pens up in the hills. She saw him take his rain gear and leave earlier today. He won't come back during the night.

I picture him all alone in the middle of nowhere four or five miles away, like a scarab beetle in his black raincoat, sliding through groves of holly oaks under the flashing, the booming, and the rain.

Belote games are underway. Someone asks the artist to be a fourth. He says yes and sits down at a table.

Like I always do at this time of year, I smoke a pipe or two. But they're very bitter-tasting.

At last, we all go to bed. We've exhausted every other possibility. The storm's still carrying on, but you can't really call it a storm anymore: it's weather going on and not slowing down. When I crawl into bed, it's still hammering away on the anvil of the surrounding country. Everything's sparkling.

I fall asleep...but not for long. I wake up. I'm going to see Catherine.

But it turns out I'm up too early. It's still raining. My American Army raincoat got torn last night on my way back from the château. I'm mending it when Catherine comes downstairs. She lights the stove, gets the coffee going, and lifts the sewing out of my hands. She's tender as can be.

We make some plans, nice ones, nothing important, simply because the thunder keeps rolling in the distance and rattling the windowpanes. I'm thinking about those deep, wide, exposed valleys where lightning is circling around. Catherine is too, for reasons of her own.

I arrive back at the château, soaked to the skin. I dry myself next to the stove. A few people ask what I've done with my beard. The thunder's stopped, but the rain's still coming down in torrents, and the sky's so dark I have to switch the van's headlights on again when I leave.

When I get back from D., the boss sends for me. The cook has made me a snack. It turns out I have to leave again right away, and I won't be back by noon. To make a long story short, it's a matter of driving four game wardens down the road to four spots the boss shows me on the map. From where I drop them, one at a time, they'll go and inspect the pens and see how the animals have weathered the storm.

He takes off ahead of me on his motorbike. He's warned me that the road is bad. In fact, it's nothing but a dirt track. But I'm glad to have something to do. There's no thunder. The rain is heavy, warm. It's not letting up. It feels like it could last for a lifetime.

I'm coming back alone in the dark after I've run myself ragged through muck all day long. We've been to godforsaken places. Lots of times when the van's been close to keeling over into a ravine, we've had to hoist it back upright and stuff tree branches under the spinning wheels.

When I'm still a good mile from the château, I see the boss in my headlights. He's standing beside his motorbike. What's the matter? Nothing serious: He's covered in slime up to his eyes. His wheels are jammed inside the mud flaps. We load his machine into the van, and he climbs in beside me.

We say a few words about the rain and the nice weather.

When we get back, he comes with me to the guardhouse. We're amazed to find it full of people. Something strange, they say, has happened in the village. Somebody's strangled that old lady, Sophie! Why? She's penniless. All she has is a couple of goats. She's eighty years old. It's not possible. But yes, it is.

I'm going up to the village. The boss says, "Wait." And he comes with me.

Some gendarmes are already here, and the doctor's car. People tell us she isn't dead. The whole village is milling around. It's one hell of a mess.

We go into Catherine's, the boss and me. And here I learn the artist is the murderer. Old Man Bertrand, hunched over because of the rain, bumped into him right in front of Sophie's around four in the afternoon. They saw each other face-to-face. The artist was bareheaded, and he took off running without saying a word.

A minute later, the artist's cap turns up in the hands of a gendarme. He asks me if I recognize it. I say yes. They found it next to Sophie. They've already carried out a search here. He shows me the artist's switchblade—he left it behind—and the two packs of cards—mine still unopened. The officer asks if the artist made his living with cards. Yes.

In reality, his name is Victor André: born in Algiers, father and mother unknown.

My boss talks to the officer. They're both feeling uneasy. After this, I'm told I'm free to go.

Now the doctor comes in. He announces point-blank that Sophie is dead. "More from shock than anything else," he adds. That guy wasn't even capable of strangling a chicken. Everybody's in agreement, even so, that he's a murderer. "A madman," says the doctor; but there's no suggestion of a *motive.*

Roadblocks have been set up. They've already put the word out by telephone. He must be up in the hills. "He's still a danger," they're saying. There are isolated farms out there. If he knocks on somebody's door in this kind of weather, they'll ask him to come inside. I point out that he didn't take his knife. People give me funny looks: not exactly sidelong but not straight in the eye either.

Somebody tells the story of a guy who killed seven people at the Richards' farm in 1912 in this district. And he wasn't a hefty guy, and he wasn't armed. He killed them with a cudgel. He was probably crazy too. Twenty-five francs is all he got out of it. They guillotined him at D. The gendarme has steam coming off his back like a wet horse. He's in no hurry to leave. Still, he decides it's time to send out a search party.

This doesn't fall on deaf ears.

My boss taps me on the arm and says, "Come on!" He brings me back to the château, up to the big hall where I saw him for the first time.

He pulls off his boots and puts on some slippers. He loads a pipe; so do I.

He asks if he was a close friend. I tell him I don't know just what he was. It's strange, but I couldn't care less. I only found his name out a few minutes ago.

In the boss's opinion, I should be joining the search party.

"I've brought you over here to make your mind up."

It takes me a second to catch his meaning. Instead of telling him I'd already made my mind up, I answer, "Yes, I agree!"

"I'm going to make you take a gun," he says.

I don't answer.

"I know you don't want to. You're refusing. And I'm the one who's making you."

"You understand: He's a pal. I'm not going to knock him off because he's done something stupid. All the more so, since the old lady gave up the ghost for different reasons."

He's listening closely. He drops the theatrical tone and he murmurs, "What you've just said is excellent."

He goes to a cupboard and pulls out a double-barreled rifle. He hands it to me and I take it.

I point out, "I don't even know if it's loaded."

"Neither do I. When you left in the dark to join the other men (who are armed with hunting rifles, you can be sure), and after I'd insisted and forced you to go, I also made you take this rifle. The same as I would have made a friend take an umbrella. We had nothing in mind, either of us. Maybe I did think about a kind of moral safeguard. Just while you were leaving. Instinctively. Because I like you. Because I have a high opinion . . ."

I say, "It's time to go."

And I do.

At the door, I add, "I'll give them to you tomorrow anyway, but there are three pots of crocuses for you in the garage, behind the gas tank."

"I know. You can give them to me when you get back."

I climb up to the village. In the square there are still five or six men, streaked with rain, lifting their hurricane lamps. I catch a glimpse of them heading off to the open fields in the direction of the plateau. I'm going to try a different strategy.

I pass by Sophie's house and I keep going. It was in this

direction that he took off on the run. At the end of the roadway you come to some clearings. On one side, they slope up toward the hills. On the other, they overhang a steep ravine.

If he thought he'd killed the old lady, he would have turned uphill. If he realized he didn't even have the strength to do her in, he would have turned downhill. I go by the fact that he was running when he left the scene of the crime. I turn downhill.

I have no need for a lantern. On the contrary, I let myself sink like a sounding lead. I take a while to get to the bottom. The undergrowth is dense. I'm not worried about the noise I'm making; the sound of the rain hides it. And there's no way he would have stayed in these thickets. I'm not worried about the rain either. Or the stream at the bottom. I cross over and get a foothold on a path.

I'm trying to find my bearings. It's hard. Then I hear the bell ringing from the church. What are they doing up there? Could they be idiotic enough to be raising a general alarm? No, it's tolling for some sort of benediction. It tells me where I am. The highway's over there—toward the village. All I have to do is head in the opposite direction. For sure, that's the way he turned.

I'm glad to notice that the path rises gently in the direction I've decided to follow. He must have been glad to notice it, too, after he'd reached the bottom here, with the highway on one side (which must have horrified him) and this forest path, rising *ever so gently*, on the other.

If he thought the gendarmes would be keeping watch on the highway (and I don't believe he did), it wouldn't have had much effect on him. Where he's come to, gendarmes don't matter. What matters is this path. The artist definitely needed to climb somewhere higher, without wearing himself out.

I understand very well what he did. I'm in his skin. There's no way he would have lasted more than five minutes with his fingers clutching Sophie's neck, trying to make them do his bidding. With his head full of grand ideas (*not within everyone's grasp*) and no means to put them into action. Obliged, from now on, to get people to take him at his word! He came out running, with the idea of hurling himself into anything at all, so long as he fell into it with his own weight. (This is why certain individuals—especially women—throw themselves off bridges into rivers. They're not trying to reach the water; they're trying to reach everything that's missing from their lives. They know it's not in the water—*on the contrary*—but how can they resist the pleasure of moving effortlessly, at last, toward anything at all, by their own weight? The most delectable part is the time it takes you to fall.)

Once you're down there the pleasure is over; you'd like to come back up. But it's too late. The artist has had luck all his life. And this time again, he's had some luck. I'm happy for him.

He threw himself down the steep slope of the ravine, through the thick brush. If it had been daylight, if there weren't this goddamned night rain but only a little moon, I bet I would have seen his footprints. He must have rolled down the slope like a wild boar chased by a pack of dogs. And landed on the path where I am.

Once he was here, he found himself back in the land of the living. (This matters. You can say what you like, but he's a lucky guy. I get a lot of pleasure from imagining that even in this place, *after all is said and done*, he's *made the most of life*. For thirty seconds, life was good. Who can pride themselves on having had any more than that or even as much?

I'm talking about what a man worthy of the name calls a good life.) As a general rule, we're dupes, all our lives, to go chasing after good times like these. He had one. I'm glad for him.

And glad to sense, while I'm groping my way forward, that the path keeps on rising gently (he couldn't have resisted this: impossible). What's more, it's a gravelly path without any kind of mud: a Jacob's ladder for the well-heeled. He is coddled, the lad. That is to say: The God of our fathers never abandons his creatures.

And I climb, too, following in his footsteps. But certainly not with the same companions. For me, there's no pomp and ceremony. I have to listen to all the sounds around me and take them into account. It's not that I'm expecting to find him all of a sudden, right in front of me. I'm hoping he's covered some ground. But me: I'm climbing simply by trial and error through the sound of the rain on the leaves of the scrub oaks (it's like the sound that silkworms make before they molt, when they're eating mulberry leaves on a silk farm), and I'm keeping an ear out for the sound of the stream. I can't afford to fall in and break my neck.

The two of us, we aren't in the same company. We aren't in the same company anymore. I can smell the pine boughs I'm passing under, and I hear the muffled breath of the rain on the needles. This scent, this catlike purring: They were here when he passed through. But he couldn't have given a damn! They would have been the last thing on his mind! My eyes are useless in this darkness, but I do have my nose and my ears. I'm always in touch with life here on earth. I've done nothing to banish earthly existence to the underworld. I can't know what any of this was like for him: the pine grove without scents or sounds; the rain not making anything wet, not pattering on these empty stretches of scrub oaks that, for him, didn't exist. We're no longer in the same night. That's all I know. Are there pine groves in his night? Or something else you could call by the same name? Rain or something close? What does it smell like? What does it do? I can't know what it's like. If from now on his mind's going to be full of things completely foreign to me and controlled by nothing I'm familiar with, it wouldn't be worth trying to catch up with him. No one could catch up with him. But he does have a body, arms, legs. And all I can think of is the way he'll have to use these implements, these tools that serve only one well-defined purpose. They can't do anything other than remain here on earth. They don't fit in with his scheme. The funny thing is, six months ago his hands knew more than his head; now it's the other way around. What's more, this is what he wanted. And this is what I have to contend with.

And now I'm arriving at the plateau. I'm forewarned by the low background sound and the thousands of raindrops freely pelting down.

I make out some lanterns far off to my left. Then more show up. They've found their way to this place too. It's true, it's been easy so far.

I watch them doing something completely idiotic: They move forward in a continuous line. They think they're waging war on the Prussian army. But we're a far cry from France facing a foreign enemy.

I keep them in sight. They don't realize they're doing something of great importance. Or rather, yes, they're convinced that they are. They're puffed up with pride. They have their finger on the trigger. They're out to avenge the death of the half-witted old woman. When she was alive, they wouldn't have spared her a crust of bread. Now they're grim and determined because they're looking out for themselves. They wouldn't shy away from a cannonball. They're far from guessing the importance of what they're doing.

I only have to flee from them to be going in the same direction as the artist.

I'm sure the gendarmes are getting the men from the village to move into clever formations, like a lobster trap or a fishnet. What do they think they're trying to catch? Even a fine paper filter would have too coarse a weave.

They don't realize that the artist made it here, at the end of the day, *with utterly useless hands.* And that night fell right afterward. What can a few lanterns, more or less, matter to him? If he's taken off in the opposite direction, it's because the shadows and the dark have more and more to offer him, with every step.

What they're setting up on the plateau, in slow motion, is a wide-meshed net for big game fish. But at any other time, my artist is … What's that old line? "A breath, a nothing." I bet it wasn't fat Nestor or two-hundred-pound Ferréol who crushed his hands up on the mountain but likely just Ironwire: Ironwire the lightweight. When it comes to making themselves happy, men don't need to use sledgehammers. And when someone's been reduced to all but nothing, what paper filter can catch the last remnant of them *that still has value*? If that remnant is what you're after, my fine sirs … But I'm insulting you by believing you have the slightest interest in it. So charge ahead with your lantern in your hand and your finger on the trigger for as long as you like in order to make the honor roll in the daily newspapers.

I have better things to do on this leafless plain. I'm still obliged to be alert to the sounds around me and to the sounds

I'm making (it's too soon though to keep an ear out for the sound of rapid breathing). In no time, I could lose you. The rain gives you cover and blots you out, and the darkness shrouds you.

Now it's good. I'm rewarded for my efforts. We're alone, the artist and I. Each step brings me closer to him. I know we're going to settle this business in a friendly fashion.

At first, I walk quickly in a general direction. I don't have to be careful anymore like I did in the ravine. Down there, I couldn't afford to take a false step, left or right; here, the ground is firm all around. But I don't have the slope of the path to draw me on, that irresistible need to climb. I was following it like a dog on the prowl. Up here, nothing's clear-cut anymore.

How happy he must have been, at long last, to reach a place where nothing was clear-cut anymore.

Suddenly, I hear something suspicious ahead of me. It's a little below eye level. The rain is beating down on something lying across my path. I stop. I listen. I curse the sound the rain's making when it hits me. I think it must be echoing and making my presence known, but it's leaving out the essential thing: Yes, I'm here, but I'm here with good intentions.

Whatever it is that's in front of me doesn't seem to give a damn. I'm scared. If it is him, has his new company turned him into stone or a tree? Is this the fate of those who no longer have their home here on earth? I'm afraid he might be that far gone.

I come closer. *I take it upon myself* to be the first one to hold out his hand. It's a wooden gate; the rain's beating on it. I caress it. I stroke it like an owner strokes his dog.

Now I can give a familiar name to what's in front of me.

There are the sounds of horse's bellies gurgling and a tile roof pattering in the downpour. I pick up a faint smell of rain-soaked manure. It's a house.

I walk around it; I feel its wall. I come to a gilded door frame, and I freeze like a bird facing a snake.

I have to give myself time to come back from a great distance. I won't be able to fathom the viewpoint of the people in here right away.

At last, I knock. Somebody opens up. I say what I have to say. A child coughs at the far end of a room lit red by a kerosene lamp. As I'm leaving, they're barricading themselves in and dousing the light.

I walk fast. That door really did me in. I don't give a damn.

Tonight, without me here, this plateau would be beautiful!

I have too much of a presence. My American waterproof jacket is crackling like sheet metal in the rain. I look like I'm taking part in a religious procession. And it's only me. Full of good intentions but with nothing to show for them.

For the first time in my life, I'm exploring for a foreign body.

I've already found one: the house. A while later, I find another one. It's still not what I'm looking for. It's a valley. I must have crossed from one side of the plateau to the other, and now I'm on the opposite rim.

I listen to the rain talking about the trees it's encountering down below. It's pounding on roads and beating on roofs. It's silent over stubble fields, plowlands, grasslands. It rumbles on top of sheds. It shifts the soil in gardens like a spade. I can smell the faded cabbage leaves it's unearthing.

I turn away from this, just like he turned away. I start walking again, in the opposite direction.

Finally, I've found what I'm looking for.

First, I heard a space ahead of me where the rain was talking in low tones. I moved ahead one step at a time. I realized there was a hollow there, a sort of bowl that I'd skirted around, where the vegetation was denser, taller. I smelled junipers, bay laurels, walnuts; trees with wine-dark sap. To begin with, I stayed stock-still for a while, till the rain landing on me started to talk low too. As long as I wasn't sure I belonged in this place, I didn't budge. Then I descended into the bowl. But God himself must have been in awe of me.

I moved closer to the first bush until I touched it. Then I entered its branches little by little. So slowly, not one of them made a sound.

My American raincoat has become my skin: sensitive and wary. Like this, I've passed through the first bush (a juniper) and come nearer to the second. It's a cluster of walnut shoots grown up around an old stump. I pass through them imperceptibly.

I'm being cautious as much for him as for myself. I've always been shy. I don't like to disturb people. If the guy is nice, even less so.

The scent of the underbrush is strong and bitter. But I know the smell of his wet jacket. That's what I'm searching for.

I'm listening too. The bay whistles softly, the juniper crackles, the shoots of the walnut snap, the rain up on the plateau murmurs. It's the kind of concert that arises as soon as there's a human around. In the house back there, there was a stove roaring, a child coughing, a bed squeaking in the alcove. If I'm not mistaken, there should be, close to me now, within a radius of fifteen to twenty feet, a silent, foreign body.

And I'm wrong. I hear someone breathing. This is a lot more complicated than I thought.

I stay motionless for a long while. It's the breathing of a runner. I can't believe it's his. But I smell his wet jacket, and I even hear the sound of the rain on that jacket.

I recognize absolutely everything. He hasn't changed.

I don't move. He's three steps in front of me. Together, we go on the most amazing excursion. He retraces the path he took here from the village, a hundred times. He strangles the old half-wit a hundred times. He fails a hundred times, runs into the street, hurls himself into the ravine, breathes hard on the ascending trail, runs across the plateau, stumbles into the search party's lanterns, stumbles into the house, stumbles into the valley, slides underneath the bitter-smelling underbrush. And I don't get tired, I stay with him. If he had the time to listen, he'd hear me breathing hard next to him, but no sooner has he hidden here underneath the laurels than he takes off again, heads back to Catherine's bistro, comes out, closes the door, crosses the square, turns into the alleyway, climbs up to Sophie's place and assaults her. I strangle her too, alongside him. Then he comes back out, collides with Old Man Bertrand, races down the street, crosses the open fields, hurls himself into the ravine as though from the height of a bridge, lands down on the path, stumbles into the peace-loving trees, the pines that are budding in the first warm rain of springtime, the forests of scrub oaks that have shed their dead leaves in the downpour and are lifting up—at the very tips of their massive branches—tiny green buds. I'm running alongside him, one yard away, with all my strength. I'm going nowhere. Neither is he. We're spinning nonstop in a bitter bowl made of earth, junipers, boxwoods, and everything we've done, and we're doing it over and over, endlessly, with an irresistible urge to sleep.

And I fall asleep on my feet, leaning against a sapling.

It's not so much the sunlight that wakes me up as it is his gaze: fixed on me. Days of love are better than nights of love. He doesn't move while I prepare myself. I fire my two shots full in his face. I see them hit their mark.

Friendship is beautiful!

In the end, the gendarmes congratulated me.

Right after, I wrap things up in twenty-four hours.

Catherine is tender but accepting.

I'm going down on foot to the highway. I'll forget that guy like I've forgotten others before him. The sun is never so beautiful as on a day when you take to the open road.

TRANSLATOR'S ACKNOWLEDGMENTS

MANY FRIENDS have given me help and encouragement along this road.

Isabelle Génin, maître de conferences at the Sorbonne Nouvelle—Paris 3, provided detailed commentary on my drafts, corrected numerous errors, and sharpened my interpretation of the myriad *"expressions et locutions"* that pepper these pages. Jacques Le Gall, a consummate Giono scholar, offered essential insights into obscure passages and penned a lucid introduction.

I'm deeply indebted to Edwin Frank, my editor at NYRB, for his acumen, commitment, and moral support.

Jacques Mény, the president of Les Amis de Jean Giono, continues to endorse my efforts. Grégoire Lacaze, linguist at l'Université Aix-Marseille, has taken a lively, scholarly interest in various aspects of my work.

The following listing doesn't render sufficient gratitude to my readers, but to each of you I extend heartfelt thanks: Roo Borson, Wendell Block, David Friend, Peter Sakuls, Simon Swale, Tim Brook, Joyce Zonana, Colin Mooers, Kate and Chris Harries, Nick Thompson.

Claude Boutterin has contributed a fine drawing.

Debbie Honickman has shared in every stage of this labor of love, reading my drafts aloud and helping me smooth and clarify the prose. In 2019, during a sojourn in Haute-Provence

212 · TRANSLATOR'S ACKNOWLEDGEMENTS

subsidized by the French government's Centre national du livre, we made an exploratory, revelatory trip to the regions— the Trièves and the Diois—where the action of the novel takes place.

For her warmth and inspiration, and in particular for a conversation during a drive from Banon to Manosque along roads that read like pages from her father's books, I dedicate this translation to Sylvie Durbet-Giono.

—P.E.

OTHER NEW YORK REVIEW CLASSICS

For a complete list of titles, visit www.nyrb.com.

J.R. ACKERLEY My Father and Myself
RENATA ADLER Pitch Dark
RENATA ADLER Speedboat
AESCHYLUS Prometheus Bound; translated by Joel Agee
ROBERT AICKMAN Compulsory Games
LEOPOLDO ALAS His Only Son *with* Doña Berta
CÉLESTE ALBARET Monsieur Proust
DANTE ALIGHIERI The Inferno; translated by Ciaran Carson
DANTE ALIGHIERI Purgatorio; translated by D. M. Black
JEAN AMÉRY Charles Bovary, Country Doctor: Portrait of a Simple Man
KINGSLEY AMIS Lucky Jim
KINGSLEY AMIS The Old Devils
KINGSLEY AMIS One Fat Englishman
KINGSLEY AMIS Take a Girl Like You
ROBERTO ARLT The Seven Madmen
U.R. ANANTHAMURTHY Samskara: A Rite for a Dead Man
IVO ANDRIĆ Omer Pasha Latas
WILLIAM ATTAWAY Blood on the Forge
W.H. AUDEN (EDITOR) The Living Thoughts of Kierkegaard
ERICH AUERBACH Dante: Poet of the Secular World
EVE BABITZ Eve's Hollywood
EVE BABITZ Slow Days, Fast Company: The World, the Flesh, and L.A.
DOROTHY BAKER Young Man with a Horn
J.A. BAKER The Peregrine
S. JOSEPHINE BAKER Fighting for Life
HONORÉ DE BALZAC The Human Comedy: Selected Stories
HONORÉ DE BALZAC The Memoirs of Two Young Wives
HONORÉ DE BALZAC The Unknown Masterpiece *and* Gambara
VICKI BAUM Grand Hotel
SYBILLE BEDFORD A Favorite of the Gods *and* A Compass Error
SYBILLE BEDFORD Jigsaw
SYBILLE BEDFORD A Legacy
SYBILLE BEDFORD A Visit to Don Otavio: A Mexican Journey
MAX BEERBOHM The Prince of Minor Writers: The Selected Essays of Max Beerbohm
MAX BEERBOHM Seven Men
STEPHEN BENATAR Wish Her Safe at Home
FRANS G. BENGTSSON The Long Ships
WALTER BENJAMIN The Storyteller Essays
ALEXANDER BERKMAN Prison Memoirs of an Anarchist
GEORGES BERNANOS Mouchette
MIRON BIAŁOSZEWSKI A Memoir of the Warsaw Uprising
ROBERT MONTGOMERY BIRD Sheppard Lee, Written by Himself
ADOLFO BIOY CASARES Asleep in the Sun
ADOLFO BIOY CASARES The Invention of Morel
PAUL BLACKBURN (TRANSLATOR) Proensa
CAROLINE BLACKWOOD Corrigan
CAROLINE BLACKWOOD Great Granny Webster
LESLEY BLANCH Journey into the Mind's Eye: Fragments of an Autobiography
RONALD BLYTHE Akenfield: Portrait of an English Village
HENRI BOSCO Malicroix
NICOLAS BOUVIER The Way of the World

JEAN D'ORMESSON The Glory of the Empire: A Novel, A History
CHARLES DUFF A Handbook on Hanging
BRUCE DUFFY The World As I Found It
DAPHNE DU MAURIER Don't Look Now: Stories
ELAINE DUNDY The Dud Avocado
G.B. EDWARDS The Book of Ebenezer Le Page
JOHN EHLE The Land Breakers
CYPRIAN EKWENSI People of the City
MARCELLUS EMANTS A Posthumous Confession
EURIPIDES Grief Lessons: Four Plays; translated by Anne Carson
J.G. FARRELL The Siege of Krishnapur
ELIZA FAY Original Letters from India
KENNETH FEARING The Big Clock
FÉLIX FÉNÉON Novels in Three Lines
M.I. FINLEY The World of Odysseus
THOMAS FLANAGAN The Year of the French
BENJAMIN FONDANE Existential Monday: Philosophical Essays
SANFORD FRIEDMAN Conversations with Beethoven
MARC FUMAROLI When the World Spoke French
CARLO EMILIO GADDA That Awful Mess on the Via Merulana
WILLIAM GADDIS J R
WILLIAM GADDIS The Recognitions
BENITO PÉREZ GÁLDOS Tristana
MAVIS GALLANT A Fairly Good Time *with* Green Water, Green Sky
MAVIS GALLANT Varieties of Exile
GABRIEL GARCÍA MÁRQUEZ Clandestine in Chile: The Adventures of Miguel Littín
LEONARD GARDNER Fat City
WILLIAM H. GASS In the Heart of the Heart of the Country and Other Stories
THÉOPHILE GAUTIER My Fantoms
GE FEI Peach Blossom Paradise
JEAN GENET The Criminal Child: Selected Essays
JEAN GENET Prisoner of Love
ANDRÉ GIDE Marshlands
ÉLISABETH GILLE The Mirador: Dreamed Memories of Irène Némirovsky by Her Daughter
FRANÇOISE GILOT Life with Picasso
NATALIA GINZBURG Family *and* Borghesia
NATALIA GINZBURG Valentino *and* Sagittarius
JEAN GIONO Hill
JEAN GIONO A King Alone
JEAN GIONO Melville: A Novel
JEAN GIONO The Open Road
JOHN GLASSCO Memoirs of Montparnasse
P.V. GLOB The Bog People: Iron-Age Man Preserved
ROBERT GLÜCK Margery Kempe
EDMOND AND JULES DE GONCOURT Pages from the Goncourt Journals
PAUL GOODMAN Growing Up Absurd: Problems of Youth in the Organized Society
EDWARD GOREY (EDITOR) The Haunted Looking Glass
JEREMIAS GOTTHELF The Black Spider
A.C. GRAHAM Poems of the Late T'ang
JULIEN GRACQ Balcony in the Forest
HENRY GREEN Doting
HENRY GREEN Living
HENRY GREEN Loving

HARVEY SWADOS Nights in the Gardens of Brooklyn
A.J.A. SYMONS The Quest for Corvo
MAGDA SZABÓ Abigail
MAGDA SZABÓ The Door
JÁNOS SZÉKELY Temptation
ANTAL SZERB Journey by Moonlight
SUSAN TAUBES Divorcing
ELIZABETH TAYLOR Angel
ELIZABETH TAYLOR A View of the Harbour
TEFFI Other Worlds: Peasants, Pilgrims, Spirits, Saints
TEFFI Tolstoy, Rasputin, Others, and Me: The Best of Teffi
GABRIELE TERGIT Käsebier Takes Berlin
HENRY DAVID THOREAU The Journal: 1837–1861
ALEKSANDAR TIŠMA Kapo
TATYANA TOLSTAYA White Walls: Collected Stories
EDWARD JOHN TRELAWNY Records of Shelley, Byron, and the Author
LIONEL TRILLING The Liberal Imagination
KURT TUCHOLSKY Castle Gripsholm
IVAN TURGENEV Virgin Soil
JULES VALLÈS The Child
MARK VAN DOREN Shakespeare
SALKA VIERTEL The Kindness of Strangers
ELIZABETH VON ARNIM The Enchanted April
EDWARD LEWIS WALLANT The Tenants of Moonbloom
ROBERT WALSER Little Snow Landscape
ROBERT WALSER A Schoolboy's Diary and Other Stories
MICHAEL WALZER Political Action: A Practical Guide to Movement Politics
REX WARNER Men and Gods
SYLVIA TOWNSEND WARNER The Corner That Held Them
SYLVIA TOWNSEND WARNER Lolly Willowes
JAKOB WASSERMANN My Marriage
ALEKSANDER WAT My Century
LYALL WATSON Heaven's Breath: A Natural History of the Wind
MAX WEBER Charisma and Disenchantment: The Vocation Lectures
C.V. WEDGWOOD The Thirty Years War
SIMONE WEIL On the Abolition of All Political Parties
HELEN WEINZWEIG Basic Black with Pearls
GLENWAY WESCOTT The Pilgrim Hawk
REBECCA WEST The Fountain Overflows
EDITH WHARTON The New York Stories of Edith Wharton
KATHARINE S. WHITE Onward and Upward in the Garden
PATRICK WHITE Riders in the Chariot
T. H. WHITE The Goshawk
JOHN WILLIAMS Augustus
JOHN WILLIAMS Butcher's Crossingt
JOHN WILLIAMS Stoner
HENRY WILLIAMSON Tarka the Otter
RUDOLF AND MARGARET WITTKOWER Born Under Saturn
GEOFFREY WOLFF Black Sun
RICHARD WOLLHEIM Germs: A Memoir of Childhood
JOHN WYNDHAM Chocky
STEFAN ZWEIG Beware of Pity
STEFAN ZWEIG Chess Story